BRIDES OF WATERLOO

Love forged on the battlefield

Meet Mary Endacott, a radical schoolmistress,
Sarah Latymor, a darling of the *ton*,
and Catherine 'Rose' Tatton, a society lady
with no memories of her past.

Three very different women
united in a fight for their lives,
their reputations and the men they love.

With war raging around them, the biggest
battle these women face is protecting their
hearts from three notorious soldiers…

Will Mary be able to resist
Colonel Lord Randall? Find out in

A Lady for Lord Randall
by
Sarah Mallory

Discover how pampered Lady Sarah
handles rakish Major Bartlett in

A Mistress for Major Bartlett
by
Annie Burrows

What will happen when Major Flint
helps Lady Catherine 'Rose' Tatton
discover her past? Find out in

A Rose for Major Flint
by
Louise Allen

AUTHOR NOTE

I was thrilled when Louise Allen and Sarah Mallory asked me if I'd be interested in working with them on a mini-series of stories to commemorate the two hundredth anniversary of the Battle of Waterloo.

I've mentioned this pivotal battle in a couple of my books before, but never actually taken any of my heroes or heroines to the battlefield itself.

My journey with *Brides of Waterloo* began in April 2012, when Louise Allen and I met up in the grounds of Ickworth House in Suffolk, where several historical re-enactment groups had set up camp. I was taught how to make cartridges, watched a cannon being loaded and fired (and learned how to protect my ears from the blast!), saw what an infantryman would have carried in his pack, and what the inside of an officer's tent would have looked like.

Over the next few months we spent hours e-mailing each other as we created the fictional unit known as Randall's Rogues and shared pictures of what we thought our heroes should look like (all for the purposes of continuity, of course!). We even met up to double-check all those little details which ensured that our heroes and heroines could walk in and out of each other's stories with ease.

If you'd like to see pictures of our day at Ickworth, or find out more about the background research for this series, you can visit our Facebook page: facebook.com/WaterlooBrides.

A MISTRESS FOR MAJOR BARTLETT

Annie Burrows

First published in Great Britain 2015
by Mills & Boon, an imprint of Harlequin (UK) Limited,
Large Print edition 2015
Harlequin (UK) Limited, Eton House, 18-24 Paradise Road,
Richmond, Surrey TW9 1SR

© 2015 Annie Burrows

ISBN: 978-0-263-25567-6

Annie Burrows has been writing Regency romances for Mills & Boon® since 2007. Her books have charmed readers worldwide, having been translated into nineteen different languages, and some have gone on to win the coveted Reviewers' Choice Award from *CataRomance*.

For more information, or to contact the author, please visit annie-burrows.co.uk or you can find her on Facebook at facebook.com/AnnieBurrowsUK.

Visit the author profile page at millsandboon.co.uk

To Louise Allen and Sarah Mallory.
It has been a great experience working with
you two on this trilogy.

Chapter One

Sunday, 18th June—1815

'Limber up, fast as you can!' Colonel Randall rode up to Major Bartlett and pointed to a spot to the rear. 'We are heading to the ridge up yonder. You will recall we came in that way yesterday, past a place—what was it called?—Hougoumont. The French are massing their heavy cavalry between the château and the Charleroi road. Take up your position between the two infantry squares up there. And be quick about it!'

Major Bartlett kept his face impassive as he saluted. Quick? That was going to be a relative term given the sodden state of the ground.

'Right, lads,' he said, turning to his men. 'You heard the Colonel. *At* the double!'

The speed at which they turned the gun carriages and started ploughing their way across the field had much more to do with the shells exploding all around them, spraying them with mud, than willingness to obey their commanding officer. The sooner they got to higher ground, the sooner they could start inflicting some damage on the Frenchmen currently trying to blow them to kingdom come. Not that Major Bartlett had any complaints. He had a rather elastic attitude to obeying orders himself. In any other unit his tendency to interpret orders to suit himself would have got him up on a charge—indeed, had done so on several occasions. Only Colonel Randall had appreciated that his ability to think on his feet, rather than dumbly obeying orders, could be an advantage, taking him into his unit and giving him promotion.

Still, when he glanced across the ridge, and saw that his team had beaten Major Flint's to reach their designated position, he felt a twinge of pride in his men. They'd worked with a swiftness and efficiency *he'd* drilled into them, even if, at this moment, they'd worked the way they had because their hides depended on it.

Flint's guns were ready to fire mere seconds after his own. Even Rawlins, who'd only been promoted a matter of days before, had his guns in position not long after. And just as well. The French cavalry were approaching at the trot.

The first salvo his men fired mowed down the leaders. But they kept coming. Big bastards. On big horses.

'Dear lord, they'll charge right over us!'

Major Bartlett whirled round. Had one of his own men dared say that?

'Not Randall's Rogues, they won't,' he snarled. 'Remember our motto—always victorious!' By any means. Particularly when sent behind enemy lines, where his, and his men's, talents for causing mayhem had so often been given free rein.

'Aye,' roared Randall, drawing his sword and holding it aloft. '*Semper Laurifer!* Ready, Rogues… Fire!'

The guns roared again. Horses and men fell. Smoke swirled round the scene, blotting out the sight of the dead and dying, though Bartlett could still hear their screams and groans.

And then he heard cheering. From the infantry squares behind him. The cavalry charge was over. This one, anyway. He cast a quick, appraising glance over his men. All of them steadily reloading, preparing for the next attack, not wasting their time cheering, or capering about and having to be pushed back into position.

At this point, between cavalry charges, their orders had been to retreat into the infantry squares for cover. But his men, seasoned veterans, knew as well as he did that if they didn't stay right where they were, the squares would break and scatter. They'd seen it happen elsewhere already today. The infantry—with little or no experience—were watching the way the Rogues calmly went about their business as though those huge French horses were no more than skittles to knock down. Their staunch disregard of danger was probably the only thing giving them any hope.

Hope—hah! It was the one thing neither he, nor his men, had felt for a very long time. They were the damned. Doomed to death, one way or another. They just preferred to take as many of the murdering French to hell with them as they could. At least they could die like men, if they did so in defence of their country, instead of dancing on the end of a rope.

'Here they come again, lads,' he heard Randall shout.

And then came the thunder of hooves. The roar of the guns. The smoke, and the screams, and the mud, and the carnage.

And his men reloaded and fired. And loaded and fired.

And still there was no end to the French.

The next morning

Lady Sarah Latymor rubbed her eyes and peered up at the manger above her head. Could she really make out wisps of straw sticking through the grating, or was it just wishful thinking?

In the stall next to hers, she could hear Castor shuffling about, lipping at whatever provender Pieter had placed in his own manger. She reached out her hand and laid the palm against the partition. Being able to hear her horse, Gideon's last gift to her, moving about in his stall during the night, had been all that had kept her flayed nerves from giving way altogether. But it looked as though the worst day of her life was over now. She could, at last, make out the pale rectangle of her hand against the planking. Dawn was definitely breaking. And Brussels was quiet. Though Madame le Brun had warned her that French troops might overrun the city during the night, they'd never come. Which meant the Allies must have won. She could come out of hiding.

And continue her quest.

To find out what had really happened to Gideon. He *couldn't* be dead. He was her twin. If his soul had really departed this earth, she would feel it, wouldn't she? Her stomach twisted and dropped, just as it had when her brother-in-law Lord Blanchards had broken the news. While her sister Gussie had broken down and wept, Sarah had stood there, shaking her head. Grown more and more angry at the way they both just accepted it.

Blanchards had brushed aside her refusal to believe that the hastily scrawled note he held in his hand could possibly be delivering news of that magnitude. He'd practically ordered her to her room, where he no doubt expected her to weep decorously, out of sight, so that he could concentrate on comforting and supporting his wife.

Well, she hadn't wept. She'd been too angry to weep. That anger had simmered all night and driven her, on Sunday morning, all the way to Brussels, the only place where she was likely to be able to find out what had really happened to Gideon. Had driven her about half a mile along the road to the Forest of Soignes before she'd been beaten back by a troop of Hussars, claiming the French had won the battle, and were right on their heels.

Hussars, she snorted, sitting up and pushing a hank of hair off her face. What did they know?

As if in agreement, Ben, the dog she'd teamed up with in the wake of the Hussars' cowardly scramble to safety, sat up, stretched and yawned.

'Did you have a lovely sleep, Ben?' she asked as the dog came to swipe his tongue over her face in morning greeting. 'Yes, you did. You marvellous, fierce creature,' she added, ruffling his ears. 'I could feel you lying at my feet all night long and knew that if any Frenchman dared to set one toe inside this stable, you'd bite him with those great big teeth of yours.' She'd felt safer with him to guard her than she would have done had she had a loaded pistol in her hand.

'Woof,' Ben agreed, settling back to give his ear a vigorous scratch with one hind paw.

'Well, I may not have had a wink of sleep,' she informed him as she flung her blanket aside, 'but at least I didn't waste all those sleepless hours. I have,' she said, reaching for the jacket of her riding habit, which she'd rolled up and used for a pillow, 'come up with a plan. We're going to find Justin.'

She frowned at the jacket. Pale blue velvet was not the ideal material for rolling up and pillowing a lady's head. Especially not a lady who'd taken refuge in a stable. She shook it, brushed off the straw and slid her arms into the sleeves.

Ben stopped scratching, and gave her a hard stare.

'It's no use telling me that now the battle is over, I should go to the authorities and ask them for details,' she informed him testily. 'They would simply order me to go home, like a good girl, and wait for official notification. Which would get sent to Blanchards. Well,' she huffed as she went to rummage in her saddlebag—which she'd draped over the stall door in case she needed it in a hurry—and came up with a comb, 'they *did* send notification to Blanchards, didn't they? And much good it did me.'

She raised a hand to her head, discovered that most of her braids were still more or less intact and promptly thought better of attempting anything much in the way of grooming.

'And anyway,' she said, shoving the comb back into the saddlebag, 'if I walked into headquarters, unescorted, they'd want to know what I was doing in Brussels on my own. And don't say how would they know I'd come here on my own, Ben, it's obvious. If Blanchards had come to Brussels with me, *he* would be the one at headquarters asking the questions. See?'

Ben shuffled forward a little and licked his lips hopefully.

'Yes, I do have more sausage in here,' she told him, dipping her hand once more into the saddle-bag. 'You may as well have it,' she said, breaking off a piece and tossing it to the straw at his feet. Her stomach was still coiled into the hard knot that had made eating virtually impossible since the moment Blanchards had told her Gideon was dead. Though she'd still packed plenty of provisions when she'd run away from Antwerp, thinking it might take her a day or so to locate Gideon, or his commanding officer, Colonel Bennington Ffog.

She wrinkled her nose as Ben disposed of the sausage in a few gulps. Why she'd thought, however briefly, that Bennington Ffog might be of any use, she couldn't imagine. It would be far better to find her oldest brother, Justin.

'Now, Justin might be cross with me,' she said as she pushed open the stall door and ventured into the aisle, 'but he won't send me back to Antwerp without telling me what I need to know first. He might be the stuffiest, most arrogant, obnoxious man,' she said, peering out into the stable yard to make sure nobody was about. 'He may give me a thundering scold for leaving the safety of Antwerp, against his explicit orders, but he does at least understand what Gideon means to me.'

With Ben trotting at her heels, Sarah made her way to the pump, where she quickly rinsed her face and hands. Ben took the opportunity to relieve himself and have a good sniff round.

When she made for the stable again, though, he was right beside her.

'Good boy,' she said, pausing to pat his head, before reaching for her riding hat, which she'd set on one of the doorposts.

'The only problem is,' she said, holding her hat in place with one hand, while thrusting as much of her hair as she could under it, 'I'm not entirely sure where to find him. However,' she added, deftly securing everything in place with a hat-pin, 'Mary Endacott will.'

Ben dropped down on to his haunches, tilting his head to one side.

'Yes, I know. She doesn't like me. And I don't blame her. But you have to admit, since she's lived in Brussels for years, and knows everyone, she's bound to know who we can ask for his direction if she doesn't already have it. And what's more,' she added, when he didn't look convinced, 'she's the one person who is likely to want to know it just as much as I do, since the poor girl is in love with him.'

She lowered her head to fumble the buttons of her jacket closed as her mind dwelt on the last time she'd seen Mary, when Justin had been ordering her to leave Brussels, too. If she'd done as he'd told her…

No. Mary wouldn't have left, not even had they still been betrothed. The school she ran was her livelihood. And Justin had forfeited any authority he might have thought he had over her the minute he broke off their relationship in such a brutal fashion.

Besides, she wasn't the sort of woman to give up hope and sit about weeping, any more than Sarah was. Even after Justin had said all those horrid things, Mary would want to make sure he'd survived the battle, even if he didn't want to have anything more to do with her.

She lifted her head, squared her shoulders and strode out of the stall on her way back to the water pump. This time she saw Pieter shambling across the yard, rubbing his eyes sleepily.

'Be so good as to saddle my horse,' she said.

He hesitated for a moment, only tugging at his cap and making for the stable once he saw Ben come trotting out and joining Lady Sarah at the pump, where she was now filling her water bottle.

'I'm so glad I found you yesterday,' she said, bending down to stroke Ben's head as he lapped up the water splashing to the cobbles. 'At first I just thought stumbling across the regimental mascot was a sign I was in exactly the right place, at the right time. But today I'm thankful that having you with me means I won't have to face Mary alone.' It wasn't going to be easy. Mary had no reason to greet her warmly. Yet what was the worst Mary could do? Show her the door? Or not even let her inside? What was that, compared to what had already happened? If Gideon really *was* dead.

Which she *wasn't* going to believe until somebody gave her some solid *proof*.

She mounted Castor and, with Ben trotting at her side, that determination carried her as far as the Rue Haute, where Mary's school stood. But then doubts started assailing her from all sides. If Mary wouldn't speak to her, then who else could she turn to?

'At least I won't have to knock on the front door and beg for permission to speak to her,' she observed, drawing Castor to a halt. For Mary was standing outside alongside a horse, talking to a group of bedraggled-looking men who stood with their mounts.

But even though this meant she'd overcome the first hurdle she'd imagined, Sarah's spirits sank. For Mary was, as always, looking neat as a pin.

Whereas she must look exactly as though— well, as though she was still wearing the same gown in which she'd spent a whole day on horseback, fighting her way against a tide of refugees fleeing the very place she wanted to reach more than anywhere on earth. And crawled through the mud to rescue Ben, and ended by sleeping in a stable because the landlady, upon whose compassion she'd relied, refused point blank to permit a muddy, fierce dog inside her house.

No, you couldn't feel your best in a gown you'd been wearing for two days, especially when you'd put it through all that. Besides which, women like Mary, petite, pretty women with pert little noses, always did make her feel like a gangly, beaky beanpole.

It was Ben who came to her rescue, for at least the second time in as many days, by letting out a series of joyful barks and bounding right into the group of men milling about on the front path. Because she'd been staring at Mary and wondering how on earth she was to persuade her to help, she hadn't been paying the men much heed. But now she noticed, as they bent to ruffle Ben's shaggy head rather than scattering in terror, that they were wearing the distinctive blue jackets of artillerymen. The blue jackets of her brother's unit, their facings and insignia only just recognisable under a coating of dirt of all kinds.

Randall's Rogues. Here? What could that mean?

Forgetting her own qualms about how Mary might treat her, Sarah urged Castor forward.

'What is it? What has happened?' A chill foreboding ran a finger down her spine. 'Is it Justin?' Mary's lips thinned as she glanced up and saw Sarah. But after only a moment she appeared to relent.

'We don't really know. Nobody can find him. They think…they think…' She gave an impatient little shake of her head. 'Can you believe they came here to look for him?'

Only too well. Because none of these men had been at the Duchess of Richmond's ball and therefore couldn't know their Colonel had broken things off. To them, Mary's school must seem the obvious place to look.

'So, we decided we had better go and search the battlefield for him, in case…'

She could tell, from the way she seemed to

brace herself, that Mary feared the worst. Sarah couldn't bear to think of Mary giving up on her brother. Not in that way.

Besides, she *refused* to believe she could have lost two brothers in the space of as many days.

'He isn't dead,' said Sarah firmly. 'He's indestructible.' At least, he would have been, had he been carrying his grandfather's lucky sword. The one that protected its wearer during battle. The one he'd accused Mary of stealing because he couldn't find it.

An icy hand seemed to clutch at the back of her neck.

'You cannot possibly know that,' said the ever-practical Mary.

'Yes, I can,' she insisted, even though she knew she was being totally irrational. Even though he might not be carrying the Latymor Luck, after all.

'Why else would fate have led me to Ben? And why else would we have arrived just as you are setting off to search for Justin?'

Mary's expression turned from one of barely repressed despair to barely concealed contempt.

But the men all perked up.

'She's got a point,' said one of them. 'Dog has a good nose. Best chance of finding Colonel Randall, since he's not where we all thought he was.'

'Aye, for the colonel's own sister to turn up here, right now…it must mean his luck is still holding,' said another.

Mary only shook her head, closing her eyes for a moment as if summoning patience.

'I think you would be better returning to Antwerp,' Mary said to her. 'You are in no fit state to come with us.'

'I have been looking for Gideon and I will not, cannot, give up my search,' Sarah replied, struggling to control her emotions now. 'I cannot go back until I know what has happened to my brothers.'

Mary sighed, clearly reluctant. 'Oh, very well, I suppose you had better come with us, then. But try not,' she snapped as she mounted up, 'to get in the way.'

Get in the way? How dare she assume…?

But then, of course, Mary only saw what everyone else did when they looked at Sarah: a spoiled, empty-headed society miss. For which she had only herself to blame. She'd taken such pains to appear to be the model of decorum, always doing exactly as her parents or guardians told her without demur and observing every rule of etiquette. She'd even overheard Lord Blanchards remark that he couldn't understand how a woman with

Gussie's strength of mind could possibly be related to such an insipid girl.

'Here,' said Mary, producing a large, scented handkerchief from her pocket. Then gave her a little lecture about why she might need it.

'Thank you,' Sarah replied, pasting on a polite social smile to disguise her true feelings. Mary might say Sarah would need to hold a scented hanky to her nose for her own sake. But was she also hinting that everyone could tell Sarah hadn't stopped to bathe that morning? She'd thought the odour of dog and horse were disguising her own stale sweat pretty well, but perhaps that dainty little nose was more efficient than it looked.

It was some consolation that Ben, who'd been so delighted to see the men at first, didn't stay with them when they mounted up, but came back to her and loped along beside her own horse.

Of course, that probably had more to do with the scent of sausage still lingering round her saddlebags, but at least he *appeared* to prefer her to the others.

Even though it was early in the morning, the road from the Namur gate was already crowded with wounded men struggling back to Brussels for treatment. And little groups, like hers, going searching for loved ones.

The closer they got to the scene of the previous day's battle, the more gruesome the sights became.

Not to mention the smells. Some of it was gunpowder. But underlying it was something far worse. Something which made her jolly grateful Mary *had* thought to drench a couple of handkerchiefs in scent and share one with her. Though at the same time, Mary's foresight only made her even more aware of her own shortcomings.

'Steady, there,' she crooned, over and over again, patting Castor's neck when she needed to urge him past a pile of what she'd identified, from the briefest of glances, as bodies, both horse and human. Although the words were almost as much for herself, as her horse.

She tried not to let her eyes linger on what lay beside the roads. It put her in mind of a butcher's shop. So many men, reduced to so many cuts of meat...

A dog ran across the road in front of their little party, a long trail of what looked like sausages dangling from its jaws.

She clenched her teeth against a sudden surge of nausea. Sweat prickled across her top lip. Ben, who'd been darting from one side of the road to the other, in an agitated manner, lifted his head and watched the other dog as it ran down a fork in the road ahead.

Sarah closed her eyes, just for a minute, breathing deeply to try to clear her head which had started spinning alarmingly.

I must not faint. I must not faint.

'Are you all right, miss?' One of the Rogues had noticed her lag behind. Sarah forced her eyes open, to see that the rest of the party had reached the fork in the road. Oh, lord, she hoped they weren't going to have to go past the place where the scavenger dog had taken its obscene booty. Thank goodness she hadn't taken any breakfast, or she would be bringing it straight back up.

She couldn't go that way. She *wouldn't* go that way!

'No, not that way!' She raised her arm and pointed to the other fork in the road. 'We must go that way,' she said, in as steady a voice as she could muster, considering her whole body was shaking.

'Begging yer pardon, miss, but down along there is where Colonel Randall ought to be, if he's anywhere,' said the soldier, pointing the other way.

Mary had turned in her saddle and wore the

look she'd seen on so many faces during her life. The look that told her she was an exasperating ninnyhammer.

'You said yourself,' Sarah replied haughtily, 'that you've already looked where you thought he ought to be and couldn't find him.'

At that moment Ben, who'd been running back and forth with his nose to the ground, suddenly let out a bark and ran a few paces down the road she'd just indicated. Then turned and looked over his shoulder as if to ask why they weren't following him.

'Even Ben thinks we ought to go that way,' she insisted.

And though they hadn't wanted to listen to her, they all seemed to have complete faith in Ben's instincts. To a man, they turned and followed him.

Leaving Mary no choice but to do so, too.

Sarah's stomach lurched again. Only this time it was from guilt. What if she was leading them in the wrong direction, simply because there didn't seem to be so many gruesome sights this way?

Mary was right to despise her. She wasn't strong and brave. Or even sensible. She should have just admitted that the sights and smells were proving too much for her. Except that, to admit to such weakness, in front of Mary and those men...

She didn't just have the Latymor nose. She had the wretched Latymor pride, too. That made her go to any lengths rather than admit she might have made a mistake.

Not that it had done her much good. For things were no better on this road, than they had looked on the one the scavenging dog had taken. The bright colours of uniforms lay stacked in heaps where the men who wore them had fallen, smeared now with mud and blood, and worse.

And there were pieces of uniforms, too, containing severed limbs. And bodies without heads. And horses screaming. And men groaning.

And Sarah's head was spinning.

And her heart was growing heavier and heavier.

Because she was finally seeing what war really meant. Men didn't die from neat little bullet wounds. Their bodies were smashed to pulp, torn asunder.

Oh, lord—if this had been what happened to Gideon, no wonder they hadn't sent his body to Antwerp. Justin might be overbearing, but it was always in a protective way. He wouldn't have wanted her, or Gussie, who was in such a delicate condition, to be subjected to the sight of Gideon, reduced to…to…*that*.

Just as it finally hit her that it might be true,

that Gideon might really be dead, one of the men gave out a great cry.

She looked up, to see Ben go bounding across a field to a sort of tumbledown building, round which even more bodies were stacked than by the side of the road.

'He's found him! The blessed dog's only gone and found him,' cried one of the men. And they all went charging up to the ruin.

Chapter Two

She heard somebody say *charnel house.*

Sarah's stomach lurched. She drew Castor to a halt as Ben scrabbled at the door of the barn until he found his way in.

'Justin is in there,' she cried in an agony of certainty. In the charnel house. Which meant he was dead. 'I know he is.'

'We shall see,' said Mary calmly, dismounting.

Sarah slid from her own horse, her legs shaking so much she had to cling to the pommel to stay upright.

'Here,' said Mary, thrusting her reins into her hands. 'You stay here and…and guard the horses while I go and see.'

Then, in a rather kinder tone, added, 'It might not even be him.'

But Sarah knew it was. Ben had scented…something. He'd ignored heaps and heaps of dead bodies. The dog wouldn't have barked so excitedly for no good reason.

And the Rogues hadn't come out yet, either.

It was her brother in there. In there, where Mary was going, her face composed, her demeanour determined and brave.

While the prospect of seeing Justin, her strong, forceful brother, lying lifeless—perhaps even torn to bits like so many of the poor wretches she'd seen scattered in heaps along the roads...

And then any pretence she was guarding the horses fled as blackness swirled round the edges of her vision. Eddied up from the depths of her, too, as the extent of her uselessness hit her. What point had there been in snatching up that bag of medical supplies when she'd fled Antwerp? Bridget, her old nursemaid, had told her she would need it. And Bridget had a way of *seeing* things. So yesterday, she'd imagined she was riding to Gideon's rescue, armed with the very herbs that he needed. But the truth was that Gideon was beyond anyone's help. And that she was so overset by the thought of seeing any of her brothers chopped and hacked about that she would have been no more use to Gideon than a...than a...

Actually, she would have been of no help to

Gideon at all. Just as she wasn't being of any help to Justin.

They were right about her—those people who wrote her off as a weak, empty-headed nuisance. All she'd done by coming here was create problems for everyone else. Gussie and Blanchards would be worried sick about her, and even though she'd promised Mary she wouldn't get in the way— Sarah groaned. She was growing more and more certain that she was either going to faint dead away, or cast up her accounts.

Well, she wasn't going to do it in front of Justin's men. Only a couple had stayed in the barn with Mary. The rest had come outside again, probably, she suspected, to keep an eye on their rather suspiciously magnificent horses.

There was a half-collapsed wall to her left, which would shield her from view if she was going to be sick. Which would conceal the evidence from the stalwart Mary, too, when she eventually came out.

If her legs would carry her that far…

They did. But only just. The effort of clambering over the lowest, most broken-down portion of the wall proved too much for both Lady Sarah's legs, and her stomach, which both gave way at the same time. She hadn't even gained the privacy she'd sought, either, because there was a group of peasant women busily ferreting amongst the rubble so they could rob the men who'd been partially buried under it.

They paused for a moment, but only a moment. With mocking, hard eyes, they dismissed her as being no threat as she retched fruitlessly, then calmly went back to stripping the corpse they'd just exhumed.

Or what had appeared to be a corpse. For suddenly, as the women turned him to ease the removal of his shirt, the man let out a great bellow, which both startled and scattered them.

Sarah gasped as he uttered a string of profanities. Not because of the words themselves, but because they were in English. His jacket, the one they'd just torn from his back, was blue, so she'd assumed he was French. But not only was he English, but his voice was cultured, his swearing fluent.

He was an officer.

And he was trying to get to his feet, though his face and shoulders were cloaked in blood.

Instinctively, she got to her feet, too, though with what aim she wasn't sure.

Until she saw one of the peasant women hefting a knife.

'No!' Sarah's fist closed round one of the stones that had once been part of the wall and, without thinking of the consequences, threw it as hard as she could at the woman who'd started to advance on the wounded man. She couldn't just stand there and let them rob him of his very life. It was unthinkable!

She'd been of no use to Gideon, but by God she wasn't going to stand back and let those women casually despatch another Englishman before her very eyes!

'Leave him alone,' she screamed, throwing another stone in their direction.

Rage and revulsion at what they were doing had her quivering with outrage now, instead of despair.

The women paused, eyeing her warily.

The man, too, turned his head when he heard her shout.

He stretched his hand towards her.

'Save me,' he groaned, then swayed and slowly toppled forward.

Oh, no! If he landed face down in the mud, that would finish him off as surely as the peasant woman's knife. Sarah flung herself in his path, arms outstretched as if to catch him. Though, of course, his weight proved too much for her. She landed with a wet thud on her bottom, the unconscious, half-naked officer half on top of her.

But at least he was still breathing.

For now. The peasant women were still hovering. And her legs were pinned in place by his dead weight.

Well, this was no time to hold her pride too dear. Throwing back her head, she screamed for help.

At once, there came a familiar, deep throaty bark.

The women ran for it as Ben came bounding over the wall, barking and baring his fangs, and looking gloriously, heart-warmingly ferocious.

Once he was satisfied the women weren't going to come back, Ben turned and licked her face just the once, then started nosing at the man who lay face down in her lap.

Because the women had managed to strip the officer of everything but his breeches and one boot before they fled, Sarah could clearly see that his back was a mass of bruises. His hair was matted to his scalp with blood, which was still oozing from a nasty gash. She didn't know how he was alive, but he was. He was.

And Ben seemed terribly excited by the fact. He kept nosing at the man, then prancing away, and barking, only to come back and nose at him, and lick him as though he knew him.

And it suddenly struck her that the Rogues uniform was blue. And that her brother was lying not ten yards away.

Was this another of his men? One of his officers, if the tone of his voice was anything to go by.

Oh, dear. Justin had refused to introduce any of his officers to her, when she'd tried to show a sisterly interest in his brigade, on the day of a mass review of all the Allied troops mustering around Brussels. He'd told her that they were decidedly not gentlemen and she was to have nothing to do with them. Gideon's commanding officer, Colonel Bennington Ffog, had gone so far as to describe them as the very dregs of humanity. They'd both be appalled if they could see her sprawled on the ground with his head in her lap.

Just as the thought occurred to her, she heard a scrabbling noise and looked up to see two of the Rogues who'd escorted her and Mary out here, pushing their way through the lowest bit of wall.

The first one to reach her knelt down and, without so much as a by-your-leave, turned the officer's face so he could peer at it closely.

'Strike me if it ain't the Major,' he said, confirming her suspicions.

'How'd 'e come to be out here?'

'Damned if I know,' said the First Rogue to reach her. 'Last I 'eard 'e'd come to and was going to make for the field hospital.'

'Well, 'e went the wrong way,' said the Second Rogue on the scene grimly. 'Looks like 'e 'ad a second go round with more Frenchies, too, else I don't see 'ow 'e come to get buried under that wall.'

'Lucky you come over this way, miss.' They'd been talking to each other, but now they both turned to her with what looked like gratitude. 'Else we'd never have guessed 'e was 'ere.'

'No.' She shook her head. 'No, I…really…' She'd only stumbled on him because of her appalling squeamishness. She didn't deserve their gratitude.

'Aye, but it was you as drove off them filthy bi-biddies, what would have finished off the Major,' said his companion, hunkering down beside her.

'It was Ben,' she said glumly. They hadn't been scared of *her* at all.

'You was the one that called him, though, wasn't you?'

Yes. Oh, very well, she had done one thing right today.

'And you stopped 'im from falling face down in the mud and like as not drowning in it.'

That was true, too. She felt a little better. Until she recalled that she hadn't been strong enough not to get knocked to the ground.

'Any way you look at it, you've saved Major Bartlett's life.'

'Major Bartlett?' She looked down at the motionless man whose head she cradled in her lap. This poor, broken, battered wretch was all that was left of Major Bartlett? He'd been so *handsome*. So full of…of, well, himself, actually. He'd been lounging against a tree, his jacket slung over one shoulder, watching her and Gideon ride past, on the day she'd learned who he was. She hadn't been able to help peering at him, her curiosity roused by Justin's vague warning.

And as if he'd known she was wondering what kind of things he'd done, to make Justin think she might be corrupted merely by talking to him, Major Bartlett had grinned at her.

And winked.

Oh, but he'd looked like a young lion, that day, basking in the sun, with his mane of golden curls tumbling over his broad brow.

So vitally *alive*.

Just like the last time she'd seen Gideon. Her

twin had been laughing as he preened before her mirror, telling her what a fine sight he was going to make on the battlefield. How she wasn't to worry about Frenchman wanting to shoot him, because they'd all be too busy riding up to enquire who'd made his exquisitely cut uniform.

Had anyone, she wondered, her lower lip quivering, held Gideon in their arms as he was dying? Or had he been left face down in the mud, because the only woman anywhere near was too worried about her reputation to go to his aid?

Her eyes welled with tears.

The Second Rogue cleared his throat. 'No need for tears, miss. You done well, leading us 'ere.'

'Aye, saved both 'im and yer brother, I reckon,' hastily put in the other, as though equally appalled by the prospect of being landed with a weeping female.

'Saved? My brother?' She blinked rapidly a few times. They weren't talking about Gideon. They didn't know him. They meant Justin. 'Your Colonel...is he...?'

'Stopped a bullet, but Miss Mary, she reckons as how she knows someone what can patch him up.'

'Oh, thank God. Thank God for Mary, anyway.' *She'd* been worse than useless.

'Aye, she's doing a grand job with 'is lordship, in there,' he said, jerking his head towards the barn, 'by all accounts.'

'Can you stay 'ere and keep an eye on the Major while we go and sort out 'ow we're going to get 'im and the Colonel back to Brussels?'

Exactly where they thought she might go, when she was pinned to the ground by a heavy, unconscious male, she had no idea.

But they were still crouched there, watching her, as though waiting for a response.

Did they really think she would try to wriggle out from under their major and leave him lying in a pool of mud?

With a little shock, she realised that it was what most people who knew her would expect. And what Justin would demand.

But she wouldn't leave a dog in a state like this. In fact, she hadn't. Yesterday, when she'd seen Ben trapped underneath an overturned wagon, she'd thought nothing of crawling under it to untie him from the broken axle, after pacifying him with bits of sausage, because she'd recognised him as the regimental mascot. And Randall's Rogues never left one of their own behind. Not that she was one of them, except by virtue of being Lord

Randall's sister, but if she couldn't turn her back on a dog, even a dog she feared might bite her, simply because he belonged to her brother's regiment, then she definitely couldn't do any less for one of his officers. It wouldn't even be as hard, in some ways. The dog had been so frantic with fear she was half-afraid he would bite her. This man could do nothing to her. He wasn't even conscious.

'Of course I can,' she snapped. 'I shall be fine.' Even though mud was steadily oozing up through the fabric of her riding habit, chilling her behind. Well, she wasn't going to take any harm from sitting in a puddle for a few minutes, was she? She was as healthy as a horse. Nor was it as if she was ever going to be able to wear this outfit again, after what she'd put it through the day before.

And at least she was shielding this poor wretch from one minor discomfort. Without her lap to lie on, he would have been frozen, never mind at risk from inhaling mud and drowning in it.

The two Rogues looked at each other and a message seemed to pass between them because, as one, they got to their feet.

'Dog will stay on guard,' said the Second Rogue. 'Dog. Stay.'

Ben promptly lay down, head on his paws,

just as though he completely understood the command.

'We'll get some transport fit for you, don't you worry,' said the First Rogue gruffly, before vaulting over the wall with his comrade.

She wasn't the least bit worried about how she was going to get back to Brussels. It was this poor man that needed all the help he could get. And her brother. Justin.

Oh, dear. Justin would be furious if he could see her now. Even Gideon had warned her to stay away from Major Bartlett. Although, Gideon being Gideon, he'd explained exactly why.

'For once I agree with Justin,' he'd said with a slight frown, when he'd caught the major winking at her. 'He's such an indiscriminate womaniser they call him Tom Cat Bartlett. The only reason he's out here in the Allée Verte this early in the morning is no doubt because he's slinking away from the bed of his latest conquest.'

On hearing that Bartlett was a rake, she'd put him out of her mind. She detested rakes. And she would never have willingly gone anywhere near him again. She sucked in a short, sharp, breath. For here she was, cradling his head in her lap, comparing him to her beloved brother Gideon, who'd warned her against him.

And yet, weren't they both soldiers, too? Wounded in the service of their country?

He certainly didn't *look* like a rake any more. If the men hadn't told her, she wouldn't have recognised him. The once-handsome face had become a grotesque, smoke-blackened, bloodied mask through which wild green eyes had stared at her.

Beseechingly.

Her heart jolted.

The poor man was in such a state that he'd thought she, who'd have just lost her breakfast beside the same wall that had buried him, if she'd been in any state to eat any, could help him.

He must be out of his mind.

'All right, miss?'

She looked up to see the two Rogues had returned, looking mighty pleased with themselves.

'We've got one of those French sick wagons,' one proclaimed. The other nudged him in the side, with a quick frown.

Oh…oh, dear. They'd obviously stolen it. Well, what could she expect, when robbery with violence was, according to Gideon, what Justin's men did best?

'Can't very well drape him over the back of an 'orse, miss. Jolting a man with a head wound would finish 'im off for sure.'

'Yes. Of course. I quite see that,' she said mildly, employing the vague smile that had stood her in good stead in so many awkward situations. It worked again. The men made no further attempt to justify their actions.

They just manoeuvred Major Bartlett off her lap and into the vehicle they'd parked on the other side of the wall—far more gently than she would have expected from men who acted and spoke so coarsely, and who'd just committed who knew what violence in order to ensure their officers had the best transport back to Brussels.

They'd no doubt go and fetch Mary now, so that she could oversee the journey and then their nursing. So Major Bartlett was off her hands.

She glanced down, then, and winced at the state of them. But there was a small stream not far away, she thought, where she could rinse them. Behind that thick border of rushes.

As she dabbled her bloodstained hands in the water, she wondered what she should do next. Gideon must be dead, she supposed, even though her whole being revolted against the notion. And Justin didn't need her to stay and nurse him. Mary would do a much better job. Besides, seeing his sister, when he came to himself—*if* he came to himself—would make him so furious it would probably cause an immediate relapse. He hadn't wanted her to come to Brussels at all. Had ordered her to leave, more than once.

There was nothing for it but to go back to Antwerp and explain herself. Her shoulders drooped as she pictured the scold Blanchards would give her for worrying his poor wife at such a critical stage. Gussie had suffered a couple of miscarriages early in her marriage and then, for some inexplicable reason, failed to become pregnant again for a worrying length of time. The Marquis of Blanchards was naturally very protective now that it was looking as though his wife might finally be about to present him with an heir. And his patience with Sarah had been wearing thin even before she'd run away. He hadn't minded taking her to Paris, when Gussie had suggested the trip. No, it wasn't until Bonaparte had fled Elba, and most of polite society had scurried back to England because France was no longer safe, that he'd begun to look at her sideways. For Gussie wouldn't have been so determined to go to Brussels if Sarah's twin hadn't been stationed there. Nothing, now, would prevent him from packing her off to England, where he could return her to Mama's care.

And he'd do so in such blistering terms that

Mama would marry her off to the very next person who applied for her hand, no matter what Sarah thought of him.

But what did it matter who they chose to take her off their hands? Without Gideon, she was only going to be able to live half a life, wherever she was. Whoever she was with.

Her head bowed, she made her way laboriously up the bank, picked her way though the mud and clambered over the wall.

'Ready, now, are you, miss?'

The First Rogue was standing at the rear of the wagon, his arms folded across his massive chest.

'If you will excuse me,' she said, lifting her chin and gesturing for him to step aside, 'I need to let Mary know that I am returning to Antwerp, so that she can inform Justin when he recovers.'

'Antwerp?' The man gave her a quick frown.

'Yes. If you wouldn't mind going to fetch my horse.'

The man gave her a dirty look and muttered something that sounded a bit unsavoury. She shrugged and went to look inside the wagon.

Only the Major was there.

'Just a moment,' she said. 'Before you go and fetch my horse—' which he'd shown no sign of doing as yet, anyway '—could you tell my why Justin isn't in here? And where is Miss Endacott?'

'Miss Endacott was adamant we wasn't to move the Colonel,' the Rogue growled. 'Not yet a while.'

'But the Major must have treatment. At once! Why, he's already been lying out all night, with an open wound. Somebody needs to clean him up and stitch him up.'

She'd been about to leave both men to Mary's care. But would Mary have the time to do anything for Major Bartlett if Justin was too poorly to even move? Besides, he'd begged her to save him. *Her.* Not pretty and practical Mary Endacott, but her.

Well, there was no question of riding off and leaving the Major behind, not now. She couldn't simply abandon him, hoping that somebody would do something for him. No matter what kind of man he was, he didn't deserve to be left untended. Perhaps to die of neglect. She wouldn't wish that fate on *any* man.

With half her mind troubled by the thought that might have been exactly what had happened to Gideon, she scrambled up into the back of the wagon.

'I will stay with the Major until we can get him

to a hospital,' she informed the rather startled Rogue.

She'd seen makeshift hospitals springing up outside the Namur gate. Wounded men had been staggering, or been carried, towards those with medical expertise even while the battle had been raging.

'I'll go and fetch your horse then, miss,' said Rogue One. 'Wouldn't do to leave a fine animal like that out here. Someone's bound to try to steal him.'

The other Rogue, who'd been leaning nonchalantly against the side of the wagon, shook his head as Rogue One darted off.

'Terrible amount of thieving goes on after a battle,' he observed drily as they waited for Rogue One to fetch not only Castor, but also the two horses they'd ridden to the battlefield, and tether them to the sides of the wagon. 'You wouldn't credit it.'

'Oh, wouldn't I?'

They both glanced up at the tart tone of her voice, then grinned at each other.

'Now look, miss,' said the one she'd come to think of as the First Rogue. 'The road is mortal bad. No matter how careful we drive, won't be able to help jolting the Major. You must do what you can to cushion his head.'

'Need both of us up here, see,' said the Second Rogue, 'making sure nobody thinks they can swipe this cart off of us to carry their own wounded.'

Which was all too real a threat, since it was clearly what they'd just done.

'Heaven forbid,' she said, smiling her vague smile again, then going to the head of the stretcher, just as they'd suggested.

She watched out of the corner of her eye as the First Rogue climbed into the driver's seat and took the reins, while the Second Rogue got up beside him and draped his musket across his knee.

She'd half-hoped Ben would jump up into the wagon with her, but he chose to run alongside, snarling at anyone who got too close.

It didn't seem to take half as long returning to Brussels as it had coming out. Which was probably because concentrating on the Major's welfare kept her mind, and her eyes, off the sights and smells that had disturbed her so much before.

Not that trying to prevent an unconscious man's head from coming to further harm was without

its own perils. Even though the wagon was well
sprung, it couldn't compensate for the churned-
up state of the road. Every time they went over a
particularly deep rut, Major Bartlett's head would
jolt no matter how firmly she thought she was
holding it in her hands.

Pretty soon, she wondered if the only way to really protect him would be to kneel on the floor,
wrap her arm about his neck and sort of cradle
him to her bosom.

The thought of doing so made her blush all over.
But then she chided herself for being so missish.
He wasn't taking liberties, after all. The poor man
had no idea where his nose would be pressed.

Just imagine if this had been Gideon, she told
herself sternly. Wouldn't she have cradled him to
her bosom, to prevent further injury during the
trip back to Brussels?

The sad fact was, she'd never know.

Her vision blurred for a second or two. But
she resolutely blinked back the tears, sniffed
and reminded herself that though Gideon was
past helping, this man wasn't. By some miracle,
he'd survived. So even though she hadn't found
Gideon, her search for him *hadn't* been a total
waste of time. She might not be good for much,

but she could at least prevent the Major from coming to any further harm as the wagon bounced along over the bumpy road.

It was one small thing, one practical thing she could do to stem the tide of death that had swept Gideon from her. Gritting her teeth and consigning her gown to perdition, she wrapped her arms round Major Bartlett's neck and held his bloodied head as tight as she could.

Chapter Three

The scene that greeted her when they reached the makeshift hospital was one of chaos.

She clambered out of the wagon, and went to the driver's seat to speak to the Rogues.

'This is awful,' she said, indicating the men with terrible injuries who were lying groaning all over the ground, flies buzzing round open wounds.

'Aye, well it's like this, miss,' said the First Rogue. 'Surgeons are too busy hacking off the arms and legs of the poor b-blighters they think they can save to bother with the ones who lie still and quiet, like our Major. They put those to the back of the queue. And by the time they get round to them, well, mostly there's no need for them to try anything any more.'

'We can't leave the Major here,' she said, appalled. 'Do you know of some other hospital we can take him to? A proper, civilian hospital? Where he can get the treatment he needs?'

The First Rogue scratched his chin. 'Hospitals in town are all full as they can hold. Saw them laying the wounded out in the park and all along the sides of the streets, too. And that was before we come out 'ere. Gawd alone knows what it'll be like by now.'

'Well, what about taking him back to his lodgings, then? His man could help, couldn't he?' Justin's own body servant, Robbins, was always tending Justin when he was wounded. Gideon had told her so.

'His man's used up,' said the Second Rogue brusquely.

She'd heard Justin apply that term to the butcher's bill after a battle. He didn't speak of his troops dying, but of being used up.

'What are we to do with him, then?' It never occurred to her, not for one moment, to simply mount Castor, ride away and leave him. In some weird way, it felt that if she just left the Major's fate in the hands of providence, it would be tantamount to submitting to the horrid inevitability of death itself.

Which would somehow dishonour Gideon's memory.

'You've got all those medical supplies in yer bags,' said Rogue Two.

'How…how did you know?'

He shrugged. 'Had a look.'

He'd gone through her saddlebags, while she'd been climbing over the wall, and throwing stones at the looters? Or had it been later, when she was washing her hands in the stream?

'I didn't take nothing,' he protested.

'Look, it's plain as a pikestaff you've been sent here to save our Major,' said Rogue One. 'If you nurse him, there's a chance he'll pull through.'

'Me? But…' She thought of the wounds covering his body, not to mention the huge tear across his scalp.

Then she saw their faces harden. Take on a tinge of disappointment. Of disapproval.

Of course, they wouldn't believe she didn't feel *capable* of nursing their Major. They had no idea how inadequate she felt. They would just think she was too high and mighty to lower herself to their level.

'I suppose I could try,' she explained. 'I mean, the little I might be able to do is bound to be better than nothing, isn't it?'

'I took a gander when we put 'im in the wagon,' said Rogue Two. 'His skull ain't broke. A lady like you could stitch him up as nice as any doctor. And then it'll just be nursing he needs.'

'Plenty of drink,' said Rogue One. 'Get all his wounds clean.'

'We'll help you with that. Lifting him and turning him and such.'

They made it sound so simple.

They made it sound as though she was perfectly capable of taking charge of a severely wounded man.

Her heart started hammering in her chest.

Perhaps she really could do it. After all, they'd said they'd help her. And now she came to think of it, hadn't she already done much, much more than anyone would ever have thought possible? She'd reached Brussels unaccompanied when everyone else was fleeing the place. She'd rescued the snarling, snapping Ben from the teetering wreckage of a baggage cart. She'd ignored the Hussars and made her own judgement about whether the French were about to overrun Brussels, and been right. She'd even stood up to those women who'd been trying to murder poor Major Bartlett. And that after riding across a battlefield without totally fainting away.

And she *could* sew.

And even though she'd never nursed anyone in

her life, she had listened most attentively to every word of Bridget's advice, because she'd believed she *was* going to be nursing Gideon. Marigold was for cleansing wounds to stop them from putrefying. Comfrey was for healing cuts. And apparently she could make a sort of tea from the dried meadowsweet flowers, which was less bitter and nasty than willow bark and almost as effective at reducing fever.

Poor Gideon wouldn't need any of that, now. He was beyond anyone's help.

But this man had fallen, literally, into her lap.

Had begged her to save him.

And there was nobody else to do it. He had nobody.

Just as she had nobody.

Well, she thought, firming her lips, he might not know it, but he had *her*.

'Very well, then,' she said, clambering back into the wagon. 'I will do my best. We'll take him to my lodgings.'

She'd already begun to prove, at least to herself, that she wasn't that fragile girl whose only hope, so her entire family believed, was in finding some man to marry her and look after her.

This was her chance to prove to them, too, that

she didn't need anyone to look after her. On the contrary!

With her head held high, she gave the Rogues her direction, then knelt down to cushion the Major's head against her breasts once more for the remainder of the journey.

Pretty soon they were drawing up outside a house on the Rue de Regence, unloading the Major by means of the stretcher with which the cart was equipped and banging on the door for entry.

'Oh, my lady,' cried Madame le Brun. 'You found him then? You found your brother?'

The men holding the stretcher glanced at her, then looked straight ahead, their faces wiped clean of expression.

Sarah blinked.

The night before, when she'd turned up frightened, and bedraggled, clutching Castor's reins for dear life, she'd told Madame le Brun how she'd run away from Antwerp to search for her twin, because she'd heard a rumour he'd been killed, but refused to believe it. She'd explained that she'd returned to her former lodgings because she hadn't known where else to spend the night, with the outcome of the battle currently raging still being so uncertain. The house where Lord Blanchards had rented rooms when Brussels had been the centre of a sort of cosmopolitan social whirl might not have been in the most fashionable quarter of town, but it was well kept and respectable. And Madame le Brun had been a very motherly sort of landlady.

It would be terrible to lie to her. Sarah hated people who told lies and she avoided telling them herself. Yet there was a difference, she'd always found, in letting people assume whatever they liked. Particularly if the absolute truth would cause too much awkwardness.

'He is very gravely wounded,' she therefore told Madame le Brun, neatly sidestepping the issue of his identity altogether.

'I shall be nursing him myself, so it will be best to put him in my room. The room I had when I was here before.' She smiled vaguely in Madame's direction, but spoke to the men. 'Careful how you get him up the stairs.'

At that moment Ben provided a welcome diversion by attempting to follow them inside.

'Oh, no. This I cannot have,' shrieked Madame le Brun, making shooing motions at the dog, who'd acquired an extra layer of mud since the last time she'd seen him. 'The stables! The stables is the place for the animals.'

Ben took exception to anyone trying to get between him and the three members of his adopted pack who were already mounting the stairs. He bared his teeth at the landlady, and growled.

In the ensuing fracas, the Rogues manoeuvred the stretcher up the stairs and into Sarah's old room. And no more questions were asked about the wounded man's identity. By the time the landlady, the dog and Sarah caught up, in a welter of snapping teeth and loudly voiced recriminations, the Rogues had got their Major on to her bed.

'Madame,' said Sarah, 'we can settle the question of what to do with the dog, who as you can see is very devoted to his master, later, can we not? What we really need, right now, is plenty of fresh linen, and hot water, and towels.'

Even though she hadn't actually ever nursed anyone before, it was obvious that the first thing they needed to do was get the poor man cleaned up.

'Oh, *le pauvre*,' said Madame le Brun, crossing herself as she caught her first proper sight of the Major's battered and semi-clothed body. 'Fresh sheets, yes, and water and towels, too. Of course. Though the dog…'

'Yes, yes, I promise you I will deal with the dog, too. He won't be any bother. But please...' Sarah allowed her eyes to fill with tears as she indicated Major Bartlett's body.

'Very well, my lady. Though I cannot think it is right for an animal so dirty to be in the room with one so badly hurt...'

'The dog it was as found him,' put in the First Rogue.

'Yes, we owe Ben a great deal,' said Sarah.

Madame le Brun grumbled about the invasion of her property by such a large, fierce and dirty dog, but she did so on her way out the door.

Sarah could hardly believe she'd won that battle. Why, only the night before, she'd cowered in the stables because Madame wouldn't let the dog in the house, and Sarah had been afraid that someone trying to escape Brussels before the French forces arrived might try to steal her horse. She'd been too timid to do more than wheedle a blanket and some paper and ink from Madame. Today she'd got the dog *and* a wounded officer right into her very bedroom.

It was a heady feeling.

Which lasted only as long as it took for her to notice that the Rogues were intent on stripping the Major of his clothes. They'd already pulled off his one remaining boot. Ben pounced on it and bore it off to the hearthrug, from which vantage point he could keep an eye on proceedings while having a good chew.

'You'll be wanting to fetch those medical supplies, I shouldn't wonder,' the First Rogue suggested gruffly, pausing in the act of undoing the Major's breeches. 'While we start getting him cleaned up a bit.'

'Yes, yes, I shall do that,' she said in a voice that sounded rather high-pitched to her own ears. She turned away swiftly and scurried out of the room, thoroughly relieved the man had offered her a good excuse for making herself scarce.

She pressed her hands to her hot cheeks once she'd shut the bedroom door behind her. Her legs were shaking a bit, but she *wasn't* going to succumb to a fit of the vapours just because she'd almost seen a man have his breeches removed.

She forced her legs to carry her to the head of the stairs and made her rather wobbly way down. She was going to have to get used to a lot more than glimpses of a man's, well, manliness in the days to come, if she was going to be of any use.

In fact, she was going to have to breach practically every rule by which she'd lived. She'd always taken such pains to keep her reputation spotless that she'd never been without a chaperon, not even when visiting the ladies' retiring room at a ball. She could scarcely believe she'd just encouraged two hardened criminals to install the regiment's most notorious rake in her bedroom—nay, her very bed.

Where he was currently being stripped naked.

Oh, lord, what would people think? Actually, she knew very well what they would think. What they would say, if they found out.

Right, then. She squared her shoulders as she marched across the yard to the stables. She'd better think of some way of preventing anyone finding out what she was doing, or they'd all be up in arms.

At least all the gossipy society people she knew from London had fled Brussels. She'd seen many of the most inquisitive in Antwerp. Even if any of them had remained, Madame le Brun thought Major Bartlett was actually her brother, so she *couldn't* let anything slip.

And as for Justin... She chewed on the inside of her lower lip, as it occurred to her he might still be in that tumbledown barn, too gravely ill to move, let alone worry about what his flighty little sister was getting up to. Actually, he might have no idea she'd returned to Brussels, if he was still unconscious. Not that she wanted him to re-main unconscious.

She bowed her head and uttered a silent, but heartfelt, prayer. And immediately felt a deep as-surance that Justin couldn't be in more capable hands. Moreover, even when he began to recover, Mary wasn't likely to mention anything that might hamper his recovery.

She retrieved the medicine pouch, then made her way back to the house, feeling sorrier than ever for poor Major Bartlett. Having to rely on such as her. Nobody, not by the wildest stretch of imagination, would ever describe *her* as capable.

A crushing sense of inadequacy made her pause outside her bedroom door. For on the other side of it lay an immense set of challenges. All wrapped up in the naked, helpless body of a wounded sol-dier.

She pressed her forehead to the door. She'd al-ready decided she wasn't going to be one of those people who thought propriety was more important than a man's very survival. But even so, it wasn't easy to calmly walk into a room that contained two rough soldiers and a naked man.

What if she tried to think of this as a sickroom, rather than her own bedroom, though? And of Major Bartlett as just a wounded soldier, rather than a naked and dangerous rake? Her patient, in fact. Yes—yes, that was better. She wasn't, primarily, a woman who'd been forbidden to so much as speak to him, but his *nurse*.

It made it possible for her to knock on the door, at any rate. And, when a gruff voice told her she could come in, Sarah found that she could look across at the Major with equanimity—well, *almost* with equanimity. Because he wasn't lying in *her* bed. He was in his sickbed. All she had to do was carry on in this vein and she'd soon be able to convince herself she wasn't a sheltered young lady who regarded all single men as potential predators, but a nurse, as well.

A nurse, moreover, who'd promised, when his men had begged for her help, that she would do her best.

In her absence, Madame had fetched water and towels. And the men had put them to good use, to judge from the mounds of bloodied cloths on the floor.

'He ain't so bad as he looked,' said the First Rogue. 'A lot of bruising and cuts to his back where the wall fell on him, but nothing broken, not even his head.'

'Really 'as got nine lives, 'as the Tom C—' The

Second Rogue broke off mid-speech, but Sarah knew perfectly well what he'd been about to say.

Well, well. Perhaps he hadn't only gained that nickname because of his nocturnal habits. Perhaps a good deal of it was down to him having more than his fair share of luck, too.

'Sooner we can get it sewn up the better,' put in the First Rogue hastily, as though determined to fix her attention on the man's injuries, rather than his reputation. 'Cut right down to the bone, he is.'

They were looking at her expectantly.

Oh, yes. They'd said that she ought to do the sewing, hadn't they?

'I...' She pressed one hand to her chest. In spite of the lecture she'd given herself, about proving how capable she was, now that it came to it, her heart was fluttering in alarm. At this point, Mama would fully expect her to have a fit of the vapours, if she hadn't already done so because there was a naked man in her room.

'You can do it, miss,' said the Second Rogue. 'Far better than us clumsy b... Uh—' he floundered '—blighters.'

'I don't know how,' she admitted, though she was ashamed to sound so useless.

'We'll direct you. And hold the Major still, in case he comes round.'

Yes. Yes they would need to do that. The pain of having his head sewn back together might well rouse him from his stupor. After all, hadn't he roused once before, when the looters had been tearing off his shirt?

'I can't...'

'Yes, you can, miss.'

She smiled ruefully at the man. 'I was going to say I can't go on thinking of you as Rogue One and Rogue Two, like characters in a play. You must have names? I am Lady Sarah.' She held out her hand to Rogue One. 'How do you do?'

He took her proffered hand and shook it. 'Dawkins, Lady Sarah.'

'Cooper,' said the other with a nod, though rather than shaking her hand, he pressed a pair of scissors into it. 'You need to start by trimming his hair back as short as you can get it, round the sabre cut,' he said.

'S-sabre cut?'

'Cavalry sabre, I reckon,' said Cooper. 'Only thing that would knock him out and slice the scalp near clean off like that, all in one go.'

I will not be sick. I will not be sick.

'Do you think he would prefer it,' she said brightly, in a desperate attempt to turn the conversation in a less grisly direction, 'if I cut it short all over? Only he will look so very odd, shorn in patches, when the bandages come off, won't he?'

'Time enough for that when he's better, miss.'

Yes, but keeping up a conversation was still a good idea. She was less likely to either faint, or be sick, if she could keep at least a part of her mind off the grisly task she was having to perform.

'Yes, of course,' she said, ruthlessly snipping away the matted curls. Lord, but it seemed like a crime to hack away at such lovely hair. Not that it looked lovely any more. She felt a pang at a sudden memory of how glorious it had looked, with the sunlight glinting on it, that day in the Allée Verte. She'd never imagined a day would come when she'd be running her fingers through it. Not for *any* reason.

'We can ask him how he wants it done when he's better, can't we? Perhaps get a barber in to do something that will disguise this hideous crop I'm giving him.'

She laughed a little hysterically. Then swallowed.

'It is amazing what a professional *coiffeuse* can do, you know.' *Snip.* 'Even with hair like mine.' *Snip, snip.* 'It is completely straight, normally. It takes hours of fussing, from a terribly expensive woman, with her special lotions and a hot iron, before Mama considers me fit to venture out of doors. And it takes such a long time to prepare me for a ball that I have gained the reputation for being dreadfully vain.'

She must sound it, too, prattling on about styling her hair, at a time like this. Except that with her mind full of hairdressers, and ballrooms, somehow it was easier to cope with the grim reality of what she was doing.

'Reckon that'll do now, miss,' said Cooper, gently removing the scissors from her fingers and handing her a needle and thread.

'Th-thank you.' She was sure her face must be white as milk. Her lips had gone numb. And her hands were trembling.

Could she actually puncture human flesh with this needle? She shut her eyes. If only she could keep them shut until it was over.

Or if only Harriet were here. For Harriet—who'd had the benefit of an expensive education—would simply snatch the needle from her hand with an impatient shake of her head and say *she'd* better take charge, since everyone knew Sarah was far too scatterbrained to nurse a sick man.

But Harriet wasn't here. And backing out of the task was unacceptable. She'd just be proving she was as weak and cowardly as everyone expected her to be.

Everyone except Gideon. *You show 'em*, she could almost hear him saying. *Show 'em all what you're made of.*

'Al…Always victorious,' she muttered, under her breath. 'That's our family motto,' she explained to the men, when she opened her eyes and saw them looking at her dubiously. She'd chanted it to herself all the way from Antwerp, the day before, to stop herself from turning back. Had whispered it, like a prayer, when she'd been cowering in the stable with her horse, to give herself heart.

'Motto of our unit, too,' grunted Cooper.

'Of course, of course it is,' she said, taking a deep breath and setting the first stitch. 'Justin—that is Lord Randall, your colonel—he took the words from our family coat of arms, didn't he? From the Latin, which is *Semper Laurifer.* Sounds like laurel, doesn't it? And we do have laurel leaves on our family coat of arms. I suppose whoever took that motto did so for the play on words. Laurel. Laurifer. After a long-ago battle. Because there have always been soldiers in our family. And I dare say plenty of earlier Latymor ladies have had to stitch up wounds. I can almost feel them looking over my shoulder now, encouraging me to keep up the family tradition.'

She was babbling. In a very high-pitched voice. But somehow, reciting family history, whilst imagining the coat of arms and all her doughty ancestors, helped to take her mind off the hideous mess into which her fingers were delving.

'G-Gideon told me that in the case of your unit, Justin, I mean Lord Randall, said you could use whatever means necessary to ensure you always won. Which sounds rather ruthless, even for him. I found it very hard to believe the things he said my stuffy, autocratic big brother got up to during the Peninsula campaign. But Gideon was so full of admiration for the sheer cheek of the way he went behind enemy lines, blowing things up, smashing things down and generally causing mayhem.'

'Confounding the French, the Colonel called it,' said Dawkins.

'And that's how you got the name of Randall's Rogues,' she said, glancing at the unconscious Major's face. He'd been with Justin, doing all those things that had made Gideon green with envy. *'I know it is far more fashionable to belong to a cavalry regiment like mine,'* he'd grumbled, *'but what I wouldn't give to have command of a*

*troop like Justin's. That's the kind of officer I want
to be. One who can take the refuse from half-a-
dozen other regiments and forge them into something unique.'*

He might not have wanted this man to get anywhere near her, but Gideon had admired him, in
a way. He was just the kind of officer Gideon had
wished he could have been.

'Not much longer now, miss,' said Dawkins
kindly, as her gaze lingered on the Major's face,
reluctant to return to the ghastly wound she was
supposed to be tending. 'You're doing a grand
job.'

'Yes,' she said with a shudder. Then took a deep
breath. 'I've decided,' she said, getting back to
work, 'that if the men in my family can go about
claiming they can do whatever they like to make
sure they come out victorious, because of a couple of words engraved on the coat of arms, then
so can I. From now on, I will be Always Victorious. In this case—' she swallowed as she set yet
another stitch '—I will do my best for this poor
wretch. If, for example, I am going to be sick, I
will do so *after* I've finished patching his scalp
back together.'

'That you will, miss,' Dawkins agreed.

Though miraculously, and to her immense relief, she wasn't sick at all. True, she did stagger away from the bed and sink weakly on to a chair while the men slathered a paste that smelled as if it consisted mostly of comfrey, on to the seam she'd just sewn.

She wished she had some brandy. Not that she'd ever drunk any, but people said it steadied the nerves. And she certainly needed it. Needed something...

'We'll go and fetch the Major's traps now, miss,' said Dawkins as soon as they'd finished covering her handiwork with bandages.

'What?' And leave her here, all alone, in sole charge of a man who looked as though he was at death's door?

'You won't be long, will you?'

'No, but—' They exchanged another of their speaking looks. Oh, lord, what news were they going to break to her this time?

'We'll be back with his things in no time at all, miss. But we can't stay after that. We have to re-port back.'

Her heart sank. When they said they'd help her, she'd thought they meant until he was fully recov-ered. But they had only spoken of lifting him and cleaning him up, hadn't they? And they weren't civilians who could come and go as they pleased.

If they didn't report to someone in authority, they would run the risk of being treated as deserters.

'Yes. Of course you do.'

'Nothing to do for him now but nursing, anyhow. You can do that as well as anyone. Better, probably.'

She leapt to her feet. 'No. I mean…I have never nursed anyone. Ever. I am not trying to back out of it, it's just that I won't really know what to do,' she cried, twisting her hands together to hide the fact they were shaking. 'What must I do?'

'Whatever he needs to make him comfortable.'

'You've got meadowsweet to make a tea to help bring down the fever, if you can get him to drink it.'

'Fever?'

'He's been lying outside in the muck, with an open wound all night, miss. Course he's going to have a fever.'

Oh, dear heaven.

'Bathe him with warm water, if that don't work.'

'And if he starts shivering, cover him up again,' said Dawkins with a shrug, as though there was nothing to it.

For the first time in her life—she swallowed—she was going to have to cope, on her own, without the aid of a maid, or a footman, or anyone.

But hadn't she always complained that nobody trusted her do anything for herself? Now she had the chance to prove her worth, was she going to witter and wring her hands, and wail that she couldn't do it?

She was not. She was going to pull herself together and get on with it.

'Give him the medicine,' she repeated, albeit rather tremulously, 'bathe him if he gets too hot, cover him if he gets too cold. Anything else?'

'Landlady will have a man about the house to help when he needs to relieve himself, I dare say.'

Yes. Of course she would. There were a number of servants flitting about the place. She *wouldn't* be all alone.

'And we'll tell the company surgeon where the Major is, so he can come and have a look.'

'Oh.' That would be a relief.

'But don't think he'll do anything you couldn't do yourself, miss,' said Dawkins.

'And don't let him tell you the Major should be in a hospital,' said Cooper vehemently. 'They won't look after him proper there.'

Coming from Cooper, that was quite a compliment. He'd been eyeing her askance every time she felt faint. His hostility had actually braced her, once or twice, just as much as Dawkins's kindness and encouragement had. Because every time Cooper looked as though he expected her to fail, it made her more determined to prove she wouldn't.

And now, to hear him say he trusted her to give the Major better care than he'd get in a hospital, made something in her swell and blossom.

'I won't let you down,' she vowed. 'I won't let him down.'

With a parting nod, the men left.

'Oh, goodness gracious,' she said, sinking on to the chair again. 'Whatever have I let myself in for?'

Chapter Four

The guns had ceased. The battle was over, then. Won or lost. Leaving the field to the dead and dying. And the crows.

Flocks of them. Tearing at his back. His head. They'd go for his eyes if they could get at them.

No! He flung his arm up to protect his eyes. And felt considerable surprise that he could move it. Hadn't been able to move at all before. They'd buried him. Tons of rock, tumbling down, crushing him so he could scarcely breathe, let alone fend off the crows.

Who had dug him out of his grave? He hadn't been able to save himself. He'd tried. Strained with all his might. He'd broken out into a sweat, that was all, and dragged blackness back round him in a smothering cloak.

But he'd be safer under the earth. Crows

wouldn't be able to get their claws into him any more. Or their beaks.

'Put me back in the ground,' he begged.

'Don't be silly,' came a rather exasperated-sounding voice.

'But I'm dead.' Wasn't he? Above the ringing in his ears he'd heard the other damned souls all round him, begging for mercy. Begging for water.

Because it was so hot on the edge of the abyss.

Or was it powder caking his mouth, his nostrils, so that everything stank of sulphur?

'Is it crows, then, not demons?' He'd thought they were wraiths, sliding silently between the other corpses scattered round him. But he'd seen knives flashing, silencing the groans. Sometimes they'd looked just like battlefield looters, not Satan's minions.

But whoever, or whatever it had been before, they'd got their claws deep into what was left of him now.

'There are no crows in here,' came the voice again. 'No demons, either. Only me. And Ben.'

Something cool glided across his brow.

He reached up and grabbed hold of what turned out to be a hand. A human hand. Small, and soft, and trembling slightly.

'Don't let them take me. Deserve it. Hell. But

please…' He didn't know why he was begging. Nobody could save him. He'd begged before, for mercy, just like all the others. Or would have done if he'd been able to make a sound. He'd understood then that he wasn't even going to be permitted one final appeal. He'd had to stay pinned there, reflecting on every sin he'd committed, remembering every man he'd killed, every act of wanton destruction he'd engineered.

'Nobody's going to take you. I won't let them.'

The voice had a face, this time. The face of an angel. Though—he knew her. She was…she was…

His head hurt too much to think. Only knew he'd seen her before.

That's right—for a moment, just one, the power of speech had returned. And he'd begged *her* to save him. It had something to do with the darkness ebbing and hearing the sound of birdsong, and working out that he couldn't be dead yet, because birds didn't sing in hell, and that if he wasn't dead, then there was still hope. And though there had been all those great black creatures clawing at him, tearing at his clothes, he'd found the strength to make one last, desperate stand.

And *she'd* been there. She'd driven them away. Told them to leave him be. And they'd gone, the whole flock of them. Flapping away on their great ugly wings. And he'd fallen into her arms...

Hazy, what came next. She'd carried him away, somehow, from the mud and the stench. Pillowed on cushions of velvet, soft as feathers.

Was she an angel, then? There seemed no other logical reason to account for it. Beautiful women didn't suddenly materialise on battlefields and carry dying men away. Which meant he'd been right in the first place.

He was dead.

'Did you fly?' How else could she have carried him here? Besides, she was an angel, wasn't she? Angels had wings. Only hers weren't black, like the crows. But blue. Palest blue, like sky after the rain had washed it clean.

'Oh, dear, oh, dear,' the angel sobbed.

'Why are you weeping? I'm not worth it.'

'I'm not weeping.' The angel sniffed.

'If I'm dead, why does it still hurt so much?' he groaned. 'Look, they know my soul belongs to their master. That's why they're clawing at me. Perhaps you should just let me go. No need to cry, then.'

'No! And it's not claws. It's your wounds. Here, try to drink some more of this. It will help with the pain.'

Her arm was under his neck, lifting his head. And she pressed a cup to his lips.

More? She'd given him a drink before?

Ah, yes. He did remember wishing someone would give him something to drink. The thirst had been worse than the pain, in that other place. He'd understood that bit in the bible, then, about the rich man begging Lazarus to dip even one finger in water and cool his tongue. And known, too, that like the rich man he deserved his torment. He'd earned his place in hell.

But his throat was no longer raw. His tongue wasn't stuck to the roof of his mouth. And he could speak.

So she must have given him water, before. Couldn't have been anyone else. Nobody else gave a damn.

'I was so thirsty.' And now he was tired. Too tired to drink any more. Or speak. Or even think.

It was the longest night of Sarah's life. He'd been lying there quietly enough until the Rogues left her on her own with him. But from the moment the door shut on them, it seemed to her, he hadn't given her a moment's peace.

Not that it was his fault, poor wretch. He couldn't help starting to come out of his deep swoon. Or being thirsty, or hot, or uncomfortable. Only it was such a tremendous responsibility, caring for someone as ill as that. It was almost impossible to get more than a sip or two of the meadowsweet tea between his lips. And sponging him down didn't seem to help for more than a minute or two. And then only at first. As the night wore on, his fever mounted and he started muttering all sorts of peculiar, disjointed things about hell, and demons, and thrashing about in the bed, as though trying to dig his way out from under some crushing weight.

And it was downright scary when he started speaking to her in that clear, lucid voice, in such a bizarrely confused manner.

The only thing that calmed him was to answer him as though he *was* making sense. To assure him that he wasn't already in hell, whether he deserved it or not. And to promise she wasn't going to let him die.

She would have promised him anything if only he would lie quietly and let her sleep. She was so *tired*. She'd hardly slept the night before, in the stable, she'd been so scared. Nor the night before that, she'd been in such a state over the report of Gideon's death.

Yet, when Madame le Brun came in to ask how

her brother was getting on, and if she wanted to take a short break, she found she was unable to leave him for long.

She was glad to have a meal, for she hadn't eaten a thing all day. And she did feel better for a wash and a change of clothes. But once she'd seen to her immediate needs, she couldn't rest for worrying about the Major.

Not that she must think of him as the Major, she decided, as she went to take Madame le Brun's place at his bedside. If he really had been her brother, she would have thought of him as… What was his first name? They called him Tom Cat, so the chances were it was Tom. Well, that was what she must call him, for now. The truth would come out soon enough. The truth about his real identity. And his real name if it wasn't Tom. And it wasn't as if it would make any difference to him what she called him, the state he was in tonight.

His eyes flicked open, yet again.

'It's so hot. Are you sure…?'

'Quite sure. This isn't hell. It's Brussels,' she said, dipping the cloth in a basin of tepid water on the bedside table, then smoothing it over his face, his neck and his chest. Though it didn't seem to be doing much good. His skin felt hotter than ever.

'But you are my guardian angel, aren't you?' he said hopefully. Then groaned and shook his head.

'Can't be. Wretches like me don't deserve guardian angels.'

'Everyone has a guardian angel,' she put in hastily. 'Whether they deserve one or not.'

And if that were true, then she was exactly the sort of guardian angel someone as sinful as Tom probably would get. The sort who wasn't sure what she was doing. And who was terrified of the responsibility. The sort who simply didn't measure up. Second-best.

She was even wearing second-hand clothes. Madame le Brun had insisted she couldn't nurse Major Bartlett wearing her muddy riding habit and had lent her one of the *femme de chambre*'s gowns. Jeanne wasn't as tall as Sarah—well, very few women were. And Jeanne was a bit more stout. So that the gown both hung off her, yet was too small at the same time. It was a perfect example of all that was wrong with her situation.

If only she hadn't been in such a hurry when she'd left Antwerp. If only she'd stopped to pack at least a nightgown. Irritably, she dashed away the single tear that slid down her cheek. How could she be crying over the lack of a nightgown, or anything else of her own to change into come morning, when poor Major Bartlett—no, she had to think of him as Tom—was fighting for his very life?

It was everything that had happened over the last few days catching up with her, that was what it was, *not* the lack of decent clothing. Ever since the night of the Duchess of Richmond's ball she'd done nothing but dash from one place to another, in a state bordering on panic. Leaving a trail of personal possessions in her wake.

She could weep when she thought of the trunks and trunks stuffed full of clothes she'd bought during her brief stay in Paris, all stacked in her cramped little room in Antwerp.

If only she could write to Gussie and ask her to send her things here. But that simply wasn't possible. For one thing she didn't want Gussie to know exactly where she was, or what she was doing, because it would worry her. And anyway, Gussie wouldn't send what she needed. She'd send Blanchards instead, with strict instructions to bring her back to safety. Which would mean poor Major—poor Tom—would be left to the care of strangers. Well, technically she was a stranger, too, but he'd asked *her* to look after him. Not Madame le Brun. Or anyone else. Not even Mary Endacott.

And he was staring at her in a fixed, glazed way as though she was his only hope.

'Drink this,' she said, in as calm a voice as she could, holding a cup of meadowsweet tea to his lips. Meek as a lamb, he opened his mouth and swallowed.

Because he trusted her. He didn't care that she had no experience. Was too feverish to notice what she was wearing. Unlike that day in the park, when he'd run a connoisseur's eye over the riding habit she'd just obtained from Odette, the brilliant dressmaker they'd discovered in a little street off the Place de la Monnaie.

Oh, my goodness! She'd placed an order with Odette only last week—and Blanchards had been in such a hurry to get them on to the barge bound for Antwerp last Friday that he hadn't let her go to collect it. She placed Tom's empty cup on the bedside table, watching his eyelids droop, though her mind was on all those gowns awaiting collection from the shop. She could very easily send a message to the modiste, requesting immediate delivery of everything that was ready and include a list of all the other items she needed, too. Stockings and stays and petticoats and so forth. No doubt the bill for doing her shopping would be steep, but then when had she ever had to worry about money? Not even the management of it. Justin, as head of the family, took care of all that side of things, so that all she had to do was send her bills to whomever he'd appointed to take care of her day-to-day needs. At the moment, it was Blanchards.

That thought brought a grim sort of smile to her lips as she went to the writing desk and turned up the lamp. He'd already written, in response to the explanation she'd scrawled as she'd been cowering in the stable, with Castor in the next stall and Ben at her feet. And his letter had been so horrid and unfeeling she'd crumpled it up and thrown it in the kitchen fire on her way back from fetching the medicine pouch. He'd totally ignored her attempt to reassure Gussie she was safe. He'd accused her of having no consideration for her sister's delicate condition, of *flitting off to Brussels on a wild goose chase,* and ordered her to come back, without once acknowledging it might be the depth of grief she felt over losing Gideon that had sparked her rash behaviour.

He hadn't let Gussie know she wasn't in Antwerp at all. Because of his over-protective nature, he'd simply told his wife Sarah was *with friends* and would *return soon.*

Oh, but she could just see his face, when her

bills started turning up in Antwerp. He would be so vexed with her for disobeying his order to return. Doubly vexed at not being able to tell Gussie why he was annoyed, since he'd kept Sarah's whereabouts secret.

Well, she sniffed, that served him right for keeping secrets from his wife. No man should try to deceive his wife, not even if he thought it was for her own good. Indeed, she was teaching him a valuable lesson.

As well as proving that she could manage without him. That she could manage *fine* without him.

Tom blinked at the angel's fierce profile as she dipped her pen into the inkwell and wrote something down. Her golden hair glowed, the way he'd seen angels in churches glow when the sun shone through the stained-glass windows.

'You've even got a halo,' he said.

She looked up, startled, and dropped her pen.

'I'm disturbing your writing. Is it important?' But, of course, it must be important. Anything an angel wrote was bound to be important. 'Sorry.'

'You don't need to be sorry. It's just a list.'

'Of my sins?' Then he *would* be sorry. 'Have you got enough paper?'

She came close. Floated towards him on a violet-scented cloud.

'I have plenty of paper, thank you.'

She sat on a chair next to his bed. The wicker work creaked.

He was in a bed. She was on a chair. He frowned.

'This is a strange sort of hell.'

'That's because it isn't hell,' she said in that clipped, practical voice he was coming to recognise. 'It's Brussels.'

'Not hell? Why not?'

'Never you mind why not,' she said sternly. 'Come on, drink some of this.'

'Why?'

'It will make you feel better.'

'Just looking at you makes me feel better.'

'I wish that were true,' she said tartly. 'Then looking after you wouldn't be half so much work.'

'Why are you doing this, then?'

'Because...I...I...well, if you don't get well again I will never forgive myself.'

'Not your fault.'

'I will feel as if it is if you die on me,' she said glumly.

'You don't want me to die?'

'Of course I don't want you to die. How can you even ask?'

'Better dead. Nothing to live for really. Just got into the habit.'

'Well it's about the only habit of yours, from what I've heard of you, that I *don't* want you to break.'

'You're crying again. Didn't mean to make you cry.'

'Well, then stop talking about dying and concentrate on getting better.'

'And now you're angry.'

'Of course I'm angry. Hasn't there been enough death already? Stop it, Tom. Stop it right now.'

He reached out and found her hand.

'Sorry. Will try and do better.'

'Promise me?'

'If it means that much to you,' he said slowly, hardly able to credit that anyone could really care that much whether he lived or died, 'then, yes.'

After that, every time he felt the pit yawning at his back, he reached for the angel. She was always there. Even when he was too exhausted to drag his eyes open and look for her, he could tell she was near. He only had to smell the faint fragrance of violets for a wave of profound relief to wash through him. For it was her scent. And it meant she hadn't left him.

He'd thought he would always be alone. But she

hadn't left him to his fate. And had promised she wouldn't.

'Hush,' she whispered, smoothing that cool balm over his burning face and neck. 'Don't fret. You are going to be fine. I won't let anything happen to you.'

He doubted her only the once, very briefly. When he thought he saw the brigade surgeon hovering over him like a great vulture.

She couldn't have saved his life, only to turn him over to that ghoul, could she? The man liked nothing better than cutting up poor helpless victims, to see what made them tick. Oh, he said he was trying to cure them, but he spent far too much time writing up his findings in all those leather journals. The journals that were going to make his name some day. His findings, he called them.

Cold sweat broke out all over him at the prospect of falling into his hands. He'd cut him up, for sure. Lay his kidneys out in a tray.

'Lieutenant…' He had to screw up his face. 'What's the name?' Foster, that was it. 'Angel…' He thought he didn't care whether he lived or died, but the prospect of being dissected in the name of science?

'Don't let him cut me up.'

* * *

Lieutenant Foster straightened up, and gave Lady Sarah a hard stare.

'You can see how confused he is. Doesn't know his own name. Seems to think he's a lieutenant. This is often the case with head wounds. Even though the skull itself is not fractured, injury to the brain can leave a patient with no memory, or impeded memory, or even physical impairment.'

'But he is going to get well, isn't he? I mean, he won't die, now?'

'There's no telling, with head wounds. Men can appear to be getting well, then suddenly collapse and die,' he said, looking more animated for a moment or two. 'Delicate organ, the brain. All you can do is keep him as quiet and as still as you can. Let nature take its course.'

The surgeon's eyes flicked round Sarah's room—no, the sickroom—lingering for a moment or two on the pile of material she'd been cutting up for bandages, the bedside table with the bowl of water and sponge, pausing with a perplexed frown at the potted geranium on the windowsill, that Madame le Brun had brought in *to cheer the place up.*

'There is nothing I can do for him that you

can't do just as well here,' he finally declared, brusquely. And marched out of the room.

She hadn't expected an army surgeon to have the bedside manner of a family doctor, naturally, but couldn't he have spared just a moment or two to advise her? Encourage her? At least let her know she'd done an adequate job of stitching Tom's head? And congratulate her for getting his fever down?

No wonder Cooper had insisted she should nurse the Major herself and keep him out of hospital. She wouldn't trust a dog to that cold-eyed man's dubious care.

As if he could read her thoughts, Ben whined and nudged her hand with his nose.

'You are supposed to be in the stable,' she said with mock sternness, though she ruffled his ears at the same time. 'Guarding my horse.' Although Castor didn't need guarding so closely now. Since the news of Bonaparte's flight from the battlefield had circulated, the city had started to become almost civilised again, from what Madame le Brun reported. Which was both a good and a bad thing. Good in the sense that England and her allies had defeated Bonaparte's pretensions. But somewhat dangerous for her reputation, if any of her old crowd discovered she'd returned ahead of them and was holed up with a notorious rake.

'We both need to keep our heads down,' she said. 'Or we'll be in trouble. But I can't be cross with you, you clever dog, for bounding up here the minute that nasty doctor came calling. I felt so much better with you standing guard over both me and Tom. Even so, now he's gone I feel completely drained,' she told Ben, before sitting down by the bed and closing her eyes. The dog laid his head on her knee in what felt remarkably like a gesture of comfort. For a moment or two she just rested. Almost dozed. But then Ben whined and pawed at her knee.

'What is it?'

But as soon as the words left her mouth she saw why Ben had roused her. Tom was awake. He was lying there looking at her with a faint frown creasing his brow, as though he wasn't too sure who she was. Though for some reason, she felt his confusion was no longer due to fever. His eyes were clear and focused steadily on her. In fact, he looked like any man who'd just woken up in a strange place with no recollection of how he'd come to be there.

A pang of concern and self-doubt had her leaning forward to lay her hand on his forehead. But, no—the fever hadn't returned.

'He's gone?'

The Major's voice was hoarse, but for the first time, what he said actually made sense.

'The doctor? Yes.'

He reached up and seized her hand. 'You didn't let him take me. Thank you.' A little shiver went right through her at the look of adoration blazing from his clear green eyes. Oh, no wonder he had such a reputation with the ladies, if he looked at them all like that.

'Of course I didn't,' she said, a little perturbed by both the fear the company surgeon could inspire in potential patients, and the feelings Tom could provoke in her now he had his wits about him. It was a warning that she was going to have to sharpen her own.

'I promised I would look after you myself.'

The grip of his hand tightened. 'Do you always keep your promises?'

'Yes. Of course.'

His mouth tightened fractionally, as if there was no *of course* about promises. But then in his world there probably wasn't. A man of his type probably made dozens of promises he had no intention of keeping. And she'd do well to remember it.

'I am in your hands, then.'

'Yes.'

He sighed and closed his eyes. 'Thank God,' he mumbled. And promptly fell asleep, as though a great weight had rolled off his shoulders.

He trusted her.

Just as those Rogues had trusted her.

Before she had a chance to let it go to her head, she reminded herself that anyone would be preferable to that doctor, who seemed to view the injured as interesting cases rather than people with feelings.

Though Tom was making her feel as if it were more than that, by the way he hadn't let go of her hand, even though he'd fallen asleep. As though he really, really needed her.

It would wear off, once he recovered, and got to know her better, of course. Though for now, why shouldn't she bask in his apparent need? It felt good. Since there was nobody here to tell her how she *ought* to behave, and think, and feel, she could make up her own mind.

She decided that even though he was a rake, whose mere glance could send heated shivers down a woman's spine, there was no harm in just sitting holding his hand while he was asleep. Besides, she was so tired. All she wanted to do was just sit and rest for a while.

So she sat there, her hand in his, half-drowsing, until a knock on the door heralding the arrival of Madame le Brun, with a tray of food, jolted her awake.

Sarah let go of his hand to stretch and yawn as Madame placed the tray none too gently on the bedside table.

'That smells good,' croaked Tom. 'What is it?'

Sarah glanced at the contents of the tray. 'Some broth and some bread. And wine.'

'Nectar.' He sighed.

'Ah! He is awake,' said Madame, 'and wanting his dinner.'

'That is a good sign, isn't it? It must mean he is getting well.'

'Yes. But he is a strong one, that one,' said Madame, casting her eye over his naked torso with what looked like feminine appreciation. And for the first time, Sarah looked, too. At least, for the first time since the battle, she permitted herself to look at him as a man, not just a patient.

She'd thought him handsome before. When she'd seen him in the park, fully clothed. But she'd never run her eyes over his torso, the way she was doing now. With appreciation of his muscled beauty.

She blushed at the inappropriate turn her mind was taking. She was his *nurse*. She was supposed to be convincing Madame le Brun that he was her *brother*. She had no business going all gooey-eyed because he had the kind of body artists would want to sculpt in marble.

'Will you help me to sit him up?' she asked Madame with what she hoped sounded like brisk efficiency. 'Then we can feed him some broth.'

'I can do it,' he grumbled.

But he couldn't. So between them, Sarah and Madame le Brun propped the Major up on a mound of pillows and fed him soup until his eyelids started to flutter closed.

'Weak as a kitten,' he muttered in disgust as they helped him lie down again.

'But now you are eating and the fever has gone, you will be up and going around in no time,' Madame chided him gently as he drifted back to sleep.

That was good news. Before much longer he wouldn't need Sarah any more. He would be up and going around, as Madame so quaintly put it. She wouldn't need to sit over him, alternately sponging his overheated body, or covering him when he shivered.

She would be able to leave, like as not, before anyone discovered she'd had anything to do with him at all. And her reputation would remain intact. She would be safe.

So why did she feel like crying again?

Chapter Five

Stupid, stupid thing to do. Sit crying over… Sarah shook her head. She wasn't too sure actually what she was crying about.

She was turning into a regular watering pot.

With a growl of self-disgust, she got up and went to the desk. Rather than moping, she would do better to reply to all the letters which were piling up.

Gussie first. She'd wronged Gussie. Wished she could put it right. But most of all, she didn't want Gussie to worry about her.

Dear Gussie, she wrote. Then paused, chewing on the end of the quill. She couldn't very well write, *I've brought a notorious rake home with me and have been living with him. He has such a dreadful reputation Justin wouldn't introduce him to me, even though he is an officer.*

She rested her head in her hands for a moment

or two. There must be a way to allay her sister's concerns without telling an outright lie.

I am in Brussels, she wrote, with a defiant tilt to her chin. She didn't want to keep her totally in the dark, the way her husband was so determined to keep her in the dark. It simply wasn't right! But neither could she tell the whole truth.

I think I went a little mad when Blanchards told me Gideon was dead. Of course, I know, really, that Blanchards wouldn't lie to me about something like that, but then, he might have been mistaken, mightn't he? The report might have been sent in error, or something. Anyway, I felt that I couldn't believe it, the way you both did, without proof. I ended up going as far as the battlefield to search for answers and stumbled across Justin instead. He is gravely ill and needs constant care.

That would give a good enough reason for her continued absence from Antwerp, without alerting Gussie to what was really going on. Justin needed constant care right enough, but it was Mary who was giving it. They'd managed to get Justin back to his lodgings, Mary had explained via a curt note, where she would now be staying so that she could nurse him without interruption from Sarah or anyone else.

Even if Blanchards suspected she was being economical with the truth, he wouldn't voice his suspicions. His first priority was to Gussie and his heir. *His* letter had revealed that he had already hidden the news of her absence from Antwerp. He would carry on doing what he could to shield Gussie from worry.

Which was just as well, because if anyone found out that she was living with a man to whom she was not related, with no proper chaperon in place, there would be an almighty scandal. Which would reach as far as London, never mind Antwerp.

Oh, dear. She really should have thought things through. She pressed her hand to her forehead as she went over everything she'd done since Blanchards had told them Gideon was dead.

Dead.

A shudder went through her. How could anyone *think things through* when they were given news like that? Of course she hadn't thought things through. She'd just reacted.

But at least she'd done what she could, since then, to mitigate some of the damage her behaviour might have caused. She'd gone to ground, as it were.

That doctor was the only person who might possibly start spreading gossip. She frowned. But he could only do so if he knew who she was. She thought back over his visit, wondering if he'd ever once called her by name. No, he hadn't. And with the amount of injured men he'd have to attend, given what she'd seen of the battlefield, he wouldn't have time to concern himself over something as minor as her reputation even if he did know who she was.

She hoped.

So all she had to do was warn Madame le Brun that she wasn't receiving visitors, if anybody by some remote chance did happen to discover she was back in Brussels, and her secret would be safe.

'Angel? Are you there?'

At the sound of his hoarse voice, Sarah leapt to her feet and went back to the bedside. She'd let him call her that while in the grip of fever, because there hadn't seemed any point in correcting him. But now it dawned on her that even he didn't know who she really was, either.

He'd forgotten he'd ever seen her. Because she'd made no lasting impression on him.

How depressing.

'I'm here. I was only writing some letters. '

He reached out and grabbed her hand as though his life depended on it.

'Couldn't see you. Thought you'd gone. Or that I imagined you perhaps.'

'No. You didn't imagine me. And I won't go anywhere. Not until you are well enough to do without me.'

'Then I hope I never get well,' he said vehemently. Because when he was well, her family would take great care to keep her well away from a man like him.

How did he know that?

Because an image swam into his mind, of a girl on horseback, blushing because he'd winked at her. And snatches of her companion's conversation drifting to his ears. *For once I agree with Justin...*

Hell's teeth, no wonder he'd had the feeling he knew this woman, even though he was sure he'd never spoken to her before. She was Colonel Randall's precious, virginal little sister. Lady Sarah Latymor.

'Oh, don't say that!'

Bless her, but Lady Sarah looked as though she really cared. Actually, he rather thought she *did* care, for some obscure reason. Else why would she be here, nursing him, when in the normal course of things, men like her brothers protected women like her from men like him?

With good reason.

'Why not? If it is true?'

'Because,' she said sternly, 'I want you to get well.'

Of course she did. As soon as he was well enough, she could walk out of his life again. For good. For some reason the prospect of never seeing her again was so distasteful he couldn't help grimacing.

'Oh. Do you have a pain? Do you want some more of this medicine the doctor left?'

He started to shake his head, only to wince. 'I hurt everywhere, but my head worst of all. It feels as if somebody's tried to slice the top off it.'

'They pretty much did. Let me fetch you that laudanum.'

'No. Not yet. It makes me sleepy. And I want...' He squeezed her fingers, absurdly grateful to discover that she hadn't pulled her hand away from his.

'Talk to me? Just for a while.'

'Very well,' she said, squeezing his hand back. And then cleared her throat. 'This may seem a funny question for me to ask. But, do you know your name?'

Only too well. And yet… 'Why do you ask?'

'The surgeon seemed to think you may have trouble remembering things.'

Perhaps there was a God, after all. He hated feeling this weak, but he'd never got anywhere near Lady Sarah when he'd been fit and active. Now here he was, holding hands with her, in a bedroom of all places.

The thing was, if he admitted he knew who he was, then he'd also have to admit that he knew she shouldn't be in this bedroom.

Not that she was doing anything wrong. No— it was one thing *her* flouting convention to nurse a wounded man. Quite another for that wounded man to permit her to do it, if he knew that just being seen talking with him, in a public street, would have been enough to stain her lily-white reputation. He'd be up on a charge. Cashiered out of the regiment. Or maybe just shot. Because Colonel Randall had made it plain that none of his officers was fit to kiss the hem of her gown.

He wasn't. But before she returned to the safety of her oh-so-respectable family, he promised himself, he'd do more than kiss the hem of her gown. He'd taste those fastidious lips of hers.

'Perhaps,' he purred, 'I would prefer to forget some things.'

'Does that mean you don't know who you are?' She looked appalled.

His conscience, an attribute he'd never thought he possessed, gave him an uncomfortable nudge in the ribs. It wasn't fair to repay Lady Sarah's kindness by putting on an act that worried her.

Though it wasn't as if he'd set his sights on *seducing* her. He never bothered seducing women, even the ones that very plainly weren't virgins. He just bedded them if they were willing, walked away from them if they were not.

She most definitely would not be willing. But he couldn't walk away from her. He couldn't walk anywhere. In fact, even if he'd woken up to find himself in the bed of a rapacious widow, he wouldn't be able to rise to the occasion.

Lady Sarah was safer than she knew.

He gave her a rueful sort of smile, hoping it made him look confused, as well as utterly innocent.

'For today, do I have to be anyone in particular? Couldn't you just call me...' His smile turned a touch mischievous. 'Just call me *Sir*.'

Just as he'd hoped, Sarah's concerned expression relaxed into something approaching amusement.

'Well, at least you remember you are an officer in the army.'

'Yes,' he admitted. 'And I suspect I enjoy giving orders.'

She pulled a face. 'So I suppose you'd like me to jump to attention and salute you, too, wouldn't you?'

'No,' he said, with complete honesty. The last thing he wanted was to have any woman behave in such a subservient manner. He liked his women to be with him because it was what they wanted. He liked them enthusiastic, and inventive, and...

His mouth went dry. Good lord, but it was dangerous, picturing *this* girl being enthusiastic and inventive.

'What I'd really like,' he said, lowering his eyelids into a practised smoulder, since, he reasoned, there wasn't any harm in testing the waters, 'is for you to kiss me. As my nurse, don't you think it is your duty to kiss me better?'

Her face flushed as her lips pursed up in disapproval.

'That does not form part of my duties.'

'Well, perhaps you'd like to do it for pleasure, then?'

To his surprise, she didn't automatically say no.

She looked at him thoughtfully, her head tilted to one side.

His heart hammered in his chest, making his blood pound through his veins, just because she was thinking about kissing him. If she actually bent forward, and pressed her lips to his, the wounds in his head would probably burst, killing him on the spot.

But what a way to go.

'Kill me...' He shook his head. 'I mean, kiss me, Angel. And let me die a happy man.'

For a moment she looked as though she was still toying with the idea. She actually swayed forward in her seat. But then she shook her head and sat back.

'No. It won't do. You don't know who you are, nor who I am. You are confused and weak, and don't know what you are saying.'

Damn. He should have told her there was nothing wrong with his memory, in spite of what the doctor had said.

She snatched her hand away, then, as though she'd just become aware he was still holding it.

'Besides, you don't really mean it, do you? I'm not the kind of girl men want to kiss.'

'What? Why would you say that?' He wouldn't have been surprised if prim Lady Sarah had slapped his face for impertinence. But never would he have dreamed she'd think he was offering her false coin.

'Isn't it obvious? Or did the blow to your head knock all the sense out of it along with your memory?'

'Possibly,' he acknowledged slowly. One moment he'd decided he wasn't going to do any more than flirt with her, just a little, the next he was imagining her climbing on top of him and taking all sorts of liberties while he was helpless to resist. And then asking if she wouldn't mind kissing him, just to get things started. That wasn't the way to deal with a society princess. No wonder she looked so offended.

'But I do want to kiss you,' he admitted. Then, deciding to turn the conversation away from his murky motives, added, 'And to be honest, I don't understand why you think other men don't.'

'Well, just look at my face. The nose. It looks aristocratic and manly on my brothers. But on a female, well…' She shrugged. 'Anyway, I don't want men to kiss me.' She shuddered in what looked like genuine revulsion.

Which made him feel a little better. At least it wasn't him, specifically, she didn't want to kiss.

She'd always had a sort of cool air about her,

now he came to think of it. She hadn't appeared to favour any of the men who'd clustered round her.

Had a sort of untouchable quality to her that had made some of them, men like her twin brother's commanding officer, look upon her as a challenge to their masculinity.

At that moment, an immense black dog shambled up to the bed, got his front paws on to the mattress and gave his face a hearty, thorough licking.

'Good grief, it's Dog,' he exclaimed, temporarily forgetting he was supposed to have lost his memory. 'Where did you come from?' He ruffled the dog's velvety ears.

'Ben, get down,' said Lady Sarah sharply. 'Tom isn't well enough for that sort of play.'

So she knew his name was Tom. And she was calling the dog Ben, too, the way some of the men had started to do, the last few days.

'Well, at least someone wants to kiss me.' He laughed, as Dog's whole body wriggled in joyous greeting.

She pulled the dog off him. But he couldn't help noticing that for all her sharp manner, she'd glanced at his mouth—albeit briefly—with a sort of fascination. As though she wouldn't mind finding out what a kiss would be like.

Which was a start.

But if he was ever going to get that kiss, he'd have to find out why she'd shuddered with revulsion at the mere prospect. Which meant getting her to talk to him. Trust him.

But what did a man like him have in common with a girl like her? What could they talk about?

Well, there was always the dog.

'How on earth did you come to have Dog?'

'Oh,' she said, taking the hound's head between her hands and gazing into his eyes with a familiarity that caused Tom a pang of something that felt a lot like envy. 'We sort of rescued each other, on the road to the Forest of Soignes. He was tied to one of the baggage wagons, which got overturned when a band of cowardly Hussars came pell-mell along the road from the battlefield. And he was so scared. I couldn't leave him trapped like that, could I?'

Tom looked at her with new respect. He could just imagine how the dog would react, tethered and scared. It would have been all snapping teeth and frantic attempts to get free. He didn't think he knew any *men* who would have gone near Ben in that condition.

Not that he could say anything. He wasn't supposed to know who he was, let alone recall all the instances when he'd witnessed this dog in action.

Though, come to think of it, he'd already given himself away by admitting he recognised Dog. Not that Lady Sarah had taken any notice of his slip.

'And then,' she said, ruffling the dog's ears, 'he returned the favour by chasing off a nasty deserter who'd been trying to steal Castor—that's my horse—while I'd crawled under the wagon and wasn't paying attention. But you saw him off, didn't you?' she said, petting the dog's flanks. 'Yes, you did. You are a good boy.'

The thought of Lady Sarah facing such peril, with only the flea-bitten hound to look after her, made his blood run cold.

She'd crawled under a wagon to help just about the most intimidating dog he'd ever come across, then had to face a deserter attempting to steal her horse? And she was speaking of it just as though she was relating an outing to the shops. What would it take to ruffle her aristocratic sang-froid?

His imagination promptly supplied a whole slew of highly improper activities where she'd end up distinctly ruffled.

The dog's tongue lolled out in ecstasy as she patted and stroked him. He shut his own mouth firmly to make sure he wasn't doing anything similar.

'And we've been inseparable ever since. Haven't we, Ben?'

'Ever since?' He looked at the window and the sunlight streaming through it. And recalled the endless hours of confusion and fever. 'How long have I been here? What day is it, now?'

'It's Tuesday.'

'Tuesday?' She'd been nursing him for the best part of two days. Not that long for him to lie semi-conscious, after what his body had been through. Thirst and loss of blood would have weakened him to the point where he didn't know who he was, or where he was, even without the blow to the head. So he had some excuse for being right where he was.

But what was her excuse? What was she doing in Brussels at all? The civilians had all fled last Friday, from what he'd heard.

And why had nobody come looking for her?

He turned away from the window to look at her. And noted a slight flush staining her cheeks.

The hussy! She knew full well she shouldn't be here with him. Not now he was awake. Yet she wasn't making any attempt to leave.

It wasn't because she'd developed a *tendre* for

him, that was for sure. She shuddered at the mere idea of kissing.

So what was she doing with him?

If only he could simply ask her. But if he did that, they'd be dealing with truths he wasn't yet ready to face.

He lowered his eyelids and studied her awkward posture, the very self-conscious way she was petting the dog now, as an excuse to avoid looking back at him, he'd guess.

'You know,' he said with mock severity, 'since we have established that I am simply an officer in the army, with no past and no name, and therefore nothing I can tell you, it is up to you to sustain the conversation.'

Her eyes flew to his, a little spark of outrage flashing at his temerity in touching on her social obligations. Because she was the kind of girl who normally stuck rigidly to all the rules of etiquette.

Still, now he had her looking at him again. He'd made her forget her awkwardness at being here.

'And I do like the sound of your voice,' he admitted with complete sincerity. Even the hint of exasperation in it, when he'd been half out of his mind with fever, had been strangely comforting. Had sort of grounded him.

'Besides, I am too weak to strain myself with

talk. I shall just lie here and listen to you while you entertain me.'

'You…you are a complete hand!'

He nodded solemnly. 'Yes, I rather suspect I am. But what are you, apart from my guardian angel? Do you have a name? No—' He pulled himself up. If she told him her real name, then he'd be obliged to acknowledge her relationship to his commanding officer. That was, if he owned up to not suffering from memory loss. Which he wasn't ready to do, not yet, even if he didn't want her to believe in it. Hell, but this was getting complicated enough to give him a headache, if he hadn't already got one.

'Just let me guess.' He studied her face as though trying to pick a suitable name. Which he was doing. If she wasn't a Sarah, what would he call her? After a bit, he came up with, 'Helen.'

'Do I look like a Helen?'

'Helen of Troy. The face that launched a thousand ships.'

'With a nose like this I suspect Paris would have had me carved into a figurehead on one of those ships,' she said waspishly. 'You do talk nonsense.'

'If not Helen, what, then?'

She thought for a minute, and then looked as though she'd come to a decision. 'Do you know, if I had a choice, I rather think I should like to be called Elizabeth.'

So. She wasn't any more keen to face up to the truth, either, or she would have told him, in that brisk, no-nonsense voice she'd used when he'd been rambling in his fever, who she really was.

'Lizzy,' he corrected her. 'Elizabeth is far too formal for the situation in which we find ourselves.'

'No,' she said firmly. 'Elizabeth. And you may as well know that I choose the name because she ruled the whole land without ever letting anyone force her into marriage.'

'The Virgin Queen,' he said thoughtfully. 'Yes. That does suit a girl who shudders at the prospect of a man's kiss. For no man is fit to so much as kiss the hem of your jewelled gown.' He certainly wasn't. That was what made this situation so piquant.

Catching the direction of his gaze, she ran her hands over the elegantly simple gown she wore.

'This gown is hardly practical for nursing a wounded soldier, is it? Though I didn't know I was going to be doing any such thing when I ordered it. Which was before we all fled to Antwerp...' She faltered to a halt, pleating a section of her skirt between her fingers. 'I suppose that sounds as if I think of nothing but clothes, but it was no joke, I can assure you, arriving here without a clean stitch to put on.'

'I am a soldier, your Majesty. Of course I know what it is like to lose baggage when I'm on the march.'

'Oh, but you haven't! That is, I mean, two of your men brought your things round. So you can have a clean shirt whenever you want one.'

Was she hinting she wanted him to cover himself up? He supposed he really ought to. Men didn't loll about, shirtless, when a woman was in the room, not unless that woman had no morals to speak of.

'I hated not having clean clothes of my own,' she said, as though it was a crime. 'People say I'm terribly vain, you know. And I do spend a lot of time shopping. But can I tell you something? You won't tell anyone else?'

'My Queen, I am your loyal subject. I shall regard your confidence as though it were a state secret,' he said, dipping his head in a mock bow. Then wincing at the hammer blow that rang through his skull.

'Idiot,' she said with a concerned frown. 'Lie still! And listen. My secret is when I dress well,

I feel as though it takes attention away from how very plain I am.'

'Plain?' He studied her face. To him, at that moment, it looked like the most adorable face in the world. He supposed it must be because he felt he owed her his life or something, because, in all honesty, her nose *was* just a touch too prominent for a female. And her lips too prim. And her hair—it was a beautiful colour, but looked as though she'd stiffened it with some sort of lotion so that she could curl it. And those curls were now sort of fraying round the edges. But her eyes...

'You have the most remarkable eyes,' he told her. 'That blue, it's quite lovely.'

'They are my best feature,' she admitted. 'I do try to emphasise them. But—' she shrugged '—there's no getting past the nose.'

'That nose,' he said on a burst of inspiration, 'is the kind of nose born to rule. And you said you wanted to be a queen, did you not? Therefore, it suits you perfectly.'

'No wonder you're so popular with the ladies,' she said with a shake of her head.

'Am I?' A flash of shame made him look as confused as he was trying to convince her he felt. He had never once thought his reputation as a prolific lover would make him uncomfortable. What was it about Lady Sarah that made him wish he'd lived a more respectable life?

Instantly she looked contrite. 'Oh, I am sorry. I shouldn't remind you of…well, we'd agreed, hadn't we, that just for now, we can be whoever we want to be.'

His heart did a funny sort of skip in his chest. Because what she'd just said meant she wanted to be with him, just as much as he wanted to be with her.

Even though they both knew it couldn't last.

'So. You have chosen to be the Virgin Queen,' he said, settling himself more comfortably against the pillows. Which was apt, given the fact she was a lady of unimpeachable virtue.

'Because, you say, you don't want to be forced into a marriage you cannot stomach. Is there any danger of that?'

She sighed. 'Mama has been very patient with what she calls my crotchets, so far. She hasn't put any pressure on me to accept any of the offers made for my hand. But she never gives up hope. She says she wants me to be happy in marriage. But—' another one of those frowns flitted across her forehead '—I don't see how she can even use the word *happy*, in the same sentence as *marriage*, without a blush. Not when her own has made her so utterly miserable. Papa was a rake, you see.'

She gave him a considering look. One which it took every ounce of his meagre strength to hold without hanging his head.

'Mama,' she said tartly, 'was expected to turn a blind eye to his many infidelities. Which took a great deal of resolution, given that Chalfont Magna's littered with his natural children. He took great pleasure, I think, in conducting his affairs right under her nose. In humiliating her.' Her lips flattened into a grim line. 'It wasn't even as if he needed to prove his virility, particularly, since he repeatedly got her with child, as well. She presented him with two sets of twins, and two girls as well as his heir, not counting the many miscarriages in between,' she ended speaking on a shudder. 'Can you blame me for hoping I never get married?'

Absolutely not. Not when she put it like that. 'You do make it sound unpleasant,' he admitted. 'But not all men are like that.'

'No?' She pursed her lips and gave him a rather withering look. 'No,' she said again, this time with more than a hint of resolution. 'I am not going to come to cuffs with you over this, not while you are so poorly.'

Then she startled him by giving him a rather mischievous smile.

'And actually, it is rather amusing to hear you saying exactly what Mama is always telling me.'

'No!' He widened his eyes in horror that wasn't altogether feigned. Well, what man wished to hear he'd started saying the same things as a match-making mama?

'My sisters, too. Since they have married men they declare are perfect paragons, they have re-doubled their efforts to find me a man just like their husbands.'

'So, how have you foiled their plans?'

'Oh, very easily,' she said airily. 'I have become adept at it, over the years. I never argue. Never throw tantrums. With the result that nobody ever knows exactly what I'm thinking. So they assume I cannot think for myself at all. I have meekly gone through several Seasons without ever bring-ing myself to accept any of the *flattering* offers made for my hand. So many, you know,' she said, putting on a particularly vacuous expression, and fanning herself with her hand. 'How is a girl to choose?'

Tom's eyes lit with unholy amusement. 'I'm be-ginning to suspect you are an unprincipled bag-gage.'

She lifted her chin haughtily. 'How dare you speak thus to your queen, Sir Tom?'

'I most humbly beg your pardon, your Majesty. I, um, forgot myself.'

She giggled.

And then, abruptly, sobered.

'The dreadful thing is, I think you are right.' She shifted in her chair and looked him straight in the eye as though imploring him to understand. 'I had no scruples about encouraging Mama to send me to France, when she got the notion that she might stand a better chance of marrying me off if only she could introduce me to some new people. Because, you see, it was exactly where I wished to go. Because Gideon was stationed there. Gideon, my twin brother,' she explained, just as if he really might not know.

'It was *not* because everyone who was anyone was flocking to Paris, instead of London, for the Season,' she added a touch tartly.

'They actually thought I might be dazzled into marriage by some wealthy European princeling. As if becoming a princess would make marriage any more palatable!' She shook her head with scorn. 'But I shall never regret the trip to Paris, nor our subsequent removal to Brussels when Bonaparte went and invaded France, since it meant that I have managed to spend these last few months close to Gideon.'

A shadow passed across her features. But then she pinned a bright smile to her face. 'So. Now you know why I wish to be called Elizabeth. Why I admire her so much.'

The smile didn't reach her eyes. And he wished he could do something to help ease her sorrow. The sorrow neither of them could mention without destroying their truce.

'Your Majesty,' he said, taking her hand and kissing it with complete gratitude, 'you honour me with your confidence.'

Sarah could see exactly why Tom had gained such a reputation with the ladies. Even pale, covered in bruises and with his head bandaged, he was an utterly charming companion.

Of course, it was all nonsense, this declaring his devotion, as her courtier. A man like him was never going to be devoted to anyone for more than five minutes. But for the first time, she didn't really care.

There was no harm in playing along, just for an hour or so, at being whoever they wanted to be. Not when they both knew it was a game.

She'd certainly never liked the person her family had obliged her to be. And she wasn't looking forward to returning to the dull conformity of that life, either. Actually, it would all be far worse than it had been before she'd lost her head and run away. She would be in disgrace with them all. And there would be a shockingly empty, aching void in her life where Gideon had been.

So, on the whole, it was better to play the queen to Tom's courtier. To bask in his practised flattery. To laugh at his witty repartee.

Far better than the alternative. Reality, with all its pain.

Chapter Six

When Madame le Brun came in with another meal of her good wholesome broth, and fresh bread, he managed a whole bowlful before growing drowsy.

Sarah took it as a personal victory. The sense of achievement was like sunshine bursting out from behind storm clouds. He'd been so close to death when his men had brought him here. And she'd been so timid. So clueless. As she took the empty bowl and set it on the tray for removal later, she realised that, even though she would never be a queen, she most definitely wasn't the same person she'd been two days ago. Tom had changed her—or, rather, nursing him back to health had changed her. Had given her faith in herself. She wasn't the useless, empty-headed female everyone had kept telling her she was. No—she'd decided that death wouldn't have this man and she'd flung herself into the task of saving him.

Maybe that was what had made the difference— she'd never flung herself into anything before. For the most part she'd been content to just drift along, taking the path of least resistance.

She turned to him abruptly. 'Thank you,' she said, before she had a chance to change her mind.

His eyes widened. 'Thank me? Whatever for?'

'For making your own memory loss into a game. It has helped keep my own reality at bay.' Suddenly she saw, too, why she'd been so keen to play along, even though she'd suspected he wasn't as confused as all that. Little things, like the way he'd recognised Ben, then tried to cover his moment of spontaneity by turning the subject, had made her suspicious. But not suspicious enough to challenge him. For one thing, he wasn't well. For another—what would she do if she didn't have Tom to nurse? She couldn't go to Justin and ask about Gideon. Justin really was too ill to burden with her problems. Nor was she prepared to slink back to Antwerp with her tail between her legs and beg everyone's pardon for running away. So, on the whole, she was grateful to him for providing her with the excuse for staying right where she was, until she was ready to face the future.

'I don't know what I will do when this is all over, but, you know, pretending to be a queen to your courtier has been a sort of golden interlude in a time of darkness.'

'Has it? Been golden for you? I'm glad,' he said sleepily. 'I only wish I could give you many more such days.'

'Ah, but both of us have been pretending to be someone we are not today. That can't go on for ever, can it?'

He winced. She could tell that though he was in pain, he was fighting it. Trying to stay playful and flirtatious. And awake.

'I have one last command for you which, as my loyal subject, you must obey.'

He smiled and half-inclined his head.

'I shall obey without question,' he vowed, falling neatly into her trap.

'Then drink your medicine and sleep,' she said firmly.

'Unfair,' he protested.

'Not at all,' she replied sternly. 'You need to rest. Come on,' she said, measuring the drops into the glass, just the way the surgeon had shown her. 'Drink it all up like a good boy.'

'A good boy?'

She shrugged. 'That is how my nurse always

used to talk to me and my brothers when we tried to wriggle out of taking our medicine. And then she'd say that we needed our sleep. Because sleep is the best medicine of all.'

'Yes, you are right. It's just that I...' He shot her one of those melting looks that made her toes curl, even though she knew it was only put on for effect. 'I don't want today to end. I will remember it all,' he vowed with so much sincerity she really wanted to believe him. 'Every moment. Every smile you have granted me. Like treasure.'

'That's a lovely thing to say,' she said as he drank the laudanum mixture.

'But you don't believe me?' He gave her an aggrieved frown, then shut his eyes and slipped almost at once into exhausted slumber.

'The danger is,' she murmured softly, 'that I *want* to believe you. Even knowing what kind of man you are.'

She sat down at his bedside, the discarded medicine glass in her hand, just staring at him, her head tilted to one side as she tried to work out how she could feel the way she did about such a notorious rake. And why it was that the sight of his naked torso now could give her thrilling little goosebumps, when it hadn't affected her in the slightest when she'd been sponging it down. Why hadn't she reacted to the magnificent way he was put together until he'd woken up and started talking to her? It was the same body, after all.

Because, she realised on a flash of inspiration, it wasn't his looks alone that made him so attractive. She'd thought him handsome when she'd first seen him, but hadn't wanted to linger in his vicinity any longer than she had to. It was him. The man he was inside. The things you couldn't know unless you talked to him.

No wonder Justin wouldn't let her speak to him. His charm was well-nigh lethal. What woman wouldn't like a man who looked like this and who could be so playful, willing to obey her every command just as though she was a queen and he her devoted slave?

Actually, come to think of it, it wasn't just his charm that tugged a positive reaction from her. The charm wouldn't have affected her at all had she not already seen him at his lowest—if she hadn't seen him battling his demons and then clinging to the sound of her voice, or the touch of her hand, as though she was his only anchor.

As though he was just as lonely as she was.

It was just as well she knew it was all make-believe, or she might be in real danger of falling for him. Fortunately she knew just how charming men could pretend to be, if they thought it would get them what they wanted. But deep down, they were all selfish, inconsiderate tyrants.

All men? Even Gideon?

Oh, it felt disloyal to think of him in those terms. But hadn't he always been as self-absorbed as any of the males in her family? True, he'd been more willing to spend time with her. To talk to her. But he'd never dreamed of putting her wishes first. She had always been the one supporting him. She'd been rescuing him from the consequences of his scrapes since they'd both been in the nursery and she'd unlocked windows to let him in when he'd sneaked out to steal apples. She'd even been distracting his company commander so that he could do whatever it was he'd been up to in Brussels before that last battle.

Even the plan to come to France—supposedly on the hunt for a husband—had come about because she'd sensed, from the letters he'd written, that he needed her. In between the descriptions of the social whirl in which his regiment was involved she could detect a sort of malaise. She'd wanted to help him. And so she'd fostered Gussie's and Mama's hopes, so that she could be at hand to help when whatever it was she could sense coming actually came.

Only she'd been too late. Or not in the right place at the right time. Or something. She'd failed him. He was dead, and she was left sitting here watching over…

As if he knew she was thinking of him, Tom moaned. His eyes flickered under his lids. He flung his arm out, throwing off the sheet.

She leaned over and felt his forehead. It wasn't unduly hot.

'Can't get out,' he muttered, fighting to get free of the sheet, which had become twisted round his legs. 'Mustn't let them get me.'

Poor Tom. He must just be having a nightmare.

'Angel!' He reached out blindly. For her.

She caught at his flailing hand, and held hard. 'Shhh. I'm here. You are safe.'

'Violets.' He sighed and settled down again.

She sat back, pushing a stray tendril of hair from her forehead. She was bone weary and ready for bed herself. She glanced longingly at the pallet bed she'd had Madame le Brun bring in here, in case Tom's fever mounted again during the night and he needed help.

She smiled at the irony. Today he'd been addressing her as *your Majesty*, but his need of her meagre nursing skills meant she was going to have to sleep on a pallet like a chambermaid.

She'd just pulled all the pins from her hair and started attacking the snarls with a comb when Tom cried out for her again.

After settling him and going back to her preparations for bed, only to have him cry out for her again, and again, she finally gave up all thought of getting a decent night's sleep.

In fact, the only way she might snatch even a few moments would be to lie down next to him.

She chewed on her lower lip, a little shocked at herself for even considering such a thing. But then he cried out again and reached for her, and, instead of merely holding his hand and stroking his brow, she clambered on to the bed beside him and gathered him into her arms. After all, it was only like the time she'd held him close, in the French ambulance, to prevent him jolting his poor head. It wasn't an attempt at seduction. It might be unconventional, to get on to the bed and cuddle him like this, but it wasn't *really* improper.

When he sighed and stilled, as though finally he felt safe, she knew she'd done the right thing. Which brought a warm glow of satisfaction deep inside. It even helped to soothe her own bone-deep loneliness. Because nobody had ever needed her like this before. Not even Gideon.

She held Tom more tightly. Holding someone

who was clinging to her was very comforting, she discovered. She'd never just cuddled anyone, as far as she could recall. Or been cuddled, either. Once, she recalled Bridget cuddling Gideon, after he'd fallen and scraped his knee. The old nurse in charge of the nursery had reprimanded her. Said he wouldn't grow up to be a proper man if she mollycoddled him.

So no more cuddles. For either of them. For Mama only visited the nursery briefly, at nights, to see them safely tucked up in bed, and Papa not at all.

'What a pair we are,' she said, shifting so that she could lay her head on Tom's chest. 'Like two survivors of a shipwreck, clinging together in the wreckage.'

There were certainly no words that anyone could say that could bring her the slightest bit of comfort over losing Gideon. Nothing to compare with just being held like this, as though she was as necessary as breathing. So she wasn't going to worry about the propriety of it. Not when she was so tired.

Not when it felt so good.

Tom didn't want to wake up. There was a deliciously fragrant, warm woman in his arms.

Why, though? He never slept with women. Once he'd taken his pleasure, he got out of their beds as soon as decently possible.

Though to say she was in his arms wasn't strictly accurate. They had their arms round each other. She'd got one leg over him, too, keeping him warm with the flow of her skirts. Which was odd. He must be losing his touch if she was still clothed, while he was stark naked. She was cradling his head to her breasts, too—his head which hurt like the very devil.

He glanced up through the mass of golden curls pillowing his cheek and cursed under his breath. It was Lady Sarah Latymor in his arms. She had spent the night in bed with him!

Didn't she know the difference between sitting decorously at his side, mopping his brow and spooning liquid into his mouth to quench his raging thirst, and holding him in her arms?

Probably not. In her innocence, she'd sought to soothe him, that was all. She'd done so every single time he'd reached for her, when the nightmares had come rolling in, swamping him, smothering him. He'd got so he'd dreaded closing his eyes for fear of what would assault him next.

And, oh, it had felt good when she'd first clambered on to his bed and rocked him. It had taken him back to his childhood and the way he'd wished there'd been someone, anyone, to come and rock him to sleep as a child. Though there never had.

Looked like she'd rocked herself to sleep, too. Poor girl must be exhausted. He didn't think he'd been an easy patient to look after. But she'd never given up. Never left him to the nightmares, or the fever, nor even fled the impropriety of being alone with him once he'd come to.

He wished he could lie here like this for ever.

Actually, no, he didn't. He wanted to kiss her, not just lie here. Her lips were parted slightly. If he moved just a touch, if he raised his head, he could steal a kiss and she'd never know. If he was gentle enough, she wouldn't wake, she was sleeping so deeply.

He huffed out an irritated breath. She might not know, but he would. He'd feel as if he'd betrayed her. She hadn't climbed into his bed for *that*.

He was a bit disgusted with himself for being tempted to steal from her what should be freely given. What kind of man even thought about repaying all her care of him by treating her with such disrespect? She deserved better.

Whereas he deserved the physical agony which clawed at just about every part of his body. The pain he suffered was just sentence.

Everything hurt. His head, particularly, pounded...

No, actually, the pounding was coming from the region of the door.

One of the household servants?

No. They wouldn't enter until given permission to do so. Whoever this was had flung open the door and come striding across the room.

'Bartlett? They tell me you're...'

Bartlett's instinct was to bury his nose deeper between Lady Sarah's breasts and close his eyes, to blot out the furious face that belonged to that voice. The face of Major Flint.

He stifled a groan. He couldn't have been discovered by anyone worse. Because Major Flint just happened to be this girl's half-brother. An illegitimate half-brother, but nevertheless he would still count her as family. Particularly since Flint owed his career to her legitimate brother. Colonel Randall, so rumour had it, had recognised the Latymor nose—the nose which was the bane of Sarah's life—and given Flint a field commission on the strength of it.

He was finished.

Flint's shocked cry roused Lady Sarah, who leapt guiltily from the bed, pausing only to fling a sheet over the lower half of his body. As if Flint hadn't seen a naked man before.

'What the hell,' said the clearly shocked Major Flint, 'are you doing here?'

Ah, well, it had been good while it lasted. Perhaps Flint would save him the bother of facing Colonel Randall by simply running him through where he lay. It wouldn't be a bad way to go. At least his last day on earth had been spent with her. Lady Sarah. In a kind of...what had she called it? A golden haze. Unreal. Too perfect for such as him. A day never to be repeated.

'You!' Lady Sarah sounded appalled. Had she really thought she could get away with this? Had she really thought that telling the landlady he was her brother would prevent the truth coming out, in the end?

'You're Adam Flint! Justin wouldn't introduce you to me at the review.'

Bartlett forced his eyes open, to take his last look at her. She sounded really distressed now. Apologetic.

Naturally. Something twisted inside him. It had been all very well caring for him when she'd thought she could keep it secret. But now her behaviour was about to be exposed. She'd crumble in the face of Flint's fury. Flint was a hard man.

He'd grown up in the gutter, gone into the army like so many of his kind, but then risen through the ranks by his own merit—until the day his half-brother had started taking an interest in him. He was one of the few officers tough enough to be able to control such men who ended up in Randall's Rogues, probably because he was, really, one of them. He'd make mincemeat of a fine lady like Sarah.

'He wouldn't introduce *any* of the Rogues,' Flint snapped. 'And for good reason. None of us should be associating with you. Let alone him.' Flint stabbed an accusing finger in his direction.

Couldn't argue with that. Ramrod Randall knew his men were scum and the officers leading them fit only to lead scum. Naturally he wanted his precious little sister guarded from them all. He'd even tried to get her to leave Brussels altogether when she'd shown too much interest in the Rogues. It had only been because her twin, the one who was in a fashionable cavalry regiment, kept her busy with a far more acceptable set of people that he'd relented.

'I know the reason he wouldn't introduce me to *you*,' she said, self-consciously tidying her unbound hair into a hasty plait. 'You're my natural brother. I'm not supposed to know any of you exist, let alone associate with you.'

That's right, she'd told him there were dozens of them. She'd told him her mother was obliged to ignore them all.

And she hated it. She'd spoken of what her mother had suffered. Why hadn't he seen that she suffered, too? That she hated the hypocrisy of having to behave as though she was ignorant of her father's behaviour.

'And stop shouting. Poor Tom's head hurts.'

Poor Tom? That sounded as though she cared for him. And wasn't afraid to let Flint know it.

A great hollow opened up inside of him. Somewhere in the region of his heart. A hunger. Yearning.

'Poor Tom's head,' Flint growled, 'is going to be ripped from his shoulders. Now get your cloak and bonnet. I'm taking you home this minute. For you can't stay here.'

Farewell, Lady Sarah. It was a privilege to know you. Albeit briefly...

But far from meekly going to the peg on which her cloak hung, Lady Sarah stood her ground.

'I *am* home. This is *my* lodging.'

'Well, then, I'll take you to your brother.'

'You can't do that,' she said triumphantly. 'Mary Endacott says he's too ill to be disturbed.'

She was like a little terrier, standing up to the farmer's prize bull, he marvelled, as the battle raged over his bed. Dodging, and yipping, and nipping with her sharp little words. While Major Flint, more used to applying brute force to those under his command, bellowed and raged with increasing impotence, confused by her speed and nimbleness.

He felt like weeping. She was still defending him. The way she'd done from the first. Not just from strangers, and his injuries, but now from her very family. The ones who cared about her and her reputation.

Nobody had ever fought for him before. Defended him. They'd all been more inclined to condemn him without a shred of evidence. Any trouble in the vicinity? Bound to be Tom's fault. So he got the punishment whether he'd been involved or not.

'Bartlett!' Major Flint was bending over him, bellowing right into his face just as though he was a raw recruit who could be intimidated by such measures. He hadn't been intimidated by such tactics when he *had* been a raw recruit.

Out of habit, he adopted the same measure he'd

done then. Widened his eyes as if bewildered as to why he was up on a charge. Though he couldn't resist taunting Flint just a bit, as well.

'Sir?'

'Don't *sir* me, Bartlett. We're the same rank, damn it.'

Yes, damn it, they were. Both of them had ended up as majors in Randall's rag-tag unit of misfits. And neither of them had been able to inherit the land, or title, or wealth that their noble fathers had enjoyed.

There was a vast gulf between them. She was on one side, a lady of unimpeachable virtue. And he was on the other. A rake and a rogue. They'd held hands across the gulf for a short while, but now it was time to let go.

The argument raged on above him, while he went under a wave of utter misery. He'd known he couldn't, in all conscience, stay here with her for long. Though why it mattered to him so much he couldn't say. He'd never even felt the merest twinge of regret when the time had come to part from any other woman.

'Leave him alone,' Lady Sarah insisted, snagging his attention once more. 'He has no idea who he is, what happened.'

What? Where had she got that notion? A dart of

shame speared him. Yesterday. When he'd been trying to stave off reality, that's where. That puerile game he'd started, hoping to prolong his time with her. In the hopes of snatching a kiss or two.

'He doesn't know you.'

He took a breath to explain. Then thought better of it. He wasn't going to contradict Lady Sarah, not when she was doing her best to defend him. Major Flint might have been the closest thing Tom had ever had to a friend, but over the last couple of days, she'd earned his loyalty, too.

'He seems to think he's a lieutenant.'

He frowned. Now that was…no, actually he couldn't think where she'd got that notion from at all. He'd never said anything about his army rank. Had deliberately kept reality out of all their conversations.

Which meant…his heart took a great bound. She was making it up. Lying. For him. She said he was too weak to move? He wouldn't move, then.

She said he couldn't remember who he was? He wouldn't make her look a fool by arguing. Besides, his memory *had* been a touch hazy, at least when he'd first come round.

'Perhaps in his mind he is back when he first joined the army,' she finished on what looked like a burst of inspiration.

When Flint's scowl turned in his direction, he therefore did his best to look confused. She'd put her reputation on the line for him. So he'd do whatever necessary to back her up.

'Have you seen the head wound?'

'Yes, of course,' she said, turning a bit pale. And stunned him still further by describing it in all its gory detail. Including an account of how she'd stitched it up.

To think of this sheltered young woman doing *that* for him.

'He is going to get better,' she was insisting now, with tears in her eyes. 'He *must*.'

Flint was looking at him with a thoughtful frown now. Was looking at Lady Sarah differently, too. She wasn't the woman they all thought she was, that was why. Her own brother seemed to think she couldn't cross the road without an escort, but in the last couple of days she'd come to Brussels alone, tamed a fearsome dog, seen off a deserter, scoured the battlefield for survivors, stitched him up and nursed him back from the brink of death.

Flint had just opened his mouth to say something, when the dog scratched at the door to be let in. Sarah ran to let him in with what looked like relief. She drew a lot of comfort from that dog, he'd noticed, though she went through the motions of chiding him whenever he came indoors—if the landlady was anywhere near.

For once, the dog didn't take a blind bit of notice of her. Instead, it flung itself joyously at Flint, who took great pleasure in making the animal sit at his feet.

Bartlett couldn't blame him. It was the first time, since setting foot in this room, he'd had the slightest bit of control over any of the occupants.

'How the devil did Dog get here?'

'His name's Ben,' she corrected him and gave a brief account of her adventures.

Major Flint straightened up from scratching Dog behind his ear. 'This animal,' he said sternly, 'is coming back with me now. And so are you,' he informed Lady Sarah. 'Pack a bag. I'm taking you to Randall's house.'

'I won't go.' She sat on the end of his bed, placing one hand possessively on his leg. 'You would have to carry me kicking and screaming all the way.'

Thwarted again, Flint changed tactic. 'Then I'll have *him* moved.'

'That could kill him!' Tears sprang to her eyes.

He stirred guiltily. He wasn't as ill as all that. And he should tell her he wasn't worth a single one of her tears. He should sit up, get dressed and go with Flint. And nip this—whatever it was that was happening between them—in the bud.

'How do you know,' she said, abruptly changing tack, 'that Gideon is dead?'

'Because I was there,' said Flint tersely.

'Are you certain?'

'Certain I was there, or certain he's dead? Yes to both. You don't get up after wounds like that.'

Bartlett's mouth firmed as he promptly changed his mind about leaving her. He might have caused her to shed a tear or two, but he wouldn't let them run down her face, the way Flint was doing, had he a handkerchief to hand. Or the strength to wield it. How could the man speak of her twin's death in such a callous manner?

'Was he shot? Was it quick?'

For God's sake, tell her it was quick, Bartlett silently willed Flint. Whether it was the truth or not.

'Sabre wounds.'

Bartlett almost groaned. How could the idiot say that, when he knew full well that she knew exactly what sabre wounds looked like, having just treated his own?

She must have felt the same, because suddenly she was on her feet, pointing at the door.

'Get out,' she screamed, making the dog shrink

into Flint's leg in surprise. 'Get out—and if you come back here again disturbing Tom then I'll use his pistols on you!'

His pistols had been stolen. But Flint didn't know that it was an empty threat. Not that it was all that much of a threat. Flint wasn't a man to quail at the prospect of having a slip of a girl waving a pistol at him. Not when he was accustomed to facing down whole columns of enemy infantry during a battle and packs of drunken deserters in the aftermath.

Nevertheless, Major Flint turned and stalked out, clicking his fingers so that the dog went trotting after him.

Sarah watched the dog leave as though it was betraying her. Tears were still rolling down her cheeks. And she was trembling.

'Ben went with him,' she said. And sat down abruptly on his bed as though her legs had no strength left in them.

He nearly had done, too. Thank goodness he hadn't. She shouldn't be alone, not when she was so upset.

'Ben is his dog,' he explained, reaching out to take the little, trembling hand she'd rested on his leg and giving it what he hoped she'd find a comforting sort of squeeze.

'No—' she shook her head '—Gideon told me he belonged to all the Rogues. That you'd adopted him when you found him on some farm where you stayed.'

He bowed his head. Swallowed. Her need to hear the truth was greater than his need to prolong his pretence of memory loss. 'It was Major Flint who took the trouble to tame him. And though the creature accepted the rest of us as part of Flint's pack, I suppose you would call it, he clearly feels he belongs to Flint.'

'Oh,' she said. 'Yes, I see. It was foolish of me to think…'

He held her hand a bit tighter.

'You were magnificent,' he stated resolutely.

'Me?' She gave a convulsive shiver. 'Look at me. I'm shaking like a leaf. It was horrible. Horrible. That was the first time I've ever stood up to someone like that. Face-to-face. I didn't know I could. And now I just feel sick.'

'It is always like that after a battle, for everyone. It's odd. You can do incredible, awful things while the battle rages, without turning a hair, but then after, well, tremble like aspens.'

'I wish I hadn't had to. That was the first time I've ever spoken to Major Flint and it was as though he was my enemy. And he's my—' she gave a little hiccup of a sob '—he's my b-brother. And he's taken Ben. I thought we were a team,' she said, gazing at the door through which they'd just gone. 'I don't care if he is Major F-Flint's d-dog...I...'

She bowed her head and gave in.

Normally, the sight of a woman in tears would have made him run a mile. But not when that woman was Lady Sarah. He knew there was nothing he could do to assuage the grief Major Flint had just inflicted, one way and another. But he could at least hold her while she wept.

The way she'd held him during his darkest hours.

Chapter Seven

Tom struggled to a sitting position, then scooted up until he could kneel behind her and put his arms round her. Though he'd half-feared she might flinch away, she actually turned and buried her face in his chest.

Though he was naked, battered and bruised and practically a stranger to her.

Pretty soon he was shaking with the effort of staying upright and keeping his arms round her, and half-bearing her weight. Heavens, but he was weak. His head was starting to spin by the time her sobs subsided.

'I'm so sorry—' she sniffed '—I'm not usually such a watering pot. And all over a man taking back his own dog, of all things.'

'It wasn't just that though, was it?' he said grimly. 'You'd only just heard your twin brother was cut to pieces by cavalry sabres.'

She flinched. Pulled out of his arms. Scrubbed at her eyes with a corner of the sheet.

He'd offended her. As well as blowing any chance he could carry on feigning ignorance of his identity and his past. Exhausted and depressed, he gave up the struggle to stay upright and lay back down against the pillows.

'Oh, Tom, I'm so sorry. Here I am weeping all over you when I'm supposed to be the one looking after you.' She leapt to her feet, tidying the sheet over him and generally fussing round the bed.

'No. *I'm* sorry. I thought I could be of help. I know I can't take the place Ben had in your affections, but I thought I could at least hold you. But I can't even do that.' He tried to lift his arm from the bed. 'I'm useless. Trembling like a whipped pup.'

'Don't ever let anyone tell you you're useless,' she flung at him angrily.

'Is that what they did to you? Is that why you fought Flint over me?' That made sense. In himself, he was nothing to her. But he had just worked out that her family had no idea what she was capable of. So perhaps he'd become a sort of symbol of her prowess.

She had the grace to look abashed.

'It doesn't matter.' He shrugged one shoulder.

'I've always known I'm not worth fighting for, myself.'

'Please, don't be disappointed in me. I didn't know you when I found you on the battlefield. And I was... Oh, you can't think what a difference it made when your men put their faith in me. When they believed I was capable of nursing you. When nobody has ever thought I'm capable of *anything*.'

'Yes. I think I can.' He gave her a rueful smile. 'Nobody's ever thought I was worth a damn. And in *my* case, they were right.'

'Oh, no. I'm sure that's not true. You're an officer in the army. Artillery, no less. Which shows you have intelligence. And to rise to the rank of major, you must be, um...'

He gave a snort. 'All it shows is that I've survived.'

'Oh, no! Far more than that. One thing I do know about the artillery is that you cannot buy promotion, or use influence to gain it. You must have earned every single promotion you've ever had.'

'Be that as it may, if Major Flint had found you nursing someone like Bennington Ffog...' His lip curled as he named the man who'd been her most prominent admirer. The fop who'd been in charge of her twin's regiment. And the man after whom his own men had named the Dog. Bennington Dog, they called him, shortening it to just Ben when the animal didn't respond to the mouthful of English. Which made them swear the name was all the more appropriate. Not only did the hound have fur the exact shade of the Colonel's luxuriant whiskers, the two of them had about the same level of intelligence. And having seen the man lolloping around after Lady Sarah with his tongue hanging out, the way Ben had done the day before, he couldn't disagree with them.

Not only that, but they were both hunting mad. He'd had a notion that if he'd thrown a bone and shouted 'fetch,' the Colonel would have yelled 'tally ho' and gone off in hot pursuit.

'Not even Flint would have suggested removing you from his bed and leaving *him* to rot. Or risk moving him, rather than have you tainted by the association. If Flint had found you in *his* arms, he'd have been talking about making it right by marrying him.'

'Oh. Yes. I hadn't thought of that.'

'Well, you should.' He seethed. Nobody thought Bennington Ffog was unsuitable—though he had less brains than his horse—because he had money and breeding. Whereas even Flint didn't want *him* anywhere near her. 'Your brothers would prefer to see me dead than married to you.'

She gave a bitter little smile. 'That's what you think. I think they'd prefer to see me married to *anyone* than being…being…oh, why are we talking about marriage? You don't want it, any more than I do.'

'It isn't a question of wanting it, or not. I haven't anything to offer a woman. Let alone a lady. I can't marry.'

Her eyes flicked down over his naked torso with a certain sort of gleam.

Good God! She seemed to think he *did* have something to offer a woman. His heart beat a little harder. His plan to get her to let him kiss her didn't seem so far-fetched, after all. She was attracted to him. How that could be when she'd seen him at his very weakest, when he could hardly sit up for five minutes, when he was covered with cuts and bruises, he couldn't think.

But she'd definitely given him a hungry little look. Even if she had swiftly wiped her face clean of expression and resumed her mask of polite, ladylike respectability.

She already looked on him as a kind of symbol of rebellion. How far, he wondered, could he get her to rebel? Against the narrow confinement of her life? Against the injustice of having to put up with men like Bennington Ffog slavering over her?

'I'm sorry I got cross. I don't want to fight with you, Tom. I just…' She rubbed wearily at her forehead.

She probably didn't want him slavering over her, either. She was only just beginning to change her mind about kissing him. He'd better not push his luck, after that one slim sign of encouragement, or she'd bolt like an unbroken filly. He'd have to persuade her to trust him, before making another move.

What? What was he thinking? He never bothered to *persuade* a woman to trust him, or attempted to woo her gently. But then no other woman was like Lady Sarah. Wasn't she worth making an effort for?

Besides, he wasn't going anywhere. And neither, to judge from her spirited resistance to Flint's orders, was she.

And his aim wasn't full congress. He knew he could never be with her, in that way. All he wanted was a kiss. Just one. Willingly given.

'You've worn yourself out looking after me,' he said, reaching up to soothe the little frown line pleating her brows. She didn't slap his hand away, but closed her eyes and sort of sank into his caress. The innocent little gesture of gratitude made his heart skip more than it would have done had another woman come in here and stripped naked.

'If I had any decency about me,' he growled, 'I'd offer to leave here and go to a hospital or something. That would be the honourable course to take. But I'm not going to.'

Her eyes flew open. She regarded him with frank curiosity. 'Because you aren't an honourable man?'

Hell, no. He wasn't in the slightest bit honourable. Or he wouldn't be planning ways to gain her trust so that he could take advantage.

'More to the point,' he said with what he hoped was a disarming grin, 'because you haven't *asked* me to leave. For some reason, which I suspect has nothing to do with me at all, you want me right where you've got me.'

She flushed. Moved away a little, so that her forehead was out of his reach. He let his hand fall back to his side.

'You're right.' She lifted her chin. 'I do want you to stay here with me. It may be terribly shallow of me, but while I'm looking after you, while you have to depend on me for everything, I feel as if my life has some purpose, for once.'

'Well, I'm happy to stay as sick as you like, for as long as you feel you need to nurse someone.'

'Oh, Tom, don't say that. I want you to get well. You *have* to get well. To show everyone that…and to myself that—' She broke off, shaking her head. 'It's terribly selfish of me, isn't it? To be nursing you just to prove a point?' She peeped up at him from under lowered lashes.

He reached out and took her hand.

'I'm sure you have perfectly good reasons for everything you do. I know, better than anyone, that people are apt to judge others on their actions, without pausing to consider what their motives might be.'

She gasped. Clasped his hand a little tighter. 'That's very generous of you.'

He gave a wry smile. 'Not really. But after the way Major Flint jumped to all the wrong conclusions about us, because of what he saw—me naked, you clasped in my arms—' he quirked one eyebrow suggestively '—he assumed guilt. People always assume the worst. Though how he could have thought the worst of you…' He scowled, not only because Flint had suggested it, but also because he minded that Flint thought it.

He'd never cared what anyone thought of any

of his women before. Not that Lady Sarah was his woman.

Perhaps he felt protective towards her because no other woman had ever gone to such lengths on his behalf before. Even if it was only to prove a point.

'Tom, you have got to stop thinking I'm some kind of angel. I'm not. I stumbled into looking after you for a whole series of stupid, selfish, reasons. Not one of them was the slightest bit angelic, I assure you.'

'Tell me, then. I should like to know how you came to stumble upon me. What someone like you was doing on a battlefield at all.'

She searched his face for evidence that he condemned her for being on the battlefield. She couldn't find it. He just looked interested. Curious.

When was the last time anyone had wanted to know why she'd done anything? Been interested in hearing her side of things, rather than just passing judgement on her?

'I went to the battlefield searching for Gideon,' she said. 'Or his body. Or some answers. That was what I told myself. But I suspect it was all lunacy, really. I just couldn't believe he was dead.

They wouldn't tell me anything that would have convinced me. Not even when the funeral was to be, or where,' she said, hitching her knee up on to the side of the bed so that she could look him full in the face. And judge his reaction. She took a deep breath.

'And I was so sure that Gideon couldn't have died without me knowing it, in my heart. Our nurse always used to say we were one soul, living in two bodies, you see. And we were so close, so very close, that I thought…I thought…' She shook her head. 'How could I have been so wrong? So foolish?'

He gripped her hand tightly. 'You weren't foolish at all.'

'Oh, but I was. I realised it not long before those Hussars came charging along the road, scattering wreckage in their path. I felt just like Ben, who was howling with panic from under that broken wagon. Stuck there, with no idea where to go next. And then when that deserter tried to steal Castor—' She shuddered.

'You must have been terrified.'

'No! That was just it. Not of him, at any rate. Only of losing the horse. Not for any sensible reason, either. But because he was the last present Gideon had given me. My last tangible link to him. He had another grey, to match, and we used to go riding out together. Cutting a dash, don't you know? Golden-haired twins on matching horses. He even wanted me to have a riding habit made up in the same colour and style as his uniform, to heighten the effect. So that people would say we looked like the heavenly twins, Castor and Pollux.'

'I saw you,' he said.

'Yes, so you did,' she replied, remembering the day and him leaning up against the tree. 'You winked at me.'

He wriggled uncomfortably, opening his mouth as though reaching for something to say. But there wasn't anything she wanted to hear about that day. That time. The man he'd been then. So she plunged on hurriedly.

'Anyway, I couldn't bear losing Castor. So I went back to Brussels to find somewhere safe to hide him, in case the French really were about to overrun the town. I slept in the stable with him, because I was afraid to take my eyes off him. I'd only been under the wagon trying to untie Ben for a few moments, you see, and that was all it took for the deserter to get his reins in his hands. I never gave a thought to my own safety, or anything sensible. It was all about keeping some link, any link, to Gideon.' She hung her head.

'Even when I started to accept he really had… died…my head was still full of nonsense. When you just fell into my lap, I told myself *that* was the purpose for my being there. It made me feel better, for a while, to think that maybe some fate had directed me to you. That those feelings I had, that I simply *had* to come back to Brussels, were some kind of intuition, or something. That's how foolish I've been…'

'No. I won't hear you say bad things about yourself.'

'But I ran away from home. Worried my poor sister, who is in a fragile state of health. Angered her husband. Flouted Justin. All because I refused to accept the truth. Oh, how could I have gone about spouting all that nonsense about not sensing his spirit leaving the world? Madame le Brun must have thought I was deranged, turning up on her doorstep babbling the way I did.'

'Sometimes,' he said grimly, 'when something bad happens and you don't want to believe it, you get this shout inside. This great, overwhelming *No!* It drowns out everything else. All common sense. Even when the evidence is right before your eyes you won't see it. All you can hear, or say, or feel is that *No.*'

She stared at him in amazement. She'd half-expected him to roll his eyes, the way her older brother and sisters did whenever she mentioned her belief about her link to her twin. They always said she should have grown out of the tales her 'ignorant, ill-educated and superstitious' nurse had told her.

'I've never held all that much regard for common sense,' she told him. 'Because,' she added hesitantly, 'nobody has ever been able to explain, for all their rational, cynical cleverness, how it was that I always knew when Gideon was about to get into a scrape. How I could always sense when he was on his way home. Or how, when he was home, we only had to look at each other to understand what the other was thinking.'

'Really? That's astonishing.'

He meant it, too, she could tell. He wasn't humouring her, or even making fun of her, let alone trying to rob her of her beliefs.

'Thank you for saying that, Tom, about the *No.*' Even though everyone she knew insisted Tom was bad, what he'd just said had actually helped her untangle her muddled thoughts. Had helped her look upon her loss and confusion from a new perspective.

How was that possible, when he scarcely knew her?

'You speak as though you have felt just like I did when they told me Gideon was dead. Almost impossible to believe, it was so bad. Did something like that happen to you?'

'Yes,' he said gruffly. 'When my father died. I lost everything I thought I had. Everything I thought I was. And, even once the shout of *No* died down,' he said, giving her a very speaking look, 'I still didn't know who I was. There was no going back, yet it took me a long time to forge a new path for myself. But you will get there,' he assured her. 'You are strong.'

He thought she was strong? Then he was the only man…no, the only person ever to think so.

'And you are an adult. With a family to support you. Not a child who has no understanding of the way the world works.'

'A child?' He had lost everything when he'd been a child?

'What happened to you, Tom? How have you ended up the way you are?'

'The way I am?' He stretched his lips into a cynical smile.

'Yes, the way you are,' she retorted. 'Smiling like that as though…as though…well, it's a mask, isn't it? And don't bother arguing, I can see when someone is hiding behind smiles and attitudes, because I've done it myself, practically all my life. And because I've seen you without it—the mask. The fever tore it away. So stop talking all that rot about not being good enough and having nothing to offer. It's an excuse. You don't *want* to let anyone close. That's all there is to it.'

'Be careful, Lady Sarah,' he growled. 'Or I might start to think you'd changed your mind about staying single.'

'Don't change the subject,' she snapped. 'I can tell when someone is trying to distract me from answering the question. If you don't want to tell me, then don't. If it is some deep, dark terrible family secret, then just say so.'

He winced. 'Secret? It's no secret. My family has caused so much scandal there is no hushing it up.'

She knew exactly how that felt.

'And you have to live with it,' she said. 'Find a way to hold your head up in public, when you know full well people are whispering about the scandal behind their fans.'

'Yes, I have to live with it,' he breathed. 'I have

to live with the fact my father hanged himself. After gambling away everything he'd ever owned.'

'Oh, my goodness!' Sarah clapped her hand to her mouth in horror. 'I thought my father was an utter disgrace, but even he never forgot what he owed to his name. Not entirely.'

'Exactly,' he said with a bitter smile. 'Most men, if they should get to the point where they feel there is only one way out, would make it look like a hunting accident. So that their children could still inherit. Well, actually, there were only debts left to inherit. My grandfather had already lost the title.'

'Lost the title?' Tom came from a noble family? 'How on earth did he manage to do that?'

'Spoke out in support of Charles Stuart's claim to the throne,' he said grimly. 'Then threw in his lot with the Jacobites. So there you have it, Lady Sarah. My grandfather was a traitor. My father, well, the best you could say of him was that he was unhinged. But after two generations of scandal, nobody has any doubt that I have tainted blood.'

'You really did lose everything,' she said in a hollow whisper. 'It makes what I've lived through, what I've thought I've had to endure...' She shook her head in shame.

'None of that,' he said sharply. 'What happened

to me when I was a child doesn't make your own woes any less significant to you.'

'My woes are petty, though, aren't they? I've always had a secure home. And family. Even though I always thought that out of them all, only Gideon ever actually *liked* me.'

'From what you've told me so far, your father blighted your childhood in his own way.'

'Yes, but he was just a lecherous old goat who couldn't keep his hands off any pretty woman unfortunate enough to cross his path. And rather than having no sense of obligation to the title, he made absolutely sure,' she said with a bitter twist to her lips, 'that every single child my mother bore was his. He only left her alone when he was certain she was pregnant. By him.'

'My father's problem was the opposite of yours, then. He was totally infatuated with my mother. When she died—bringing me into the world, as it happens—he lost interest in everything else. Hanging himself was probably his way of ensuring I knew how much he disapproved of me surviving at the cost of the only woman he'd ever loved.'

'Our fathers were both as bad as each other,' she said, her lips tightening. 'How could yours abandon his child the way he abandoned you? Leaving you with nothing? Worse than nothing! He burdened you with the belief that somehow his failings were your fault. Ooh—' she clenched her fists '—I thought my father was a bad man, but to act the way yours did is downright unnatural.'

Tom had never really talked about this with anyone before. It was something everyone who knew him knew, anyway. He'd been taunted about it, frequently, but nobody had ever asked him how he felt about it. Let alone taken his part, the way Lady Sarah had just done.

She had such a generous heart, to get all indignant on behalf of a little orphaned boy, rather than react to the disgrace she'd just learned was his inheritance. In that, she was unique. Society ladies, in his experience, had always fallen into one of two camps. There were the ones who turned their noses up at him. Who even twitched their skirts aside to avoid getting accidentally contaminated.

And those who got sexually aroused by the aura of disrepute surrounding him.

Not one of them had appeared to understand exactly how he felt about it, or had even been that interested, come to that.

'What happened to you next? You were only six, you say?' Sarah curled up in the chair next to the bed and rested her cheek on her hand. 'Did you have to go into a foundling home?'

'No. Worse. My father's sister took me in.'

'How could that possibly have been worse?'

'Well, her husband looked upon me as the spawn of a weak, degenerate man, who was in his turn the spawn of a traitor. And felt it was his Christian duty to ensure I didn't follow in their footsteps. Which was his excuse for taking every chance he could to beat the evil out of me.'

'Did not your aunt try to stop him? After all, your bad blood ran in her veins, too.'

'Ah. Well, looking back, I can see she was too afraid of him to stand up to him. He was a vicious bully. But as a child, I didn't understand. I just thought she believed what he said and didn't think it worth the bother of looking for some evidence of good in me. Of course,' he said, his smile turning a little wicked, 'their attitude had a predictable effect. Since I soon learned that trying to be good didn't ameliorate their treatment, there didn't seem much point in trying. In fact, rather the opposite. If I was going to get a beating, I decided I may as well have done something worth getting the beating for.'

'Good for you.' She gave a determined nod. 'I

hope you made their lives as miserable as they made yours.'

He gave a bark of laughter. 'Well, do you know, I rather think I did. I became a regular little hellion. They couldn't keep me in school. I much preferred being out of doors with the other village lads, of whom I was pretty soon the ringleader. Before long, if there was any trouble within fifteen miles of our village, they laid it at my door,' he finished with a glimmer of pride.

'My uncle said if he didn't put a stop to my criminal career I'd end up hanging, just like my father. And so he decided the best course was to let the army have me. Only then he faced a bit of a dilemma. As the son of a gentleman, he couldn't very well have me enlist like a common man. But neither did he want to go to all the expense of buying me a commission. So he sent me off to the Royal Military Academy at Woolwich, where they trained me to become both an officer and an engineer,' he finished with a grimace.

'There is nothing wrong with that,' she retorted. 'Justin himself chose to serve in the artillery, like our grandfather.'

'Yes, but it isn't the done thing, is it? Far more acceptable to go into the cavalry, or the Guards.'

'People don't just go into the cavalry to be acceptable,' she said, a little flash of annoyance in her eyes. 'Gideon wanted to... He would have...' She stopped and drew in a shuddery sort of breath. 'He idolised Justin, but he didn't want to ape him. So Mama bought him a commission in a cavalry regiment. She was the one who wanted him to be fashionable. Gideon never cared for any of that. He's like... I mean, he *was* like me. Never happier than when on horseback. Whenever he was home we used to pack our saddlebags and just take off. We'd stay out all day,' she said with a faraway look in her eye. 'It started when we were very little. We'd slip away from the schoolroom and hide somewhere on the estate. We'd dam streams and climb trees, and make dens in the woods. Even when they sent him away to school, he couldn't wait to come home so we could play together. And tell each other all the things we couldn't put in any of the letters we wrote. Once or twice he brought friends to stay, but they only spoiled things by asking why on earth he let a girl tag along. And he'd declare I wasn't a bit like most girls. That I could stay out all day and not get tired, or complain about mud, or brambles. And he never invited them again.'

She wasn't a bit like most girls. Most women.

He could talk to her. As though she was a…a friend.

He wished he'd known her when he'd been a grubby, half-starved boy. He might not have grown up so certain the whole world was against him. He was just wondering whether to tell her so when Madame le Brun came in with a breakfast tray.

'Good morning. You are looking so much better,' she said, running her eyes over him assessingly.

'Down to your amazing cooking,' Tom replied, casting aside the temptation to confess things better left unsaid. He gave the landlady the benefit of his most flirtatious smile. 'And having my every whim catered to by two such beautiful women.' He leaned back and tucked both hands behind his head. 'You are making me feel like a sultan in a harem.'

To Sarah's amazement, the landlady, who must have been fifty if she was a day, blushed and laughed in a very girlish way, then shook her finger at him, in mock admonishment. She then spent rather longer than she needed, flitting about the room setting things to rights. When she left, Sarah shook her head at Tom.

'What?' He shrugged and widened his eyes in

mock innocence. 'Flirting does no harm. She enjoys it.'

He'd got in the habit of flirting with women, he realised, as he took a spoonful of the eggs Madame had brought. All women, no matter what their age. Making them blush and simper gave him the upper hand. By making them react to what he was doing, rather than letting them get in first, he controlled them. Kept them in their place.

Flirting was the quickest way to discover whether they'd be willing to lift their skirts, too. If a woman was amenable, his next objective was normally to find out how quickly. If she wasn't, he always moved on to the next likely prospect without hesitation. It was a ruthless method. A foolproof method that got him bedded more frequently than any other officer in the Rogues. Or any other unit in which he'd served.

Maybe that was why he'd toned things down with Lady Sarah. He didn't want to try and control her, or keep her in her place. It felt more important to get to know her—right down to the very bones of her. And flirting too brazenly would only put her on her guard against him.

Oh, he still wanted to kiss her, make no mistake. More than that. Much, much more. Though he didn't want it to be like the crude encounters of his past, that satisfied a momentary itch. He wanted…he wanted…

All of a sudden the words of the marriage vows popped into his head. *With my body, I thee worship…*

A chill curled its fist round the back of his neck. He wasn't contemplating *marriage*. It was just that Sarah was the kind of girl who deserved marriage. Yes, that was it. She should have someone who loved and cherished her, and all the rest of it. Hadn't she already roused all sorts of similar responses from him? Feelings of protectiveness, and friendship, and loyalty. The chill receded. Now he knew where the sudden understanding of the marriage lines had come from, there was no need to panic. He wasn't in danger of doing anything stupid, like falling in love with her, and proposing marriage himself.

Men like him didn't fall in love.

Didn't know how.

Chapter Eight

Sarah took her dish of chocolate to the writing desk and gazed out of the window as she sipped at it. Another funeral procession was snaking along the street. Every day, more young men were dying of wounds inflicted in the battle that had taken Gideon from her. Her nose felt hot. Though she blinked rapidly, she couldn't prevent a single tear sliding down her cheek. Though why should she even try to hold it back? She'd lost Gideon, and to know so many more young men were dying was utterly tragic.

She *wasn't* upset by the fact that, though Tom was now well enough to flirt with the landlady, he'd started treating her more like a…like a sort of sister. Yes, a sister, that was it. They'd just spent the morning talking with each other exactly the way she and Gideon used to. Sharing thoughts openly. Trusting the other with cherished beliefs and the pains of their past.

She delved into the top drawer and pulled out a handkerchief. She blew her nose as quietly as she could, glancing at Tom in case he'd noticed her distress.

But he was lying back on the pillows, his face ashen, his breakfast tray tilting at a dangerous angle.

She got up quickly and saved it before it went crashing to the floor. Didn't pause to look back, but went with it to the door.

'I will leave you to sleep,' she said, keeping her face, and in particular the evidence of her tears, averted. 'You look exhausted.'

She would be a fool to sit about all day, waiting for this connoisseur of women to look at her *that* way. It wasn't going to happen. Men didn't find her attractive. Oh, plenty of them had shown an interest in marrying her, once they knew who she was, who she was related to and how much wealth she had at her back. But as a woman? No. She had less appeal, apparently, than a fifty-year-old Belgian landlady.

It was all very well Tom saying he was willing to stay sick for as long as she needed him. But he didn't mean it. As soon as he was strong enough to walk, he would reclaim his freedom. He'd told her he wasn't the marrying kind. Which meant, really, that he didn't want to be tied to one woman.

Particularly not a foolish, fey, plain one like her.

'I need to wash and change, and, well, heavens, but I have been neglecting Castor. Talking about how I used to spend all day riding about with Gideon has made me quite...' She bit down on her lower lip. It was one thing making excuses, another to embroider them to the point where they became outright lies.

'Of course,' he said with a tight smile. 'You should go out and get some fresh air. It will do you good. And in truth, I do want to sleep. There really is no point in you sitting here all day, is there?'

'None whatever,' she said with a toss of her head.

It was a relief to reach the stables, with its familiar smells and sounds.

'It's not as if I *want* him to flirt with me,' she informed Castor, giving his velvety nose a rub. 'Why would I? I detest rakes.' Though she didn't detest Tom.

'It's just as well I did want to come out for a ride, isn't it? Because the last thing I would ever do is sit about all day waiting for some man to admire me. Or pretend to, because that is what rakes generally do. Ooh,' she breathed, leaning into the reassuringly solid column of Castor's neck, 'I thought he looked full of himself, the first time I saw him. He may not have a title, apart from his army rank, but he's certainly become lord of that room. He's one of those men who are born bossy, just like my brothers. Both Justin and Major Flint expect everyone else to do what they say. In fact, they don't even always need to say anything. Just the way they walk shows they think they are lords of all they survey. Not that Tom can actually walk at the moment, but if he did, he'd be strutting about the place, turning heads. Female heads, that is.'

Castor blew heavily through his nostrils, as if in complete agreement.

'And the worst of it is, I don't really understand why I mind. I knew he was a habitual womaniser when I scooped him up out of the mud. It's more than likely that he'll have a go at getting Jeanne to kiss him while I'm out.'

Her stomach clenched into a cold knot. She half-wanted to run back upstairs, to prevent any such thing from happening.

Instead, she firmed her mouth and led Castor

to the mounting block. 'If I find he's done any such thing,' she muttered between clenched teeth as they set off, 'I shall tip his next bowl of broth over his head.'

She hadn't gone more than a few yards before revising this punishment. But only because she remembered she was the one who'd have to change Tom's bandages if she did douse them in broth.

By the time she reached the end of the Allée Verte, she'd devised and discarded a dozen plans for punishing Tom. None of which would make her feel the slightest bit better. No, the only thing that would make her feel better would be making certain, somehow, that he wasn't kissing anyone else.

Even if it meant keeping him occupied with her own lips. It went against her principles, but it was the only course she could see that would satisfy her pride. Not that she'd ever kissed a man before, but how hard could it be? Anyway, Tom's vast experience would more than compensate for her own ignorance.

If she could get him to see her as kissable, that was.

Her determination to appear amenable to kisses took a nosedive the moment she set foot in his room, for in her absence he'd washed and shaved, and put on a shirt. In her imagination, during the ride home, it had been the piratically whiskered, half-naked Tom she'd approached and snuggled up to, and offered her mouth to.

This Tom, this clothed, clean, *proper* man, didn't look like her Tom at all. He made her feel shy and nervous, and aware of how improper her plan had been. Without the four days' growth of beard, he also looked very pale, which smote her conscience. He was her patient, for heaven's sake. He'd been grievously wounded. The last thing he needed was for some inquisitive spinster to fling herself on his chest and make demands he'd shown no sign of wanting to fulfil.

'What's the matter?' he said, with a quick frown. 'Has something happened?'

Nothing she could confess. Only stupid things that had gone on inside her own head, which she hung in shame.

And caught sight of the hat she was clutching in nervous fingers.

'I don't like this hat,' she said inanely, 'anywhere near as much as the one I lost that day I went searching the battlefield.' It was either that, or blurt out her confused, contradictory reactions to seeing him properly clothed, instead of all naked and tempting. 'I suppose it doesn't matter. The riding habit it matched had to be burned, anyway.'

'Never mind your hat. Or your gown. I know that isn't what is upsetting you.'

'No. You are right.' She went to the window and stood looking out for a moment or two, gathering the strength to turn round and face him again. The new Tom. Or was it the true Tom? She blinked away her confusion. Whichever it was, it was no longer *her* Tom, that was what was upsetting her.

'It is the terrible waste of it all,' she said, instead. 'So many men, young men at that, with nobody to care what becomes of them, from the looks of it. Oh, the citizens are doing what they can. Taking them food and drink. And some of the hotels are putting straw down for them to make them more comfortable. But I just…' She wound the stings of her hat round and round her fingers. 'I wish I could *do* something.'

'You are doing something. You are nursing me. You saved *me*, Lady Sarah.'

'Yes. Thank goodness your men brought you here. I've heard some officers, ones who went back to their own billets, died while waiting to get medical attention. So I know I saved you. But you are just one. And there are so many more of them out there.' She waved her hand towards the window. Her hat caught at the potted geranium, spraying the sill with blood-red petals. 'And I feel so helpless. I dare say,' she muttered darkly, 'Mary has turned her school into a regular hospital by now.'

'Mary?'

'Mary Endacott. The woman…' She'd been about to say, the woman who was going to marry Justin. But who knew how that was going to end?

'The woman who helped me make my way to the battlefield, to search for my brother. The one who is nursing him, now. She's so capable, so organised. I'm sure *she* won't be stretched to her limits nursing just one man.'

'Lady Sarah, don't disparage yourself this way. What you have done for me is nothing short of miraculous. I never thought—'

'No. And nor would anyone else think me able to cope with anything so real as stitching up wounds or nursing a sick man through a fever. A social butterfly, that's all I am.'

'No, Lady Sarah. You are so much more than that.'

'What?' She flung her poor abused riding hat across the room in vexation. 'What more to me is there than fashionable clothes and insipid con-versation?'

'Loyalty,' he replied without a second's hesita-tion. 'To your brother. Not many society women would stir themselves out of their safe drawing rooms to go hunting for an injured brother. Nor take pity on anyone else, if she didn't find who she was looking for. Nor put themselves through such an ordeal. Most society women would have turned me over to the care of servants, rather than contaminate their fair little hands with my blood, my sweat.'

'No, I'm sure that's not true.'

'Oh, but it is. This Mary person may be more used to dealing with practical matters, if she's a schoolmistress. But don't compare your great-ness of heart to her ability to cope with things as a matter of course.'

Heavens, no wonder she wanted her first kiss to come from his lips. He might not mean the half of what he said, kissing her might mean nothing to him, but oh, how she wanted to believe he ad-mired her. He kept on making her feel as if there was something about her, apart from her title and wealth. As if he'd seen something in her that no-body else ever had.

She smiled at him sadly.

'You are so sweet, Tom, to say things like that. But—'

'I'm only saying it because I believe it. Lady Sarah, you may have led a sheltered life up till now, but these few days have shown what you really are, deep inside. And what you are is brave and compassionate, and kind. You haven't run from your fears, or hidden behind propriety. You just rolled your sleeves up and did what had to be done.'

Perhaps that was what she should do now. Roll up her sleeves, take his face between her hands and show him what she needed.

Her heart banging against her ribs, she went to the bed and sat down. Reached out her hand.

But what if he didn't really mean all those things he said? What if he didn't find her attractive?

Instead of leaning forward and kissing him, she just took the hand he held out to her and pressed it to her cheek.

'Oh, Tom.' No wonder he was so successful with women. He knew exactly what to say to make them feel good about themselves. To make their hearts melt with tenderness towards him. To want to press kisses all over his dear, battered face.

This was what made rakes so dangerous. This was exactly why she avoided them.

Fortunately, Madame le Brun came in just then, with another tray of soup and freshly baked bread, before she could summon up the courage to really make a fool of herself.

And after they'd eaten, she took care to keep the atmosphere light.

But as night drew on and the time for going to bed loomed ever closer, Sarah became more and more aware that tonight it was all going to be very different. The impropriety of sharing a room with Tom when he'd been crazed with fever hadn't bothered her very much at all. Besides, she'd remained fully dressed, since there hadn't been the time, or the opportunity, to change into her nightwear.

But tonight he was in his right mind. And even though she'd had Gaston install a screen between his bed and the pallet she was going to use, it still felt positively scandalous to come into his room in her nightgown, rather than her day clothes. Especially when she'd been thinking about kissing him, on and off, all afternoon.

Not that he'd shown any inclination to attempt anything improper, she sighed, flicking her braided hair over her shoulder. For all his talk about her being loyal and brave, and compassionate, he hadn't said anything about her being desirable.

Not that she wanted him to, she huffed as she lay down on the pallet and pulled the blankets up to her chin. Not now her fit of jealousy, or whatever it was, when she'd thought about him kissing someone else, had worn off. She *didn't* want *that* kind of attention from such a notorious rake. It would be terribly wearing, having to fend him off all the time.

And she would fend him off. Of course she would.

She turned on her side and thumped the pillow into shape. She mustn't forget that if he did attempt to seduce her, it would only be because it was his nature to try to bed the nearest available woman. She had too much pride to join the long line of women who'd fallen prostrate at his feet.

Even if he asked her to.

Which he hadn't. Wouldn't.

She turned over again, vainly trying to find a comfortable position. Which was impossible when she was so very aware of him lying there, not four feet away, clad only in a nightshirt, so far as she could tell.

But her eyelids soon grew too heavy to hold open. She hadn't slept in more than brief snatches for days. Had worked harder, and been through more than she ever had in her whole life.

And, according to Tom, had learned what she was really made of. She'd always known she didn't have what it took to be a brilliant social hostess like Gussie, she might not have any interest in all the worthy causes that so fired up her other sister Harriet, she might not be practical and clever like Mary, but for the first time in her life, none of that seemed to matter.

Loyal and brave, he'd said. *Compassionate and kind.*

Those things were all much better than being clever, or accomplished, weren't they? At least, the way he'd said it sounded as though he thought so.

Which made her almost believe it, too.

How he wished he hadn't said he didn't need anything for the pain. It was all very well hating the way it clouded his mind. And he certainly didn't want to end up craving it, the way he'd seen so many men fall victim to laudanum once it got its hooks into them.

But nor did he relish lying here, wide-awake, feeling like one enormous bruise. Everything ached. Everything.

He slid one hand under the sheet, seeking to ease the place he ached most of all. The one ache he could do something about, for himself.

He must be on the mend, if *that* could be giving him so much trouble.

It had started to sit up and take notice the moment Lady Sarah had left the room to go and prepare for bed. There was a little room, a room that had been her maid's when she'd stayed here before, she'd told him, which she was now using as a dressing room. Which was right next door. Her washstand must be on the other side of the wall from the head of his bed, because he'd distinctly heard the sound of water being poured into a basin. And splashing. His imagination had supplied the rest. He'd imagined buttons unpopping. Clothing slithering to the floor. Porcelain-white skin, all wet and soapy. Water running down her body just where he wanted to run his hands. Then, of course, she'd rub herself dry with a towel. Her face first, and then her arms, her legs, her breasts...

His breath quickened. He whipped his hand away, clenching it into a fist. What was he doing? He couldn't sully her with his lustful imaginings, when she was lying there, unaware. It felt so wrong.

He stifled a groan as the ropes of her pallet creaked. She was turning over. Trying in vain to get comfortable, because he'd taken possession of her bed. And now she was throwing the blankets off. Because she was too hot. Well, it was a hot and sultry night.

He was certainly sweating. Was she?

His mouth watered at the thought of swiping his tongue over her neck, down, over her breasts, tasting the salt of her. The woman taste of her. He wanted to lick her all over, until she moaned with pleasure.

Right on cue, she did moan. Shifted on her bed, just as though she was responding to his unclean thoughts.

He pressed the heels of his hands over his ears. Reached over his head for his pillow. Pulled it over his face.

But it couldn't block out the sound of Sarah's sudden, strangled scream.

Tom flung the pillow aside. Of course she wasn't lying there dreaming of an earthy encounter with him. He sat up as she moaned again. No—by the sound of it, she was having a nightmare.

A pretty nasty one, if he was any judge. She was whimpering now. And from the way the screen suddenly rattled, she'd flung out her hand to ward off…something.

He got out of bed, planted his feet on the floor and waited a second or two for the room to stop spinning. Then tottered the few feet to the end of the screen, rounded it and stood looking down at her. His breath caught. God, but she was lovely, lying in the abandoned sprawl of sleep. She'd kicked off all her blankets, and rucked her nightgown up to her knees. A gentleman wouldn't let his eyes linger, but he couldn't help savouring the sight of her beautiful, shapely legs.

'Lady Sarah,' he murmured gently, dropping to his knees at her side. 'Wake up.'

She whimpered again. In the feeble light that made it to this darkened corner of the room from his bedside candle, he could see silvery trails of tears streaking her cheeks, which brought him to his senses. No longer did he want to run his hands over those invitingly bared legs. He wanted to scoop her up into his arms and comfort her.

'Lady Sarah,' he said again, a little louder. 'You are having a nightmare.'

He reached down and shook her shoulder gently. Her eyes flew open wide.

'Tom!' Before he had a chance to explain that he had a perfectly innocent explanation for kneeling over her as she slept, she'd flung her arms round his neck and buried her face against him.

'Oh, Tom, it was horrible. Horrible!'

'It's over now. It was just a nightmare.' He put his arms round her. Inhaled the fragrance of sleepy woman. The scent that was normally a prelude to becoming intimate.

He gritted his teeth. That wasn't what Sarah needed from him tonight. She wasn't an experienced woman looking for a good time, but a vulnerable young lady who'd only stumbled into his life by accident. And what she needed after a nightmare was to feel safe, secure.

Actually, tonight she probably would be perfectly safe from him, even if his conscience wasn't shouting at him like a regimental sergeant-major. He simply wasn't fit enough to do her any real mischief.

'No.' She shuddered. 'It wasn't just a nightmare. It was Gideon…and…'

She went still. Her eyes narrowed.

'What are you doing out of bed?'

'You were crying out. So…'

'I woke you? Oh, Tom, I'm so sorry.'

'Lord, Sarah, you've lost enough sleep sitting up with me through my nightmares this past couple of days.'

'That's not the same. You were wounded.'

'And you weren't?'

'I meant physically.'

'Yes, but you've been through a terrible ordeal.'

'I wasn't hacked at by French cavalry, then buried for hours under a pile of rubble,' she replied tartly. 'Come on, Tom, let's get you back to bed.'

He leaned back on his heels. 'You don't think I can make it there on my own?'

'Well, I don't know, do I? This is the first time you've been out of bed. And I don't want all my hard work undone by having you go off into a swoon, or something. Then we'd have to wake up Gaston to carry you back, because I certainly don't have the strength.'

He could hear the concern in her voice though she was covering it up by saying she was only being practical.

She'd just suffered a horrific nightmare, yet she was trying to put his needs first.

Although—he glanced at her as she got her shoulder under his and helped him to his feet— perhaps doing something for him was helping her to push the nightmare aside. After all, that's what she'd been doing with him for the past few days. Nursing him had been salving her own hurt at not being able to do anything for either of her brothers.

So he let her lead him back to bed, where he meekly lay down while she tucked a sheet round his chest. The exertion of walking to her bed and back had dealt a deathblow to his arousal, thank goodness, or he wouldn't have been able to look her in the face.

'There. Comfortable?'

Not entirely.

He nodded.

'Good. Well, I should go back to bed, now.' She glanced over at the screen and gave an almost imperceptible shudder.

'Don't want to shut your eyes again, just yet?' He reached for her hand, and she took it. Clung to it. Shook her head. Then sat down in the chair beside his bed, her back ramrod straight, her eyes huge in her chalk-white face.

'And the last thing you want is to talk about it, I dare say,' he said sympathetically. 'I don't think I could talk about the ones I've had, the last few nights. They were so hellish. Bits of things that had really happened, all mixed up with horrors I didn't know I was capable of imagining.'

'Yes—' she gasped '—it was just like that. The bodies.' She gripped his hand so tightly that it was only then he became aware that formerly it had been just about the only part of him that hadn't hurt. 'Bodies everywhere. All hacked to bits. Or lying in the street, begging me for water when I didn't have any to give them. B-but they all of them had Gideon's face.' Her voice sank to a hoarse whisper, her mouth quivering with repressed pain and tears.

Propriety be damned. She needed more than just a hand to hold. Uttering an oath, he tugged her down on to his chest and wrapped his arms round her. Rocked her.

'It wasn't him,' he grated. 'He didn't go through any of that.'

'How do you know? How can you know what he went through?'

'Well, I don't, that's true. But…' He shifted uncomfortably. He'd thought he'd never speak of the things that had leapt up and leered at him through his fevered dreams. But Sarah needed to hear that what she was experiencing happened to other people, too.

'One of the nightmares I had, over and over again, was about a woman. A pregnant woman we discovered after we'd driven the French out of a Portuguese village. It was about the worst thing I'd ever seen. But she's been dead for years now.

So why did she leap out at me again last night? Right in the middle of all the things I was reliving from the battle that had just happened? It is as if the worst things, the things you won't allow yourself to think about while you're awake, jump out to taunt you when you're powerless to stop them.'

'Yes,' she breathed. 'I *had* been thinking about Gideon. That he might have lain there, alone and broken, like all the others I saw. And then, when I went to sleep, what I'd really seen got all jumbled up with the things I'd been fearing.'

She was shaking. Trembling all over, as though gripped by a fever.

His heart went out to her. He'd already established that she wasn't in any real danger from him tonight. Even if his conscience couldn't keep his lustful nature in check, in his weakened state, she'd have no trouble tipping him out of bed if he forgot himself. Besides, he wanted to comfort her, not seduce her. To repay her for all she'd done for him. Couldn't he, just once, give a woman something apart from an orgasm?

'Stay here with me for the rest of the night,' he breathed into her ear. 'Let me keep your nightmares at bay, the way you kept mine from me.'

'Did I? I didn't think so. They didn't seem to stop.'

'They didn't entirely. But somehow, the scent of you reached me even during the worst of them. The scent of violets will always remind me of you. Of the feeling of security that came from lying in your arms.' He breathed in deeply. 'For I knew the hellish landscape couldn't be real, because surely violets couldn't bloom in such a place. Even when I couldn't recall how I'd got there...' He shook his head.

'Oh, dear. The surgeon said you might never fully recover your memory.'

'I know I'd been in the thick of fighting all day. My ears were ringing. But to be honest, I can still only recall bits and pieces. The noise and the smoke. I know there was thunder, the night before we fought the battle in which I was injured. In my dreams, that thunderstorm got all jumbled up with the thunder of the guns. And the smell of the smoke became the flames from the pits of hell.'

'I'm not surprised you got dreams like that. We could hear the guns as far as Antwerp, on Friday. It did sound like a distant thunderstorm. I can't imagine what it must have been like to have actually been there.'

'You shouldn't have to,' he said fervently. A shiver went through him as her hand slid across his chest and came to rest, trustingly, over his heart.

'What else did you dream about?'

'I dreamed I was dead,' he said bleakly. 'And buried in my grave. Of course, I was only pinned down by all the stones from the wall that fell on me. But in my half-conscious, confused state, the men roaming the field by night looking for plunder became demons, collecting the souls of the damned. I wasn't totally convinced I wasn't dead until morning, when birds started singing. I knew birds wouldn't sing in hell. But even they got muddled up in my nightmares. The singing birds, and the wraith-like looters, merged into great black crows. There are always crows after battles, pecking at the bodies. I felt as though every cut of mine, every bruise, was evidence that they'd been there, feasting on my flesh.'

'Oh, Tom!' She flung her arms round his waist, hugging him tight. 'All those odd things you said make perfect sense now. It must have been dreadful.'

'I'm sorry, I'm sorry. I'm such an idiot.' Heaven help him, he'd just planted a whole new set of images in her head. 'I shouldn't have spoken about all that. It can't have helped.'

'It did, actually,' she retorted, 'because you're

a man. And a soldier. If even someone like you can have dreams like that, then it makes me feel that I'm not such a poor sort of creature, after all.'

'Everyone has nightmares after a battle,' he said grimly. 'Nobody knows how to stop them. And nobody speaks of them.' He gave a puzzled frown. 'Not usually, anyway.'

Without warning she pulled out of his arms, got up and disappeared behind the screen.

He sighed. Just when he thought he'd been making progress he went and said something that sent her running for cover. As though she didn't she trust him.

He snorted in derision. Of course she didn't trust him. Which was just as well. Every chivalrous impulse he felt towards her was almost immediately countered by an appallingly lustful one.

To his amazement she reappeared with one of the blankets from her bed draped over one arm.

'Just for tonight,' she said, climbing on to his bed beside him, on top of the sheet that covered him, 'we'll hold each other. I will keep your nightmares away from you,' she said, snapping the blanket open and arranging it over her legs. 'And you will keep mine away from me.'

She snuggled down next to him, tucked her head in the crook of his arm and draped her own arm over his waist. 'What do you say to that?' She twisted her head to look up at him.

It sounded like heaven.

It sounded like hell. It had been bad enough when she'd been across the room, with a screen and four foot of empty space between them. Now she was in his arms, close enough to kiss if she moved her face just a fraction further.

'I say yes.' He groaned and moved his own face just the necessary fraction.

His lips brushed hers lightly. Surely, just once wouldn't be such a terrible crime, would it? A kiss goodnight.

She gasped, and for a moment he thought she really was going to tip him out of bed. But then, miraculously, she pressed her own lips against his. Clasped him more tightly and wriggled closer.

'Don't do that,' he gasped.

'Am I hurting you?'

'No. Yes. It's agony,' he growled, burying his face in her neck. He hadn't been so aroused since his first fumbling encounter with a willing chambermaid. But this was no chambermaid. This was Sarah. An innocent. An angel.

He couldn't sully her. Not in his imagination and not in reality, either. He might have crossed many lines during the course of his career, but debauching respectable females hadn't been one of them.

'Go to sleep,' he bit out. 'Lie still and go to sleep.'

'But what about you?'

Yes, what about him? His aim had been to get a kiss from her, nothing more. But now he had kissed her, it wasn't enough. And if she didn't lie still and stop wriggling in that inviting way, he might forget what he owed her and attempt to go further.

'I will lie here and hold you. It is my turn. Whenever the bad things try to come back, you will feel my arms round you and know it's not real.'

'But…'

'Hush. I will keep you safe. I won't…' He shifted slightly, so that she wouldn't be able to feel his newly awakened arousal pressing into her hip. 'I would never harm you, Sarah. I couldn't.' His whole being revolted at the thought of any harm coming to her, from *any* source. 'I'd rather die.'

She went very still. And very quiet. For a moment he wondered if she knew the effect she'd had on him and was trying to decide whether it was more dangerous to stay in the bed with a randy soldier, or go back to her own bed and risk the nightmares returning.

Eventually, she gave a little sigh and snuggled back down. It seemed, for whatever reason, she'd decided to stay right where she was.

She trusted him.

His eyes stung. When was the last time anyone had trusted him? With so much as sixpence, let alone their very virtue?

Never. Nobody had ever had such faith in him. They'd all expected him to break his word. To behave badly. To let them down and cause mayhem.

His grip on her tightened as he swore to himself that he'd never do any of those things. He'd never break his word to her. Never let her down or cause her a moment's grief.

No matter what it cost him.

Chapter Nine

Lady Sarah woke with a smile on her face. Tom had been right. Whenever the dreams had threatened to turn troubling, she'd somehow sensed his arms round her. Known she wasn't alone, the way she'd been when she'd really gone to the battlefield. And though there were times when her dreams grew distressing, they never descended to the depths of horror she'd suffered before.

But even better had been his physical reaction. He'd stood to attention for her. She snuggled into his side, basking in the knowledge that he *could* feel desire for her, after all. She'd never been pretty, but these last few days, without a maid to help her, she hadn't even looked presentable. Her choice of outfits was limited to those few gowns sent to her by Odette, from that last order before they'd fled for Antwerp. Her hair was a complete mess. And her complexion must be blotchy, too, since she'd been crying on and off practically the whole time. She always looked particularly unappealing when she wept, which was one of the reasons she didn't do it often. Her nose, always her worst feature, glowed deep crimson, making it even more obvious and unattractive than ever. And her eyes, which actually were the one feature that wasn't half-bad, got bloodshot, her eyelashes all clumpy, effectively destroying their appeal.

And yet he'd been aroused. Better than that, she hadn't had to risk her pride by trying to get him to kiss her. He'd done it without the slightest provocation. Well, not deliberate provocation, anyway. She hadn't been thinking about getting him to kiss her when she'd climbed into bed with him. Not at all.

She sighed happily. He'd promised she need not fear, that he would rather die than harm her. By which, she knew, he meant he wouldn't act on the desire that his masculine body had made all too obvious.

Which, now she came to think of it, was a very unrakish thing to do. Rakes didn't care about anyone but themselves. She should know. Her father really had been a rake. Whenever he'd wanted a woman he'd just taken her—whether she was willing or not.

How could people accuse Tom of being a rake? Tom was…Tom was…just a man, an unmarried man, who enjoyed life to the full. It wasn't as if he was doing anything so very different from what her brothers and other officers did. Only, by the sound of it, more regularly and with a greater variety of women than them.

'You are awake, aren't you?'

She wriggled round at the sound of his low, gruff voice, to look up into Tom's face, and couldn't help sighing. Overnight his beard had started growing in, which made him look much more like her very own Tom again. The rather desperate, powder-blackened warrior who'd fallen into her lap on the battlefield. Though that wasn't what made her sigh. Not entirely, anyway. It was the look in his sea-green eyes. *Such* a look. Even a sensible, practical woman would want to drown in it.

And she'd never been, either.

She sighed again. 'Thank you for last night.'

'Hmmph.' He shifted as though he was in pain. 'Lady Sarah, I am glad I could be of service, but right now…'

'Yes? What is it?' She sat up, searching his face intently. He looked as though he was in great discomfort. 'Are you in pain?'

He grimaced. 'I need...I need...' He closed his eyes, clenching his fists on top of the sheet that covered him. 'Could you send for Gaston, do you think? And then give me a few moments' privacy?'

He probably needed to use the chamber pot.

She blushed and got out of bed. 'Of course.' She went to the bell pull by the fireplace and tugged on it sharply. 'Now that you are a little better, you probably want to try to get out of bed for a short while today, too.'

'And shave,' he growled, rubbing his hand over his chin. 'It is amazing how much better I felt yesterday after Gaston gave me a wash and shave.'

It was the proper thing to do—have a manservant see to his most intimate needs. The sensible thing. Yet hearing him start to think of propriety and sense saddened her. She'd much rather he wanted to do something improper, and reckless, like a bit more kissing and cuddling.

Oh, well, there was no point in refining on what wasn't to be. She might as well go to the little dressing room next door to wash and dress herself, while Gaston saw to Tom.

The moment she'd poured out her water, though, she started to get cross with herself. Why had she just meekly walked away, when it hadn't been what she wanted? Why had she allowed him to dismiss her so easily?

Her irritation made her movements jerky and brisk, so that she was ready to ring for Jeanne to do up her day gown in no time at all. Funnily enough, it never did take her very long to prepare for the day now she no longer had a personal maid in constant attendance. Since returning to Brussels she'd dispensed with all the other nonsense, such as trying to get her hair to curl and then arranging it in a fashionable style. She simply combed it, braided it, coiled it up and pinned it out of the way. And since she only had the choice of two or three outfits, she didn't have to agonise for ages about which would be the most appropriate for the events she was scheduled to attend, either.

She tapped on Tom's door. *Tom's door.* She pulled herself up short. When had it become his room? And how had he managed to make her feel like a visitor?

She felt even more like a visitor when she saw that he'd rearranged the furniture. Or had Gaston do it, anyway.

'I can see out of the window from here, without having to get out of bed,' he said hastily, when her reaction must have flitted across her face.

'Of course. It must be very boring for you hav-

ing nothing to look at all day.' Yet another sign
he was recovering. He needed something to do.
Something to look at. Other than her.

'It looks like a glorious day,' he said. 'You
should make the most of it. Go out and get some
air.'

She didn't wince. Nobody, looking at her face,
would guess how much his attitude hurt. But then
she'd had years of enduring brutal attacks from
her father, more subtle campaigns waged by her
mother, followed by the cut and thrust of society
gossip. Letting anyone know what she was thinking would have been fatal, on so many occasions.

'Well, if you really don't need me,' she said
brightly, 'I would love to go for a ride.' He wanted
her to leave him in peace, did he? Very well, then.
At least Castor would be genuinely pleased to see
her. No blowing hot and cold with him.

No wonder she preferred horses to people. They
didn't play games. Say one thing one minute,
making you think...

Not that horses could talk. But if they did, they
would be honest and open, and straightforward.

'Aside from my brief ride out yesterday I have
been woefully neglecting Castor. And after he
looked after me so splendidly, too.'

'Did he?' Tom didn't sound interested. He was

gazing out of the window with a rather wild air, as though planning his escape. From the clutches of a respectable female, no doubt. Now that he'd started to respond to her, as a man, he clearly felt it was time to put some distance between them. Why, he'd told her he didn't want to get married. He'd couched it in terms of not having anything to offer a woman. But she knew what he'd really meant was that he didn't want to get tied to just one. She knew how men's minds worked. Unless they had a title and needed an heir, or a bride with a dowry to solve their financial problems, not one of them really wanted to get leg-shackled.

She'd seen it in her father's behaviour. She'd observed it in Justin's. But most important, she'd heard it from Gideon's own lips.

That kiss, and then spending the night in each other's arms had probably scared the life out of him. He probably thought she was going to get silly, romantic ideas now. Which was why he was acting all starchy and unapproachable.

In another day or so, he would be up and about, and, to judge from the way he was acting this morning, that would be the end of their strange friendship.

All of a sudden, some imp of mischief, some

spirit of rebellion that had been fermenting over the past few days, came to a head.

She marched over to the bed, seized him round the back of the neck with one hand and planted a kiss full on his mouth.

He made a strange gasping, gurgling sound. The green part of his eyes got almost entirely swallowed by the rapid expansion of his pupils. He reached up to put his arms about her, too.

'No. That's quite enough of that for now, Tom,' she said, darting away. It would have been different if he'd started it, if he'd shown any inclination to take things further. She might have…well, actually she didn't know how she would have responded to a flirtatious, eager Tom this morning. She only knew that she wasn't going to let him think he could dictate how she should behave any longer.

Nor give him the idea that she was so desperate she was flinging herself at him. That wasn't what the kiss was about at all.

'I don't want to get you over-excited. Not in your delicate condition.'

'In my *delicate* condition?' He glared at her ferociously, as though to prove there was nothing the least bit delicate about him. Her last sight of him that morning was of him staring at her, with an expression on his face she was going to cherish for ever. As though he wished he had the strength to get up and chase after her. Although she wasn't totally sure what he would do to her, if he could catch her. Put her over his knee and spank her, as likely as kiss her, probably.

Either of which would, at least, be preferable to his indifference.

Although the day was fine and Castor had been keen to get out and gallop away the fidgets, there was too much evidence of the battle wherever she looked to be able to fully enjoy her ride.

By the time she returned, her pleasure in provoking Tom into a reaction had completely dissipated. And it wasn't just the sight of soldiers lying wounded all over the road, the broken gun carriages, splintered wagons, or the smoke rising from mounds of carcasses that had been made into great bonfires, that had done it.

It was the guilt. Guilt caused by realising that whenever she was with Tom, actually in his presence, Gideon always got pushed to the back of her mind.

So it was with a heavy heart that she finally stepped through the back door of the lodgings, later that morning.

'Ah, *ma petite*,' said Madame le Brun, bustling up towards her, wiping her hands on her apron. 'It is such sad news, is it not? To hear that your gallant officer, your beau, he has fallen in battle.'

'My...my beau?'

She hadn't had a beau.

'Who do you mean?'

'Why, that cavalry officer with all the moustaches. The colonel.'

'Oh. Colonel Bennington Ffog,' she responded dully. She'd experienced a jolt, it was true, when she'd read his name on the lists of the dead, but it was hardly more than she'd felt for any of the other names she recognised of men she'd talked to, and danced with, in the preceding weeks. Even though he had been her most frequent escort. After Gideon.

'Never mind,' said the landlady, placing her hand on the sleeve of Sarah's riding habit. 'The major, he is much more the man for you than that other one.'

Sarah felt her face flood with heat. 'The...the major? You mean you know that Tom isn't...isn't my...'

'Your brother?' The landlady gave her a knowing look. 'But no. No man looks at his sister the way that man looks at you. And I recall both your brothers. They have your nose. That one—' she jerked her thumb upwards '—he is much more handsome. And then it made me to wonder at the way you said you did not want visitors, when last time you were here, there was a constant stream of callers, and you and your sister and her husband the marquis, you were all so caught up in the going to parties and balls. It all became clear,' she said in a conspiratorial tone, 'when the other English officer came, the one with also your nose, the one with a voice loud enough to be heard over a salvo of cannon fire.'

Sarah's stomach hollowed out. She thought she'd been so discreet. She thought nobody would guess she was living in one room with a man to whom she was not married. And yet now this landlady knew. And Major Flint knew.

And how many others?

'You haven't told anyone, have you? That Major Bartlett and I… That the Major isn't…'

Madame le Brun pulled a face. 'As long as you pay your rent, what do I care what you get up to behind the closed doors?'

Was that a subtle threat? Was the woman going to increase her rent, in return for her silence?

'Besides—' she gave a wry smile '—to begin with, I wondered if perhaps he was French.'

'French?'

'Those men who carried him in, they wore the blue jackets. And they drove a French wagon. And so to begin with I did not tell anyone there was a wounded officer here at all.'

'I… Well…' Sarah recalled how the woman had fussed over her the night she'd turned up, on horseback, with only what she could cram into her saddlebags. How willing she'd been to hide her in the stables in case the French overran the city. How she'd even put up with Ben lolloping up and down the stairs, a law unto himself, once she'd seen how much comfort he brought Sarah during the long hours of watching over Tom.

And felt ashamed that for one terrible moment, she'd suspected Madame le Brun of attempted bribery.

'Thank you, Madame.'

'It is nothing,' she said with a careless shrug. 'But you—' she reached up and patted her cheek in a motherly fashion '—do not mourn too long for the other one. He was not a worthy suitor for one with such spirit as you.' She pulled a face. 'I have heard about the behaviour of your British cavalry during the battle. How all their brains belong to their horse. How they charge recklessly here and there.' She waved her arms wide. 'They do no damage to the enemy, they get themselves into bad positions and practically hand themselves and their poor horses to the other side for the butchery.'

'What?' Sarah's mind reeled. She had come to Brussels to learn the truth. But did she really want to hear exactly how Gideon had died? If it had been in that manner?

Oh, why hadn't she just stayed in Antwerp, in blissful ignorance? If only she'd never seen a battlefield, she could still picture Gideon falling down neatly, swiftly, feeling no pain and suffering for only a moment.

As it was…

'Excuse me, I must return to the Major. See how he is.' With a fixed, rather strained smile, she turned and strode along the corridor, and up the stairs.

It felt as though a cold hand was squeezing at her insides. Major Flint had said Gideon had been cut with sabres. Cavalry sabres, like the ones that had knocked Tom unconscious, while nearly slicing off the top of his head.

She most certainly didn't want to learn that her reckless, charming, rather wild twin had thrown his life away in some stupid, pointless charge such as Madame le Brun had described. And got himself butchered.

She came to a dead halt the moment she entered Tom's room and just stared at him, her arms wrapped round her middle.

He'd been reading a newspaper, by the looks of it. Pages were scattered all over the bed.

'What is it? What has happened?' He stretched out his hand to her, causing a flurry of newsprint to drift to the floor.

Sarah ran to him. Flung herself into his arms and buried her face in his shoulder.

He rocked her, stroked her hair, but didn't say a word. Didn't tell her it was going to be all right and she shouldn't get herself into a state. He just waited, patiently, until she felt ready to form words.

'Gideon,' she said, sitting up and pushing her hair off her face. 'He was in the cavalry. And Madame le Brun said…about the cavalry… There have been stories about how they all charged about in disorder and got themselves cut to pieces without doing any good. And I can't bear it. I can't bear to think of him throwing his life away in such a stupid fashion.'

'He didn't. I'm sure he didn't.'

She pulled herself out of his arms, his words

jarring deep. 'Tom…don't. Don't mouth stupid platitudes at me. Not you of all people!'

'Me of all people? What do you mean by that?'

Yes, what did she mean? Why had it hurt so much to have her fears dismissed as though they were nothing? 'I thought…I thought…' He'd kept saying she was an angel. Looking at her as though he almost worshipped her. But now he'd spoken to her just the way everyone else did.

Had it been an act, after all? The practised charm of a rake? 'I've been such a fool,' she gasped. 'I actually thought you *respected* me. That you would be honest with me if nothing else. That you wouldn't treat me as though I'm completely bird-witted!'

He took her shoulders firmly and looked straight into her eyes.

'I do respect you, Sarah. You have no idea how much. And I don't think you're in the least bit bird-witted. I think you're perfect.' He traced the line of her jaw with one finger.

She pulled back, only preventing herself from slapping his hand by an immense effort of will. This was absolutely not the time for him to finally start with the flirtatious gestures.

'And I would never lie to you, do you hear me?'

But he just had.

'I think we both know that I'm very far from perfect,' she began bitterly.

'Why can you not see what I see? Why can you not believe in yourself?'

'Because…' She shook her head irritably. 'Oh, there are too many reasons to go into them now. But if you really do mean to be honest with me, then what do you mean about being sure he didn't throw his life away?'

'Just think about it, Lady Sarah. Your brother died at Quatre Bras. It wasn't anything to do with a cavalry charge, so far as I know. No—from things I heard, he was with Colonel Randall at the time.'

'He was with Justin?' She stared at him in confusion. 'Why is this the first I've heard of it? Why didn't you tell me before?'

He let go of her. Looked down at his hands as he clasped them over his stomach. 'I'm sorry. I should have thought of it. Knowing that you only came to Brussels at all to find *him*. Your twin.' He sighed. Looked up at her, his eyes bleak. 'The surgeon was right. In part, at least. I…I don't remember all that much about the battle. Just impressions, really, of the hours immediately before I was injured. And then nothing, until I started coming round and couldn't move because I'd been buried under all that masonry.' He grimaced as if in remembered pain. 'That episode stuck in the forefront of my mind, to be honest. It was only when you talked about hearing the cannon fire on Friday, it came back to me. *That* was Quatre Bras. That was where he died, wasn't it?'

'Yes. That's right. I...' Her stomach gave a funny lurch. 'I just panicked, didn't I, when Madame le Brun started talking about the way so many of the cavalry officers died in the battle on Sunday.' She'd overreacted to him saying he didn't think Gideon had thrown his life away, too. Tom hadn't been dismissing her fears, the way others would. No, he'd really meant it. He had grounds for saying what he had. Only, it had hurt so much to think he might not be taking her seriously, after the way he'd made her think...

She shook her head. She wasn't going to waste time wondering what Tom thought of her, let alone what she thought of him. It was irrelevant! She'd come to Brussels to find out what had happened to Gideon. She shouldn't have let Tom sidetrack her so completely.

Although, it wasn't all his fault. She rubbed at her brow. 'You know, part of me still can't grasp the fact that he's dead. I came to Brussels convinced he couldn't be dead. It was only when I rode over the battlefield where I found you, and saw all the…' She shuddered. 'Saw how frail men's bodies really are.'

'Sarah.' He reached for her, took her into his arms and drew her head to his chest.

And it felt so good that she just nestled there. Listening to the strong beat of his heart under her cheek. Feeling the strength of his arms, holding her. Keeping the rest of the world at bay.

Keeping the reality of her bereavement at bay.

That was what she'd been doing, she saw. While she was busy, nursing Tom, she didn't have time to dwell on the truth. She'd been pushing it away for as long as she could. By any means.

She'd just decided to pull out of Tom's embrace and do something, when a knock came at the door. Giving Sarah the perfect excuse to untangle herself, sit on the chair by his bedside and run a hand over her hair to smooth it, before shouting out permission to enter.

It was Madame le Brun, with a troubled expression on her face.

'I know you said you do not want the visitors. But this man, he says he has come from Colonel Randall, your brother. And so I thought…' She spread her hands wide in one of those Gallic expressions that said so much.

Sarah's heart seemed to flip over in her chest. On the one hand, she did want to learn how Justin was faring. But on the other, if he was sending messages to her, here, then it meant he'd discovered where she was. And probably who she was with, too.

Which meant the fat would be in the fire.

Well, she'd survived all sorts of things so far this week. Done things she'd never imagined she could do.

Including kissing a rake. Deliberately. To shock him.

She wasn't that timid, diffident girl who would do anything to avoid confrontation. To say whatever people wanted to hear, if it meant they would leave her be.

She squared her shoulders.

'You did quite right, Madame. Send him up.'

Though as soon as Madame had shut the door on her way out, Sarah reached for Tom's hand. Somehow, nothing seemed so bad when she could hold his hand.

Not that she needed him to protect her from her own brother.

On the contrary. If Justin really did know she was here with a man they'd nicknamed Tom Cat, it was more likely *she'd* need to protect *him*.

'I won't leave you, Tom,' she vowed. 'No matter what he says. What threats he uses. Not while you need me.'

She'd got that look on her face again. The look of a lioness guarding her cub. Which made him feel much better. When she'd come in looking so bereft, after he'd just seen Bennington Ffog's name on the casualty list, he'd experienced such a bitter wave of jealousy he could still taste it. Even when she'd confessed that her heartbreak was for her beloved twin, rather than the man who'd spent the last weeks of his life practically turning cartwheels in order to gain her favour, from what he'd observed, the jealousy had scarcely abated one whit.

There just wasn't room in Sarah's heart for any man, not while it was still filled with Gideon Blasted Latymor.

Except, she had flung herself into his arms for comfort, hadn't she? Appeared hurt when she thought he didn't respect her.

Ah, but then when he'd explained himself, she'd let him take her in his arms and settled in as if she felt she belonged there.

And now she was bristling at the prospect of receiving a messenger from Colonel Randall.

He'd been half-joking when he'd said he would gladly stay ill for ever if it meant keeping her beside him. But there was no denying that whenever she thought he needed her to defend him, she forgot all about her dead twin and took up the cudgels on his behalf. And it was such a sweet feeling, having somebody thinking he was worth defending. Nobody had ever tried to defend him from anything.

No wonder he wished, so badly, that he belonged to her. With her.

The door opened then, and a short, squat man with iron-grey hair came in.

'It's Robbins, isn't it?' Sarah got to her feet and held out her hand to him, in a particularly regal fashion. With a smile Tom would describe as queenly.

Tom just about managed to bite back an appreciative grin. She'd fought Major Flint openly. But it seemed she was going to subdue Robbins with a combination of charm and hauteur.

'I have a letter here from Miss Endacott,' said Robbins, darting Tom a brief look from his shrewd grey eyes.

'Thank you,' said Sarah as she took it from him with a dazzlingly sweet smile. As though she was blithely ignorant of any impropriety in her situation.

It didn't have the effect on Robbins she'd probably intended. On the contrary, his eyes grew flinty.

'And how is my brother? The Colonel?'

'Mortal bad, miss,' said Robbins harshly. 'When Major Flint told him how you and Major Bartlett here are fixed, he got very upset. Took two of us to keep him from coming straight round here with a horsewhip.'

'Well, I'm very sorry he was upset,' said Sarah with a toss of her head. 'But would he rather I'd left one of his officers lying on the battlefield at death's door?'

'Couldn't rightly say, miss, but what I do know is that the upset made the bullet move. Miss Endacott had to call for a surgeon to dig it out. Getting on nicely he was, until then. But now *he's* the one at death's door.'

Sarah gasped as he turned on his heel and marched out.

'I never meant to cause any harm,' she said, turning pale. 'I thought I was helping.'

She looked down at the note in her hand, and tore it open feverishly.

'Oh. Oh. Mary says… Oh, it is just as Robbins

said. I thought he might have been exaggerating. Trying to scare me, but...' She sat down in the chair by his bed as though someone had cut the legs from under her.

'I didn't even wonder why he hadn't sent a letter. I just assumed he couldn't know— That Mary would be shielding him from anything that might upset him. But I should have...' She shook her head, staring wildly, and Tom thought probably sightlessly, round the room. 'Not Justin, too. I can't lose both of them.'

Tom reached for her and pulled her on to the bed, right on to his lap. It was a measure of her distress that she didn't make the slightest attempt to stop him. And it was a measure of his character that he was glad of the opportunity his colonel's relapse had given him. Not that he wanted her distressed. Just that in moments like this, she turned to him. Sought comfort in his arms.

And that might be because he was the only person here.

But what did he care?

About anything—when she was in his arms.

Chapter Ten

'What am I to do?' she said. 'What *can* I do? It's all my fault. All my fault.'

'Now you stop that right now.' He cursed Robbins soundly and colourfully under his breath. 'If Colonel Randall was really as dangerously ill as Robbins implied, surely Miss Endacott would have written to inform you before? She knows how much you care about your brothers. She was with you when you found him near the battlefield, wasn't she?'

The wild, desperate look faded from Sarah's eyes.

'You really think so?' She looked at Tom in confusion. 'But then why…?'

'Robbins is extremely loyal to the Colonel. Your brother inspires that in the men. Gutter rats, who've never had anyone to look up to. Anyone they can trust. Until he showed them that a man in authority isn't necessarily going to stamp on them, just because he can.

'I wouldn't be a bit surprised if Robbins is trying to ease the Colonel's worries by making you feel guilty enough to run back to him and stay where he can keep an eye on you.'

Her eyes filled with tears.

'No! Surely he wouldn't?'

'Oh, I think he would.'

'Oh!' She sat up a little straighter. 'What a mean, dirty, low sort of trick to play on me.'

'That's the way the Rogues work, Sarah. And, to be fair to Robbins, he probably thinks he's doing you a favour, too. Getting you away from me.'

Her mouth firmed into a tight line.

'I wish everyone would stop trying to organise my life the way they think is best for me, without even asking me what I want.'

She wriggled off his lap, got back on to the chair, and looked down at Mary's note again.

'Do you know, I think you may be in the right of it. Mary doesn't say anything about it being my fault. Not at all. Which I'm sure she would if she thought it. She doesn't like me very much. With just cause, I may add. I—' She bit on her lower lip, then took a deep breath, lifted her chin and looked him straight in the eye.

'I tricked her into going with me to the Duchess of Richmond's ball, you see. Gussie was too poorly to take me and I was desperate to find Gideon. Because he'd been—' She broke off. 'Well, I knew I couldn't attend without a chaperon. And I couldn't think who else to ask. I thought she was the one person I might be able to persuade, because she was bound to want to see Justin one last time before they all went off to fight, just the way I wanted to see Gideon.

'Only Gideon wasn't there, so it was a waste. No—' she sighed and shook her head '—it was worse than that. Justin ripped up at her. Accused her of stealing his lucky sword and insinuating herself into my good graces so she could get her hands on his title... Oh, all of it was so unjust. And it was all my fault. If I hadn't made her take me, none of it would have happened. They would still be together. They'd be getting married.'

'You can't know that.'

'Yes, I can. She told me,' she said gloomily. 'Besides, he danced every dance with her. And looked at her the way I've never seen him look at anyone else. Ever. And she looked at him the same. They were in love, Tom. And I ruined it.'

'No. If they really loved each other, nothing

you or anyone else could have done would have ruined it.'

'Oh, stop making excuses for me, Tom. I am the most selfish woman alive. And sly, to boot. Yes, sly! To think I congratulate myself on never telling an outright lie. I just hint, you see, then let people think whatever they want, particularly if it enables me to do exactly what I want. Take the ball, for example. I made Gussie think I was going with a respectable matron, rather than another single lady. And let Mary think Gussie knew I was going with *her*, when I hadn't actually spoken her name at all.'

'Well, that isn't so bad, is it? I mean, it wasn't as if you were sneaking out to meet a lover, or really misbehave, was it?'

'No. But that's just it, you see. I'm always making excuses for sliding out of confrontation, rather than standing up for myself and telling them what I really want. I even sneaked away from Antwerp, rather than telling Blanchards I needed to come here. Well, he wouldn't have let me come, you see, so rather than alert him, and have him take steps to stop me I...' She shook her head, closing her eyes briefly. 'It was Sunday morning. Gussie wasn't feeling well enough for church. So I asked him if he was going to stay with her. And let him assume I meant to go with friends. And went and changed into my riding habit, telling my maid that I planned to go for a ride, and she could take the morning off, which got rid of her. Because, you see, none of the staff Blanchards hired had ever seen me being anything but ridiculously proper, never venturing anywhere without a maid, or a groom, or some other respectable escort. They wouldn't have dreamed I could do anything so un-ladylike as saddle my own horse, let alone ride off on it without summoning my groom. But I didn't,' she said, lifting her chin defiantly, 'because he wouldn't have let me get anywhere near Brussels, either. And anyway, if he'd known of my plans and failed to stop me he would have lost his job.'

After a moment's pause, he ventured, 'You're not totally selfish. You took steps to protect that groom. And you did stand up to Major Flint.'

'Yes. Yes, I did, didn't I?' She took in a juddering breath. 'But it was the first time I've ever done anything like that. You must think I'm dreadful.'

'No. I could never think that.'

'Haven't you heard a word I've just said, Tom? I'm cowardly, and deceitful, and stubborn and wilful, and unfeminine.'

'Unfeminine? How can you say that? I watched

you charming and flirting your way through Brussels society these past few weeks.'

'Oh, no, Tom, acquit me of that. I never flirt.'

'Nevertheless, you had no end of admirers.'

'I did nothing to encourage them, though,' she insisted. 'In fact, I made sure that the only ones whose escort I accepted were ones I was sure wouldn't look upon me with marriage in mind. It's a game I've become adept in playing. Keeping Mama happy. For if she sees me surrounded by admirers, she thinks I am at least *trying* to select a suitable husband.'

'But you aren't?'

'No. Even the trip to Paris was an attempt to persuade her I was doing my best to make a good match. Between us, Gussie and Gideon and I put notions of foreign princes into her head, until she started thinking it was all her own idea to send me to meet new and more exciting men than the ones I ran across Season after Season in London. And all the time—' her shoulders slumped '—it was just a ruse to get close to where Gideon was stationed.'

'But...Bennington Ffog...'

'Oh.' She shifted guiltily. 'Well, you see, he was Gideon's commanding officer. And Gideon had asked me to be kind to him. And it wasn't as if he was clever enough to outwit me by manoeuvring me into a situation where he could get an opportunity to propose. Besides...' she lifted her chin, 'I was pretty sure he didn't have marriage in mind. I always thought he just enjoyed being more successful with me than any other officer. It suited us both.'

She shuddered. 'Oh, heavens. I'm turning into my mother! For years, she used to get her own way only by scheming and cunning. And at the time, I didn't blame her, because Papa was such a brute that I'm sure it was the only way she could survive. But what excuse do I have?'

She put her hands to her cheeks in chagrin. Screwed her eyes shut for a moment. Then drew herself up, and faced Tom with new resolve on her face.

'I'm going to change, Tom. I'm going say what I believe, from now on. Like my sister Harriet. Yes, I shall be forthright, and honest, and *good*.'

'Really?' Tom's heart sank. If she really did turn over a new leaf, where did that leave him? Discarded, most like.

As if to confirm his fear, she said, 'I shall go straight round to visit Justin and tell him that he is not to worry about me.' She waved a hand between them. 'About us.'

'No. I mean, do you think that is wise?' His heart was hammering. The Colonel was bound to make her capitulate. Not only had she just admitted she hated confrontation, but Ramrod Randall wasn't the man to brook any opposition to his will. Not that he could say so. Not after she'd just informed him she was going to stand up for herself. She'd think he didn't have any faith in her.

With the skill of an experienced soldier, he reached for the one weapon he knew he could use against her without it blowing up in his face. He'd play on her nurturing nature.

'If he is really so ill he cannot even write a letter, but must have Miss Endacott do it for him—' and, come to think of it, he must be in bad case, or he'd have torn Sarah from his arms well before now '—then do you think he is really well enough to endure a confrontation?'

'Oh.' She looked deflated for a moment, then brightened up. 'Well, perhaps I won't go right this minute. Tomorrow will be soon enough, won't it? One more night together won't make much difference, will it? From the way Robbins looked at me, and Major Flint, too, my reputation was ruined from the moment I brought you up to my room. Are you really so bad,' she said, turning on him a look of naked curiosity, 'that just nursing you is enough to ruin a perfectly innocent woman?'

'Yes.' Though he burned with shame to admit it, he'd vowed never to lie to her.

'Why? What have you done?' She leaned her chin on her hand and gazed at him with fascination.

He felt a blush steal across his cheeks. Even his ears felt hot.

'I cannot speak of such things to you. I don't want to corrupt you.'

'Fustian! Talking about the sort of things men do in the pursuit of…adventure,' she said cheekily, 'cannot possibly corrupt me. Why, Gideon used to tell me *everything*.'

'I'm sure he didn't,' Tom retorted. 'A man doesn't fill his own sister's ears with tales of his… um, exploits of a…carnal nature.'

'Oh, he didn't go into detail,' she said airily. 'But I know he had his amorous adventures. And I know Justin has them, too. And now I come to think of it, when it comes to having a wild childhood, I don't think there are many things you can have done that my own brothers haven't done in their time. Fighting, stealing, plundering hapless farmers' crops, letting bulls out of their fields, burning hay ricks, setting their terriers on to the chickens.'

'Colonel Randall did all those things?'

'Oh, not *him,* no. And the other exploits were divided up between the other three. Gideon was always getting into scrapes. But my younger brothers, the twins who are now at Eton, are positive hellions. Do you know, I don't believe you are any worse than my own brothers. What I think is that people are painting you blacker than you are, because of what your father, and grandfather did. Which is grossly unfair.'

'There may be a nugget of truth in that. But I'm still not the kind of man Lord Randall would want you to associate with.'

She cocked her head to one side and examined him thoughtfully. 'That is true. And you aren't what Mama or Gussie would call eligible, either. Not a bit. Because you don't have a title, or land, or money. Which isn't your fault. But none of that makes you a bad man.'

'I am the very last man *any* of your family would welcome as a husband for you.'

'True,' she said thoughtfully. 'But then I don't want a husband,' she added, brightening up.

'Do you know, it might turn out to be a jolly good thing to have lost my reputation. After this—' she waved her hand to encompass the cramped room and Tom's battered body lying in the bed '—even Mama might abandon her attempts to marry me off to someone respectable. I shouldn't think anyone respectable would want me, now, would they?'

'Not if they found out about it, no,' he admitted.

'I could go and live on one of the smaller estates, somewhere deep in the country,' she said dreamily. 'I wouldn't need many servants. In fact, the fewer the better, because one thing I've discovered over this last week is how much simpler life is without maids and dressers fussing round me all day long. As long as I can keep Castor, and go for plenty of rides, I won't want much else.'

Her face fell abruptly.

'Mama will be very upset, no doubt. She has such ambition for me. And Gussie will feel guilty because Mama entrusted me to her care. Which will so infuriate Blanchards that he will probably never forgive me. He will cut me out of their lives. I shall miss them,' she said sadly.

'But Harriet won't care for that. Funny, I'd always thought of Harriet as living a dreadfully dull existence with her rural dean, but one thing I will say for her—she isn't the slightest bit fettered by convention. With her radical views, I wouldn't be surprised if she didn't become a frequent visitor. Unless—' her face fell again '—she hears about my part in her friend Mary's disappointment.'

'Sarah.' Tom reached for her hand, his conscience flayed raw. She was sitting there reckoning up what her association with him would cost her, while all he'd been able to think of was ways of keeping her in his life for even one more night. Of perhaps beguiling her into letting him kiss her a few more times.

'Harry and Jack won't be allowed to have any contact with me, naturally. Until they come of age. When, with any luck, curiosity may well drive them to seek out their notorious older sister. So, it won't be the end of the world, will it? Being ruined, I mean. Only a bit unpleasant, at first, weathering all the scenes that are bound to lead up to my banishment.'

He couldn't let her do it. Couldn't let her throw her life away on his account.

'Sarah—' he began again.

'Hmm?' She turned and smiled at him. A smile of such sadness that it was like having salt flung on to an open wound.

'It isn't too late. For you. I'm certain that with Colonel Randall's influence, and his money, they could find someone to marry you and bury this incident.'

Her smile faded.

'I have no intention of letting them do any such thing,' she said indignantly. 'I haven't spent the last four Seasons deliberately avoiding matrimony to surrender now, just when freedom, total freedom, is finally within my grasp.'

'But…'

'And another thing. Since we are both agreed that my reputation is damaged beyond repair, there doesn't seem any point in playing at propriety any longer, does there?'

His heart gave a heavy thud, then began to race as though it would burst through his ribcage.

'What are you saying?'

'I need you, Tom. I don't want to wait until I have a nightmare to give me the excuse to seek the comfort of your arms. And, well, not to put too fine a point on it,' she said, blushing, 'I want to spend tonight in your bed.'

Could he really be that lucky? Was Sarah really asking him what he thought she was asking him?

Randall would kill him when he found out.

Not that that would stop him. If Sarah wanted him, then…then…his head began to spin.

'There's no point in pulling out that truckle bed,'

said Sarah, 'and having it made up when I fully intend to sleep with you, Tom. The way I look at it, if everyone thinks I'm ruined, I may as well enjoy some of the benefits, mayn't I?' she said cheerfully as she whisked out of the room to go and prepare for bed.

Even though he'd had his bed moved away from the wall, so that he could no longer hear those preparations, he could still picture what was happening next door.

He should ring for Gaston. Wash. Shave. He ran a rather shaky hand over his jaw. Let it drop to his side. If only he was a little stronger. Better equipped to make her first time memorable. The way he felt right now, she would be lucky if he could last long enough to make it even mildly pleasurable.

But then she was coming back into the room, clad in a sensible nightgown with a demure wrap over the top, a blanket draped over one arm.

A blanket? Why the blanket? What did she mean to do with that?

He got his answer when she lay on the *top* of his bedclothes and draped the extra blanket over her legs, just as she had done when she'd sought his comfort from her nightmares last night.

'There.' She sighed, snuggling down trustingly

into the crook of his arm. 'That is comfortable, is it not?'

Not. He was painfully aroused. His heart was stuttering like a stammering schoolboy. And sweat was trickling down his spine.

He managed to form a noise that was a sort of pained grunt, that she might take for agreement.

'We can hold each other all night—' she sighed with a blissful purr that made her sound like a kitten '—and keep the nightmares at bay.'

He certainly wouldn't be having any nightmares tonight. Because he wouldn't be able to get a wink of sleep, with her breasts pressed against his ribs like that and the softness of her hair flowing over his throat.

'I won't let anything bad disturb you tonight,' he grated, dropping a kiss on the crown of her head. Most particularly not him. Dear God, how could he have imagined she'd been inviting him to deflower her? He should have known her request was a completely innocent one. For she was innocent. Pure.

And he couldn't betray her by letting her get so much as a whiff of his own base desires. He would just hold her, since that was all she wanted of him. Watch over her while she slept.

Preserve the innocence she'd entrusted to him.

'Tom?'

'Mmm?' He hoped to goodness she wasn't going to expect him to carry on a lucid conversation. Not while nearly all the blood in his depleted system was raging south of his waistline.

'I still feel dreadfully guilty, you know, about Justin. I did try to take measures to prevent creating a scandal, so that nobody who cares about me would get upset. I wrote to Gussie as soon as I got here, trying to explain as much as I dared...'

'I saw you sitting at the desk, in a halo of light, writing something. You looked so fierce, and pure and bright, all at once. Just how I pictured a guardian angel should look.'

She looped one arm about his waist as she shifted into what was, for her, a more comfortable position. Lord, why had he been all noble last night and promised she need not fear him? Now he had to live up to her expectations.

He sucked in a deep, juddery breath. He'd been stupid enough to make her a promise and he couldn't break his word. Not to her. That was all there was to it.

'That only proves how very ill you were. Likening me to an angel, indeed.' She gave a very un-angel-like snort and began toying with the buttons on his nightshirt, driving him almost demented as he pictured those slender fingers sliding them undone, slipping inside, running over his chest.

Gliding lower…

'I know that now,' he said huskily. 'You are very much a woman.' A woman who was becoming increasingly more inquisitive and bold. If he wasn't shackled by that stupid promise, he'd have been trying to see just how bold she could be. She'd already shocked him by kissing him that morning, in a defiant sort of way, as though seeing how far she could go.

He twined one of her golden locks round his finger. 'But still, you shouldn't blame yourself for what happened to Colonel Randall.'

She stiffened. For a moment he thought he'd offended her. He braced himself for a haughty demand he stop playing with her hair.

'Do you know, I think you are right? I took the greatest care to guard my reputation— Oh, not that I give a fig for it, Tom, so don't worry on that score. No, but I do know that Justin wouldn't want people gossiping about me. Though heaven alone knows why he's so consumed with preserving the family name, when our father made it a byword for depravity when he held the title. Nevertheless—' she shrugged '—my presence in Brussels would have stayed secret had it not been for Major Flint.

'Not even Madame le Brun gossiped about the wounded officer I'd hidden in my bedroom, you know. She says she doesn't care about any scandals so long as I pay my bills.'

'Very practical,' he panted, wondering whether he should take hold of her hand and remove it from the vicinity of his buttons. The only problem with doing that was the temptation to guide it to where he wanted her to touch him the most. Giving her a subtle hint, then letting her explore a little wasn't the same as deliberately rousing her, was it? It wouldn't be breaking his promise if she was the one to take the lead.

Would it?

'Yes. So, if anyone is to blame for Justin having a relapse, it is him. Major Adam Flint,' she hissed, curling her fingers into his shirtfront like little claws, relieving him of the bother of doing anything about its innocently seductive exploration of his chest.

'He just marched in there, without a thought for the damage he'd cause, and blurted it all out. And not even the truth, either, I dare say. But his own version. Painting you as black as he could, and making out that I've suddenly become a…a sort of…lightskirt, or something,' she finished indignantly. 'When you are so ill you can hardly get out of bed, never mind get up to the kind of mischief he was implying you'd wrought.'

That was probably true, he reflected gloomily. He'd gone dizzy just thinking about deflowering her. If he'd attempted anything even remotely strenuous, he'd probably have passed out like a light.

'He's just like Papa,' she went on. 'He may go by the name of Flint, but every inch of him is typical Latymor male. He throws his weight around. Barks out orders left, right and centre without a care for how anyone feels about anything. Or how it's going to affect them.'

'I don't think that's quite true. He just…didn't foresee what the outcome would be.'

'Don't you take his side, Tom! Men,' she huffed. 'You always stick together, in the end. I suppose,' she added morosely, 'it comes from you being brother officers. You have great respect for him, or something.'

'Well, I do, as it happens.' He released the lock of hair he'd wound round one finger and let it slither straight to flow over his knuckles. 'I haven't always respected all the officers I've served with, in the various regiments I've gone through. But

Major Flint is competent. Good with the men. Fair. Brave.'

'Oh, don't go on about him,' she said sulkily. 'The more you praise him, the more I want to wring his neck.'

At that moment, they heard someone hammering on the street door. Since Madame le Brun had already locked up for the night, it came as a bit of a surprise when, a few moments later, they heard the sound of someone knocking on their bedroom door.

'Oh, no. What now?' Sarah got out of bed, went to the door and peered out on to the landing.

'Excuse me, but it is the other one,' panted Madame le Brun, as though she'd just run up the stairs. 'The major with the loud voice and the angry face. Demanding to see you. But, after what we said, what you told me, am I to let him in?'

'No! On no account.'

'That is what I thought, *mon chou*. Leave him to me,' she said, scurrying out of the room and down the stairs.

After a moment or two, they heard the sound of booted feet marching to take a position right under their window.

'Lady Sarah! Major Bartlett!'

'Well,' gasped Sarah, 'if that doesn't beat all! It's as if he deliberately wants to cause a scandal.'

She flew to the window. Threw up the sash, pushed the potted geranium to one side and leaned her head out.

'Haven't you done enough? Not content with upsetting Justin, you have to come here shouting our names out as though you want to make sure I'm ruined!'

'I wouldn't have to shout for you,' Tom heard the infuriated voice echo up from the pavement, 'if you'd let me in.'

'I'm in bed,' she retorted. 'Gentlemen don't come visiting ladies at this hour of the night. Come back in the morning at a respectable time.'

'You are behaving like some Billingsgate doxy,' Major Flint bellowed in the voice that had the power to make the hardened men under his command quake in their shoes. 'And I have just come from leaving your brother's coffin in the Chapel Royal.'

Sarah gasped. Went white. And then her hands, as though seeking some way to express her rage and frustration, clenched round the potted geranium.

'You...' She inhaled sharply as she formed what was probably the worst word in her vocabulary.

'You bastard,' she flung at him, along with the poor unsuspecting geranium.

Tom heard the sound of pottery shattering on the paving flags. And he grinned. At least she wouldn't have a second head wound to tend because, knowing her, if she'd actually hit her target, she would have been mortified. Would have run down to her half-brother, dispensing tears and bandages in equal measure.

Fortunately for all concerned, Major Flint beat a hasty retreat. No doubt rueing the day he'd attempted to cross swords with his doughty little half-sister.

His grin faded when he caught sight of Sarah's face, though. She looked stricken as she gazed after the Major's retreating figure.

And then it hit him. Major Flint had brought her the intelligence she'd been seeking ever since coming to Brussels.

The location of her brother's body.

Which meant her quest was at an end.

Or very soon would be. Right now, she was too shattered by the skirmish with Major Flint to think about the future. But once she'd recovered from the initial shock, once she'd realised he wasn't ill enough to need constant nursing, there would be nothing to keep her here.

This could be the last night he spent with her.

Chapter Eleven

She cried herself to sleep.

But at least it was in his arms.

As he held her, watching her finally succumb to exhaustion, he resisted the pull of weariness. If this was to be his last night with her, he wasn't about to waste it sleeping. Not when he could savour the feeling of holding her In his arms. Not when he could watch her features, softly lit by candlelight. Even when the candle guttered and went out, he couldn't take his eyes off her. She looked even more ethereal by moonlight, the planes and hollows of her face stripped of colour. He loved the way expressions flitted across her face. The way she quieted when he smoothed her hair back from her forehead whenever a frown began to pleat it.

If only dawn would never come. For soon after daybreak, she would wake, and get up and leave him. Oh, perhaps not altogether, not yet. But now that she knew where Gideon was, now that she could finally lay him to rest, and he was recovering, she wouldn't have any reason to stay.

All too soon, so far as Tom was concerned, she stirred, rubbed her eyes and stretched her arms over her head. Sat up.

One look at her face was enough to tell him she was already, in her mind, far, far away from him.

'You are going to the Chapel Royal?'

She nodded. Got out of bed. Folded the blanket over her arm. 'And then I will go to visit Justin. Straighten things out. Oh, don't worry, Tom,' she said when he must have made some movement that betrayed his despondency. 'No matter what Justin says, I won't leave you. After all, he has Mary nursing him, so why should he begrudge you your own nurse?' She lifted her chin in that defiant gesture which was becoming so familiar to him. 'It isn't as if you have anyone else to care for you.'

But it wasn't the same. He had no doubt that Mary was watching over the Colonel with such devotion because she was deeply in love with him. Whereas love wasn't even *on* the list of reasons Sarah had for taking her stand in this bedroom.

She wanted to defy her family. She wanted to prove her own worth.

No wonder she could so easily withstand the physical attraction that she was occasionally starting to feel for him. The last thing she wanted was to be hampered by whatever might be starting between them, just when she was finally breaking free of the hold her family exerted over her.

She bent down and gave him a fierce hug.

He put his arms round her and hugged her right back.

So what if she was only using him, for any, or all, of the reasons he'd just come up with? He wasn't the man to look a gift horse in the mouth. He inhaled the faint air of violets that still clung to her. Savoured the feel of her breasts, pressed against his upper body.

Memorised it all.

'I shan't be long,' she said, straightening up.

'Take all the time you need with Major Latymor. To lay him to rest. I will have Gaston wash and shave me, and try sitting out of bed for a while. But I shouldn't be a bit surprised if I need a nap before long.'

'Oh, poor Tom,' she said, looking down at him ruefully. 'I keep forgetting how very ill you are.

You really don't look at all well today. Is there anything I can get for you while I'm out?'

'No, thank you. I will need to replace the pistols that got stolen while I was unconscious. And get some new boots. I had a spare pair in the baggage the men brought here, but now they are my only pair. But all that can wait until I'm up to visiting the boot-maker myself.'

'Clothes,' she said, suddenly looking a little shocked. 'Oh, my goodness, I haven't done anything about mourning. And I'm going to pay my respects to Gideon. I have only the most frivolous blue bonnet and spencer. Getting some blacks would have been the very first thing Gussie would have done.'

'Yes, but you've been sitting over me night and day. So don't you go condemning yourself for thinking more about saving a life than what you should be wearing to do it!'

'You don't really mind what I look like, do you, Tom?' she said thoughtfully.

'You always look utterly beautiful to me,' he said staunchly.

She blushed. And lowered her eyes.

'Thank you,' she said quietly. And then stood completely still for a moment or two, as though contemplating adding something else.

But in the end, she simply shot him a brief smile, before darting out of the door.

It took next to no time to walk to the Chapel Royal. Sarah could scarcely believe that Gideon could have been so close to her and she'd not felt anything.

But he wasn't really here, was he? Not in that coffin. That was only his earthly remains. His soul was... Her breath stuck in her throat.

Somewhere else. Of course. That was why she could sense nothing of him here.

Only, when she reached further, with all her being, only a massive great nothing echoed back.

Nothing.

Her heart started beating so wildly she found it hard to breathe. She had to get outside. Out of this cold, empty chapel and into the sunshine.

She stumbled into the nearest shop and tried to concentrate on kitting herself out in black.

But it was all a blur. All that seemed real was her deep inner cry of *No. No*, Gideon couldn't be gone. *No*, she didn't want to be alone. So alone.

She'd been filling her days with activity, with purpose, all to silence that *No*.

She'd ridden to Brussels, spent the night curled up in a stable with Castor and Ben, braved Mary's hostility, even gone on to the very battlefield where she feared he had fallen and finally grabbed at the chance to save one poor wretch from the grinding jaws of death, in a vain attempt to silence that deep, instinctive denial.

But none of it had worked.

Except it wasn't exactly the same kind of *No*, any more. It wasn't a refusal to accept the truth.

It was a *No* of anger. Of protest.

All of a sudden she came to herself to find she was standing outside the door to her lodgings in the Rue de Regence. She had no idea how she'd come here, when her plan had been to visit Justin.

But it was a foolish plan, she decided, going inside. She wasn't strong enough to face Justin. And she would have to be very strong indeed to stand up to him, particularly when he was so ill and she so filled with remorse for being a cause of it.

Right now, she just needed...she needed...

She ran up the stairs to their room. Tom. She needed Tom.

He was sitting on top of the bed, clad in breeches as well as a clean linen shirt and waistcoat. He took one look at her, and held out his arms.

She flew to him. Buried her face in his shoulder, and just sobbed. With grief. With some gratitude, too, because she hadn't had to say a word.

One look at her face and Tom knew what she needed most.

'He wasn't th-there,' she hiccupped, when she eventually grew calm enough to be able to form words. 'Nothing of him at all. I couldn't…couldn't feel him any more. He's gone, Tom. Really gone.'

'Shhh.' He rubbed his hands up and down her back soothingly. 'From this world, perhaps, but he will always live in your heart.'

'Memories,' she said scornfully. 'I don't want them! I want *him*! I want my brother back. I need him. He was the only one who understood me. The only one who gave a damn…'

He tensed. 'That's not true any longer. I—' he took a deep breath '—*I* give a great deal more than a damn for you. In fact, I— Well, I've never said this to any woman before—never thought I would, either—but I think—well, I don't know any other way to describe what I feel for you. So it must be love.'

'What?'

'I think,' said Tom gravely, 'that I love you, Sarah.'

She felt her jaw gape open.

'I suppose this wasn't the best time to make a declaration of that sort, was it? For a seasoned rake, I seem to have lost my touch. To have put a look like that on your face.' He ran one finger along her jaw, with a rueful smile. 'But I couldn't just sit here and listen to you say that nobody loves you any more, when it simply isn't true.'

'But you can't!'

'Why can't I?'

'Because I'm not pretty.'

'I told you that I don't care about that. And this morning, I thought you looked as though you believed it. To me, you are beautiful. And it has nothing to do with the way you look.'

'But you can't love me for anything else. For heaven's sake, Tom, I'm such a ninny! I haven't a sensible thought in my head. No mind for study, or books. Even the very few times I've tried to do a good deed,' she said, remembering her attempt to befriend and encourage Mary Endacott to become her sister-in-law, 'it turns into a disaster. You…' She smoothed her hand over his bruised brow. 'You seem to have got me mixed up in your head with some creature you've fashioned from your imagination. Your fevered dreams.'

'No. I liked the look of you before you rescued me from the battlefield and brought me to your bed. I used to watch you, riding about the place with Gideon, or a group of your admirers, and wish I was the kind of man who had the right to form part of your court.'

'Did you? Did you really? Oh, Tom.'

'And since we've been shut up together like this…talking to you, watching you move about the room, making it feel like home, when I've never had a home in my whole life. I've never talked to another person, the way I've talked with you, this week. Never wanted to. Never had anyone show the slightest interest, if you must know. Never known this sense of connection before. You only have to raise one eyebrow, just a fraction, and I know exactly what you're thinking.'

Yes, he did seem to understand her, without her going into lengthy explanations all the time. Even just now, when she'd said Gideon wasn't in the Chapel, he hadn't asked a lot of tiresome questions about where the coffin had gone, then, or if she'd gone to the wrong chapel, the way Gussie or Harriet would have done. Her sisters, with their very down-to-earth turns of mind, would have taken her literally.

But Tom just knew she meant she couldn't *sense* Gideon.

They were in tune, in a way she hadn't been with anyone.

Not even, if she was totally honest, with Gideon.

The world seemed to tilt crazily as she admitted it. Oh, *she'd* understood *him*, right enough. Had sensed what mood he'd been in when he'd written to her, even before she opened the letter and read its contents.

But had he ever really cared about her to the same extent? While he'd enjoyed talking to her, hadn't it always been about his adventures? His ambitions?

No! Her stomach cramped into a cold knot. He had listened to her. He had!

But she'd had to explain what she felt. What she thought. He'd never simply *known*.

Not the way Tom seemed to do, instinctively.

Now it was her heart that seemed to lurch.

'I haven't anything to give you, Tom,' she whispered, guilt-stricken. 'You know how I feel about marriage.'

'I'm not asking you to marry me, Sarah,' he said with that wry grin he always used, she suddenly realised, when he was pretending something didn't hurt him. She recognised it easily, since she was in the habit of employing meaningless, vague smiles herself.

'We've already established that I could never be acceptable to your family. I just wanted you to know, that's all.'

'Oh.' She sat back and looked at him. Really looked at him. If she wasn't so set against marriage, if she didn't think it would feel like a sort of prison, she could make a very good case, with her family, for exactly why he *would* make her an ideal husband.

'They aren't as high in the instep as some families are, you know,' she said. 'I know Mama was thrilled when Gussie married a marquis, but she was almost as happy when Harriet chose her scholarly clergyman. And even Justin doesn't care that much about popular opinion. Otherwise he wouldn't be so involved in the artillery, would he?

'It isn't that,' he said, gazing at her steadily. 'You don't have any idea of how cruel the world can be to people who have stepped outside the bounds of respectability. I've lived with the stigma of being the grandson of a traitor, and the son of a bankrupt who committed suicide, all my life. The village boys used to sing a song about me, you know. *Tom, Tom, the traitor's son, Stole a cake and away did run. The cake was eat, and Tom was beat, Like as not, he'll end in the Fleet.* Which pretty much summed up my childhood,' he said with that lopsided smile. 'I was so miserable in my aunt's house I would rather go into the village and steal food than go back for meals. And I was beaten regularly, as I've already told you. And everyone always predicted I'd come to a bad end.'

'Oh, Tom. How horrid for you.' She hitched one hip on to the bed and took his hand. 'Nobody should have treated you that way, just because of what your father had done. Or your grandfather.'

'I'm not telling you this because I want you to feel sorry for me,' he said fiercely. 'I want you to understand what it would be like. I don't want to inflict that kind of public mockery on any woman. Let alone one I truly care for.' He gripped her hand so hard it made her wince.

Then, seeing it, he drew her fingers to his lips and kissed them fervently.

'These days here with you, like this, I know they are all I can ever have. And I don't mind. It's more than I deserve.'

'That's utter rot!' She drew her hand away sharply, and tucked it in her lap. 'You hold the rank of major. You've fought bravely in battle. And apart from a bit of womanising—'

'A lot of womanising,' he corrected her, drily. 'Let us be accurate.'

'Very well, a lot of womanising,' she said, blushing. 'I've never heard anything bad about you.'

'Perhaps your family have kept it from you, have you thought of that?'

'Oh. Well, yes, they do tend to keep things from me.' Nobody but Gideon had ever answered any of her questions properly. It was always, *no need for you to worry your head about such things.* Or, *not a suitable topic for ladies.*

She lifted her chin and eyed him militantly. 'Very well, then, Tom. Tell me yourself. What have you done that is so bad you don't think you are fit to marry me? Apart from having the misfortune to have been sired by a man who was an utter disgrace. Which, let me tell you, makes us just about even as far as I'm concerned. What are your vices? Do you gamble?'

'No. Do you think I could follow the course of a man I hold in such contempt? I hate watching my fellow officers losing their possessions to one another on the roll of a dice or the turn of a card. As far as I'm concerned, if a man wants to take another man's property he ought to just steal it honestly.'

'Do you steal things, then? Habitually?'

'Not now I have the means to keep my belly full, no. Not unless I'm ordered to do so by a commanding officer to bring confusion to the enemy, at least.'

'So it's just the womanising, then.' She took a deep breath and, though her face went bright red, asked him the most important question of all. 'Are you in the habit of taking women against their will? Taking no account of whether they might be virgins?'

'No!' His shock and disgust were genuine, she could tell. 'I've enjoyed a lot of women. But I've always ensured they enjoyed the encounter every bit as much as I have. More.'

'That sounds a touch boastful.'

He glowered at her.

'No. It's just the way I happen to like it. Sex is a natural appetite. And like any appetite, men have preferences. Mine are for energetic, enthusiastic encounters. I need the... Hell, I shouldn't be talking like this with you.'

She gave a small, cat-like smile.

'Tom, what you have described is not the temperament of a rake. You are just a normal, healthy male, who needs...companionship every now and then.'

'Are you actually trying to persuade me to marry you? Is that what you want? Was all your talk about staying free just words?'

'No! I— You are twisting my words,' she finished hotly. 'I'm not talking about whether I want to marry you. Or anyone.' She got to her feet and paced across the room to the window. 'I'm saying that your reasons for not wanting to marry me, or for thinking you aren't good enough, are totally stupid. That's all.'

'Is it?'

There was a coldness in his voice that sent a shiver down her own spine.

'This—' he waved his hand between them '—whatever this is, it can't come to anything. It can't survive outside this room.'

'Does that matter?' She strode back to the bed and grabbed at the hand he'd been waving at her. 'Does it matter that there is no future for us? What we have now is precious.' Her voice faded to a whisper. She bowed her head over his hand, raised it to her lips and kissed his knuckles. One by one. 'I've never cared about any other man the way I've come to care for you, these past few days. I've never felt moved, when a man said he loved me, the way your declaration just now moved me. I never wanted any man to love me.' She looked up at him, confusion clouding her eyes. 'Tom, let's not talk about this any more. About feelings, or the future. Let's just...'

'Enjoy the moment?' There was a bleakness in his eyes, even as he gave that lopsided smile, and shrugged. 'Yes. Why not? It's what I'm best at. Seizing whatever opportunities come my way.

Forget I said anything. I told you it was foolish. Ill timed. Shows how low this wound has laid me,' he said, touching the bandage over his head. 'In my right mind I'd never have done anything so crass as scare a lady away with such maudlin talk as I've been spouting these last few minutes. I don't suppose,' he said, drawing his hand from hers and looking towards the door, 'you could persuade Madame to bring me some brandy? And something to eat apart from the pap she's been ladling out?'

Sarah went to the door. 'I will go and ask,' she said, keeping her face averted, so he wouldn't see the tears that were stinging her eyes.

If he felt he was maladroit, what did that make her?

Touched in the upper works, Gideon would have said. It was the only thing to account for any of her behaviour, this last week.

The smells that assailed her nostrils, when she reached the kitchen, were so delicious they made Sarah's stomach rumble.

She paused in the doorway, watching Madame and her kitchen maid bustling about, wondering how she could feel hunger, could carry on having *any* feelings, when Gideon—who'd been her whole life—had none.

And yet there was no denying she wanted some of Madame's soup and a slice of her fresh, crusty bread.

And Tom.

'Tom has asked if he can have something a bit more, um…' She faltered, loathe to speak disparagingly of Madame's provision so far. 'Substantial.'

'Ah, that is good, no? It means he is getting stronger. Gaston said he thought so this morning, when he went up to give him the wash. But you, *ma petite*? How are you?'

Madame le Brun carried on doling out sympathy and good cheer along with the soup, and somehow had Sarah back upstairs and sitting down at the table with Tom to a meal which included some thickly sliced ham, coddled eggs and thinly sliced cucumber, as well as the soup, without once letting her give way to her grief.

It was only after she'd consumed about half a bowl of soup that Sarah's conscience reminded her she had no right to enjoy anything.

'What is it,' said Tom. 'Not hungry?'

She flung her spoon aside in disgust. 'I have no right to be. I had vowed to go and visit Justin this morning. But after the chapel, I…' She shook her head.

'You can still go. Later.'

'If I get there and find he's died, while I was wandering about the shops...I'm never going to forgive myself.'

'I shouldn't think it likely, now. And before you rip up at me about not taking you seriously, listen to me,' he said, laying his hand on the back of her wrist. 'Just listen. If he had died, or if there was any danger of him doing so, don't you think Miss Endacott would have urged you to go and sit at his bedside?'

'I don't know. I think she would rather keep me away, lest I aggravate his condition.'

'That may be the best course,' said Tom, with a particularly firm look on his face. 'You say you would never forgive yourself if he died before you saw him again, but how much worse would you feel if you went and he grew upset over us, and had a fatal relapse?'

'You are right,' she admitted shakily. The soup she'd already eaten curdled in her stomach. 'Perhaps I should stay away until he's completely out of danger,' she said in a small voice.

'Look,' he said, rather more gently. 'The fact that she has let you know he's had an operation must mean she has more hope for him, don't you think? And this may sound rather brutal, but the fact that he's survived that operation at all is the critical thing. That was the most dangerous point, for him.'

'I just feel so…' She pursed her lips, and shook her head, searching for the words to explain. 'Useless. I've always been useless, I know that, but it hits particularly hard, knowing Justin is lying there, fighting for his life, and what did I do? I went shopping, Tom. Shopping!'

'You went to the chapel first, to pay your respects to your twin. You are grieving, Sarah, you can't expect to be in any fit state to do much. Don't be so hard on yourself. Why, you have done wonders for me.'

'Yes.' She turned her hand over to grasp hold of his. 'At least *you* didn't become one of those officers who died of their injuries while waiting for a proper doctor to see to them.'

'No. I owe you my life.'

'It wasn't just me,' she put in hastily. 'Your Rogues made sure I was going to be able to look after you. They even stole a French ambulance to get you back here in comfort.'

A wry grin twisted his beautiful mouth. 'One thing you have to say for the way your brother has set up his troop of Rogues—we never leave one of our own behind.'

She bit down on her lower lip. 'That was what Major Flint did, wasn't it? He took charge of Gideon's body, since Justin wasn't able to do it. Just as though Gideon was one of his own Rogues. Oh, dear…' She shut her eyes on yet another wave of guilt. 'I really shouldn't have thrown that flower pot at him, should I? Adam had only come to tell me where Gideon was. He hadn't come to interfere, or blacken my name. Not on purpose.'

'No, but he need not have called you those foul names,' said Tom hotly. 'I could run him through for thinking, for one moment, that you would… you would…' He ground his teeth.

'I don't think,' she said mildly, 'you are quite up to running him through, are you?'

'No, but I could shoot him,' he finished grimly.

'I beg your pardon, but didn't you tell me that your pistols had been stolen?'

'A minor inconvenience,' said Tom, making a dismissive gesture with his free hand. 'I can soon buy some more.'

'Well, I don't want you to shoot him,' she said tartly. 'If you two fought a duel over me, it would be bound to cause a dreadful scandal. Not that I care,' she added hastily, in case he thought she regretted any part of their few days together.

'Well, *I* care,' he grumbled. 'You shouldn't have

to forfeit your position in society because of the selfless way you've looked after me, this week.'

'I don't give that for it,' she said, snapping her fingers. 'If you'd ever been a part of society, you'd know that mostly it is one long struggle for position. Everyone is trying to impress everyone else. Either by having more money, or more influence than anyone else. And most of them are trying to drag others down, so that they can clamber over their shredded reputations. It's brutal.' She shuddered.

'But you have been one of the leading ladies,' he said with a frown.

She pursed her lips. 'Only because of my family. I never really took part in any of the posturing and striving for position. I would gladly have stayed at Chalfont Magna all year round if only Mama would have permitted it. But she would have made such a fuss. It was easier to go along with Mama's plans—to pretend to go along with them, anyway, than openly defy her. I...' She shook her head ruefully. 'I went to all the balls, endured those London Seasons, even behaved like a pattern card of virtue at Chalfont Magna, because it all seemed so much *easier*. I didn't even speak out when Mama decided to hire a governess and keep me close under her eye, rather than risk sending me away to school. Harriet came home with her head stuffed full of radical ideas, you see. You should have heard the commotion when she swore she would never marry, because it went against her principles.'

'She is the one who is married to a scholar of some sort, isn't she?'

'Yes,' Sarah smiled. 'I don't think Mama would have tolerated him, were he not better than the alternative—which was Harriet never marrying at all.'

'Did you want to go to school, though?'

'I'm not entirely sure,' she mused. 'I never really cared very strongly about anything, or anyone, except Gideon. Wherever I was, it wouldn't have been with him, because he'd gone to Eton. I reckoned I may as well wait for him to come home to Chalfont as anywhere. The only thing is,' she added wistfully, 'if I had gone to school I may have made some friends, the way Gussie and Harriet did. None of the local girls wanted to come anywhere near. Too scared of what Papa might do, I dare say. Besides which Mama always said they weren't of our class.'

'It always looked to me as though you had plenty of friends. People who admired you. Wanted to be with you.'

She gave a bitter, sad little smile. 'When a girl from my background makes her entrée into society, she will always have crowds of people wanting to get near her. For various reasons. The only trouble was, they were all keen to get husbands, too. So all their talk was of beaus, and fashion, and things I found deadly dull. I suppose they must have found me dreadfully dull. Or cold. I know that some of them whispered that I was cold and haughty. And because I abhorred the prospect of attracting a man's notice, with a view to marriage, prim and proper, to boot.'

'You are none of those things,' he said hotly. 'You are most certainly not dull. Or cold.'

She pulled her hand out from under his, her cheeks warming. 'You have seen a side to me I have never revealed to anyone else.' She frowned. 'So far as anyone else is concerned, I am a demure, rather dull, society miss without two thoughts in her head to rub together and form a spark.'

Though, since she'd done her best to play at being a simpering virgin, too delicate and sensitive to accept the first offer some great brute of a man made her, wasn't it her own fault if people couldn't see who she really was?

'I am honoured, Sarah.'

She lurched to her feet and went to the window.

'The Mayor of Brussels requisitioned all the carriages yesterday, did you hear? They have actually begun going out to the battlefield to search for survivors at long last.'

'Sarah.' Tom's voice sounded pained. He clearly didn't like the way she'd turned the subject. But she couldn't go any further down that road. Or examine too closely why she could tell him things she'd never told another living soul, apart from Gideon.

'Wounded men keep on crawling out of the fields,' she carried on, her back to him, her shoulders tense. 'Half-crazed with thirst and pain. Heaven alone knows where the citizens will put them. Officers have been sent by barge to Antwerp, but as for the ordinary men—'

She broke off and turned to him. 'Now that you are getting better, I really do think I ought to do something. To help. You don't need me so much now, do you? It was different when you had the fever, but now...'

A cold lump formed in his stomach. She was going to leave him. She could already have left him, had he not pretended to be weaker than he actually was. And if Major Flint hadn't tried to bully her into leaving, which had made her dig in her heels to defy him.

Yet he was too proud to beg her to stay.

Too attuned to her views to attempt to forbid her.

'You must do what you think best, of course.'

She stood looking at him for a few seconds, a world of turmoil in her eyes. 'I think, what I will do, right now, is go out riding. Castor will need the exercise.'

And she needed to think.

Somewhere away from the distraction of his handsome face, and his tempting words, and his smouldering eyes.

Chapter Twelve

It had jolted her to realise she'd fallen into the habit of speaking to him the way she'd always spoken to Gideon. Was she using him as a substitute? She had started out feeling that if she couldn't nurse Gideon, doing something for another, seriously injured soldier was a sort of...not compensation, exactly. But something along those lines. The next best thing, then.

Not that anybody could ever take Gideon's place, not completely.

Though she did feel closer to Tom than any other living soul. She valued his opinion. When he said good things about her, it made her feel all warm inside. Like curling up in front of a nursery fire when a storm raged outside.

Was this love? Was she falling in love with Tom? How could she know?

Though it would explain why it had meant something, to hear him say he loved her. She rather thought she did want Tom to love her. To have been in earnest. She'd always brushed aside any declaration of the sort before, knowing men said all sorts of things they didn't mean. But Tom's blunt admission that he loved her, coupled with his assumption that nothing could come of it, had sounded genuine. And had touched her. Deeply.

Did that mean she loved him, too?

And if she did, then…

Oh, she couldn't think about that. It was all happening too quickly. And she was still broken up inside about losing Gideon. Thinking of him cut to pieces by cavalry sabres. Worried about whether Justin would survive before she had a chance to mend fences with him. Because as sure as eggs were eggs she would never forgive herself if he died, with the suspicion that she'd somehow been the cause still hanging over her.

Oh, bother Tom for talking about love at a time like this! For making her wonder if her own heart was susceptible, when all her life thus far she'd been immune.

Why should she feel obliged to love him back, simply because he'd said he loved her? She'd never before thought she ought to love a man back, just because he claimed some affection for her.

Not that she'd ever believed any of the others. She probably ought not to believe Tom, either. He'd admitted he was a womaniser. Perhaps he told all his conquests he loved them. Perhaps it was a ruse to get them to become *enthusiastic*. Perhaps that was what made him so successful. For when he said it, with his eyes smouldering the way they did, it had certainly made her want to yield. Oh, not to him, precisely. But to the feelings he was beginning to evoke inside her. That sort of slow burn. The physical, as well as the emotional, pull he exerted over her.

Lord, even in his weakened state he was the most powerfully attractive man she'd ever met. Temptation incarnate.

She still couldn't credit the way she'd felt last night, when she'd been getting ready for bed, knowing she was going to be sharing it with him. Running the soaped washcloth over her skin had made her wonder what it would feel like if he ran his hands over the same places. She'd lingered, her eyes half-closed, until the strange tingles and burning sensations that were mounting had begun to alarm her.

She might tell herself, and him, that she just wanted the comfort of being held in his arms all night, but that wasn't the whole truth. She wanted his hands, too. Touching where they shouldn't. Stroking where she had those tingles. Bringing her the pleasure he'd informed her he always ensured he gave his bed partners.

Whether she loved him or not, she wanted him. Her limbs went so weak with longing, for a moment, that she had a struggle to keep Castor under control. Angry with herself for that lapse in horsemanship, she turned back.

It would be better to exercise Castor first thing tomorrow, when it was cooler. When there were less people about, crowding the streets and providing distractions and alarms in equal measure. So that if her mind did wander, her hands grow slack on the reins, there would be less chance of Castor tossing her over his head and into the canal.

As it was, daylight was fading by the time she returned. She'd been out longer than she'd realised, while her mind had been whirling. Their room was heavily shadowed. Like Tom's expression.

She lifted her chin as she marched in.

'I want to sleep in your arms again tonight, Tom.' She'd decided, as she'd handed over the reins to Pieter, that she wasn't going to fret any longer about the rights and wrongs of it. For once in her life she was just going to do what she wanted.

'I want that, too,' he said gruffly.

'I will go and get ready for bed, then,' she said, a touch defiantly. And flounced out of the room, her heart thudding.

He would just hold her in his arms. Of course he would. She poured water into the basin, and shrugged off her dusty riding habit. Washed herself as quickly as possible, without lingering over the places that were clamouring for his hands.

Doing anything more than just cuddling would be wrong.

And exciting.

And wrong. But then the most enjoyable things always were wrong, weren't they? For girls. Climbing trees or cantering all over the estate on her pony had always held more appeal for her than behaving decorously. It was only because she hated the scenes that followed that she'd moderated her behaviour. Especially since nothing was half as much fun without Gideon to share it.

Also, she'd shrunk inside under both the force of her father's thundering fury, and her mother's tart, stinging words of disappointment alike.

But now her father was gone. And her mother

was never anything but disappointed, no matter what she did.

There were going to be scenes, unpleasant scenes, because she'd come to Brussels. Bringing Tom to her room, when she hadn't been able to find Gideon, and nursing him, rather than creeping back to the safety and respectability of the Blanchards's household in Antwerp, had just put the icing on the cake.

So the only question that mattered was what she thought of herself. She hesitated on the threshold, her hand on the door latch. She wasn't an angel, that much she knew. Nor was she a Billingsgate doxy. She might be susceptible to Tom's charm, but so far she was still completely innocent.

She was just a woman. A lonely woman without a friend in the world except the man in that bed. A man the rest of the world said was rotten to the core. Yet he was the only person who understood her. Who really *saw* her.

The only comfort she had.

And she didn't see why she should deny herself that comfort, because of what some mealy-mouthed, judgemental hypocrites might think.

And, yes, he was dangerously attractive. But then a nursery fire could be dangerous, too, couldn't it? If you stuck your hand *into* it. Or allowed your skirts to catch in the embers. Fires could be perfectly safe, as long as all you did was warm your hands at them.

And that was all she would do with Tom. Just warm her cold, lonely heart a little.

Lifting her chin, she opened the latch, and marched into their room.

'You don't look as if your ride did you much good,' said Tom when he caught sight of her mutinous expression. 'You look all hot and bothered.'

'Thank you,' she said tartly. 'That is exactly what every girl wishes to hear. That she is looking far from her best.'

'Would it help,' he said, deliberately ignoring her waspish tone, 'if I were to comb out your hair for you?'

'Comb my hair?'

He indicated the comb she held in her hand. The comb she didn't even recall picking up. She gazed at it, wondering what category permitting him to act as a sort of lady's maid came under. Would it be the equivalent of warming her hands, or shoving them right into the flames?

'You were about to tackle it yourself, weren't you? And I know how long it takes you. I've watched you wrestling with the tangles often enough. And though you've done without a maid very well,' he said in as calm and rational a tone as he could muster, 'surely, you would appreciate having someone else do it for you?'

Well, there was no harm in asking, was there? The worst she could do would be to refuse his request. But if she let him, ah, then he'd have the memory of sifting all that glorious golden mass through his fingers.

A victorious feeling soared when she plumped herself down on the edge of his bed, her back to him, and handed him the comb with what looked like resignation.

'I used to think having the maid dress my hair was the most tiresome part of the day,' she said as he deftly unbound the braids into which she'd fastened it that morning. A shiver of longing rippled through him as her tresses flowed across her shoulders and down her back in waves. All the way to her waist. 'But at least it wasn't *my* arms that ached with the effort of subduing it.'

It wasn't his arms that were aching, either, just at the prospect of plunging his fingers into all that silken glory.

'It could do with washing, really,' she added, as he started at the tip of one lock and began to tug the comb through. 'It has been getting dustier, and dirtier, every day.'

'Shall we ask Madame if she will bring a bath up here and some hot water? I could wash it for you.'

She sighed. 'Oh, that would be heavenly, Tom, only—' she shook her head '—it would also be disastrous. I haven't any of the special lotion Mama found that helps it take a curl. And nobody to put it in papers. I dare say it is very vain of me, but I have no wish to let you see me looking like a half-drowned waif with a head full of rats' tails.'

'You could never look like that,' he said, laying aside one lock and starting on another. 'A mermaid, perhaps, washed ashore after a storm. Come to steal the heart of the poor fisherman who caught you in his net.'

She shook her head and sighed. 'Tom, you do say the most preposterous things. But you do tempt me to yield. To the idea of washing my hair,' she added hastily. 'Only, don't you think it would be rather improper?'

'You are about to get into bed with me. Spend another night in my arms,' he pointed out. 'Isn't that even more improper?'

She cocked her head to one side. He could almost hear the wheels whirring in her mind as she considered her response.

'No,' she said at length. 'I don't know how it is,

but cuddling with you doesn't feel anywhere near as improper as letting you wash my hair.'

He knew why it was. He could just see her closing her eyes and leaning back. He could feel the liquid warmth anointing his fingers as he massaged her scalp. Hear the little moans of pleasure she'd give as he poured warm water from the pitcher to rinse out all the lather. She'd arch her neck, thrusting out her breasts...

The comb slipped from his fingers and clattered to the floor.

She bent to retrieve it. His eyes fixed on the curve of her bottom where the nightgown stretched over it. He'd become erect at the vision he'd just had, of her getting wetter and soapier as he rhythmically ministered to her. From behind.

Now he was as hard as a ramrod.

He groaned.

She turned swiftly, a concerned frown on her face.

'What is it, Tom? Is something hurting? Oh, I *knew* I shouldn't have let you comb my hair. Lie down and rest.'

She bent over him, laying one hand across his brow.

'I don't need to rest. I need...' He swallowed. Then, pushed to the limits of his endurance, he reached up to cup the back of her neck. 'Don't you know what you make me want, when you speak of intimacy and the impropriety of being in bed together?'

'I'm sorry!' Her face was a picture of contrition. 'I didn't mean to.'

'I know. That's the hell of it,' he gritted. Then, since his soul was bound for hell, anyway, he pulled her down to him and sipped at her lips.

She didn't resist. But nor did she respond. Not with her mouth, anyway, but she was breathing heavily. And he was shaking with the force of desire surging through him.

'Oh, Tom, you're shaking,' she whispered. 'You mustn't exert yourself.'

'It isn't that! It's because I want you so much. Can't you tell?'

'I…' She shook her head. 'I thought it was just because you've been so ill. That whenever you try to do too much, you tremble.'

'No. That's not it.'

He wanted to take her hand and place it over his arousal. He wanted to put his own hand between her legs. He wanted to tear the ties of her nightgown open with his teeth and devour her breasts.

He shut his eyes and moaned again.

'Tom,' she whispered. 'What should I do? I don't want to torment you.'

And he was a man with a healthy appetite. He'd warned her. She'd even warned herself about the risks of playing with fire. By letting him comb her hair, she'd somehow stoked his simmering urges until they were raging red hot.

And since she was the one who'd fanned the flames, shouldn't she go through with it? She didn't want him to think she was a tease. And he did look so tortured, poor lamb, that…that…

Except—would it be fair to him to let him make love to her, completely? Wouldn't he take that as a sign that she loved him back? That she belonged to him, even? No! She couldn't *belong* to a man. Not even Tom. She'd vowed never to put herself completely in any man's power, the way Mama had done.

Besides, she wasn't completely sure she was ready to commit the sin everyone assumed she and Tom were already enjoying. At the moment, she could still hold her head high, knowing that she was innocent of all their nasty suspicions. She would even be able to face Justin down, knowing she'd done no wrong. But would she be able to look *anyone* in the face, if she really did fall? She'd always been the picture of perfect propriety. How they would all laugh if they knew she'd been tumbled by the English army's most notorious rake.

But worst of all was the dread that Tom might think less of her. It was a bit ridiculous, the way he kept calling her an angel. But the way he always leapt to her defence, whenever anyone assumed she'd been intimate with him, the way he spoke of her purity almost with reverence... A shaft of ice pierced her to the core. Would he still claim to love her if she was no longer innocent? If she admitted she had desires, like all the other women he'd bedded, would he think she was no better than them?

'Perhaps I ought to sleep on the truckle bed, after all.'

'No!' His eyes flew open. 'Oh, no. Please, don't go all the way over there. Behind that screen. It will only make things worse. At least if you are here beside me I can hold you. Smell you.'

She crouched on the bed for a few moments, eyeing him warily.

He grimaced. 'I'm not an animal, Sarah. I won't ravish you.'

'I know,' she replied indignantly. 'I never, not for a moment, thought you would. It's just...' She caught her lower lip between her teeth. 'Won't it be hard for you? Having me in bed, when you want…and not doing anything about it?'

Hard? She had no idea how hard.

'I will be hard all night no matter where you sleep,' he admitted.

She glanced down, saw exactly how hard he was, blushed and looked back at his face.

'Isn't there anything I can do? To ease—' she glanced down at where the sheet tented over his engorged manhood '—your, um, discomfort?'

Oh, yes, there was plenty she could do to ease that. Two or three strokes from her soft white hands, a swipe of her tongue, and he would be done. He was that primed.

'No.' He groaned. She wasn't a whore. She was pure. Totally pure. And he couldn't debase her by teaching her how to give him relief.

'Just lie down next to me. Let me hold you. And I will be content.'

She did so, though she didn't snuggle up to him the way she'd done the last two nights. She was tense. Almost as tense as him.

Sweat broke out on his brow.

It was going to be a long night.

He'd never claimed to be a good man. Never so much as attempted any form of self-restraint.

But he would rather cut his own throat than betray Sarah's trust.

And so, for the third night in a row, he lay sleepless, tortured by the combination of a raging desire, and the presence of the woman who caused it, lying innocent and trusting, in his arms.

But not unaware. He'd destroyed something, by letting her see what she did to him. Of speaking so frankly about all the other women he'd had. Every so often she managed to doze a little and he'd pull her closer. But then she'd jerk awake and stiffen within his hold.

'Shhh,' he murmured, stroking her hair. 'You're perfectly safe. I promise.'

But every time he said it, that promise was harder to keep.

He wasn't sure which of them was the most relieved when it finally started to grow light and she had a valid excuse to get out of bed.

With her purity still intact.

He had precious little to give any woman, but at least he wouldn't rob her of that.

'I promised Castor I would take him out for a gallop early,' she said, self-consciously flicking her hair over her shoulder. 'Before it gets too hot.'

'And you always keep your promises,' he replied

gruffly. That was the kind of woman she was. A woman who should never have got so close to a scoundrel like him.

His vision blurred slightly as he watched her leave, knowing it might be the last time he ever saw her.

He'd made his decision during the night. He wasn't going to be here when she came back.

The moment the door closed behind her, he got out of bed, rang for Gaston and gritted his teeth to do what had to be done.

Major Flint was right. She shouldn't be here with him like this. Every minute her danger grew greater. He was a rake. A rogue. Thus far, he hadn't done her any real damage. People might talk, but Lord Randall was well able to quash any malicious gossip.

But as his physical strength grew, so did his desire for her. He wasn't going to be able to resist her for much longer.

Even worse, she probably wouldn't even resist him, beyond the merest moment's hesitation, either. She was growing increasingly curious about the way her body was starting to respond to his. And the way she'd kissed him two days ago had rung alarm bells in his head. She'd sort of dared herself to see how far she could go. And she was lonely. Susceptible to talk of love.

He grimaced. Love. What right had he to talk of love? What did he even know of that emotion? The only thing he knew for sure was that if he let go, if he seduced Sarah, stole her innocence, then whatever it was she felt for him would curdle. Turn to dislike. Resentment.

He couldn't bear that. Were a few minutes of pleasure worth a lifetime of regret?

He groaned, and clutched the edge of the washbasin as doubt and longing assailed him.

He had to get out of here.

Before the increasing attraction raging between them incinerated the flimsy code of honour by which he lived.

And he dishonoured them both.

He made it as far as the park.

And then realised he should have formulated some sort of plan. He'd left all his things in Sarah's room, thinking he could send for them later. But send for them and have them delivered where? Tourists were starting to flock back to Brussels, which meant that his former lodgings were probably occupied by someone else. He supposed he ought to go there and take a look.

Or perhaps he should report to Major Flint, first. Flint had clearly been left in charge of caring for the wounded. So he could get the company surgeon to look him over and pass him fit for duty. If he *would* be fit for duty by the time Flint finished with him.

They could still give him some sort of light work to do. There was always a mountain of paperwork involved in running a battalion. He could sit at a desk and wield a pen, couldn't he?

Anything, to take his mind off Sarah. To keep him busy and away from her.

Yes, he would report to Flint.

But instead of making his way straight up the Rue de Ruysbrock, misery kept him wandering aimlessly through the Park. He wasn't the only one. Other soldiers loitered in the shady walks, some on crutches, some with arms in slings, and some, like him, with their head swathed in bandages.

'Tom!' Sarah's voice. What the hell was she doing here? And bearing down on him like an avenging fury, brandishing her frivolous little ivory parasol like a battle standard.

'How could you!' Her face was livid. Her voice strident. An officer in a scarlet jacket, who'd been sunning himself on a nearby bench, opened his eyes and frowningly turned his head to see who was disturbing his nap.

'Sarah, please, keep your voice down,' he urged her. He'd left her to protect her reputation. But her words were bound to make people think he'd done the very thing he'd almost killed himself to avoid doing.

'Keep my voice down? Keep my voice down! Ooh, I...' She gathered herself, like a thunder-cloud about to burst. 'I never thought I'd hear you say anything so utterly mealy-mouthed and...and hypocritical. But then I never thought you'd abandon me, either.'

'I didn't abandon you,' he said, taking her arm and towing her towards a deserted walk. 'I left you a note.' Over which he'd agonised for what felt like hours. 'Explaining.'

'You call that an explanation? Two lines saying Major Flint was right and that you needed to think of duty. *Duty!*' She spat the word as though it was a curse. 'I had no idea where you'd gone.'

He'd had no clear idea where he was going himself.

'When I got back from my ride and saw your things packed, and your note on the pillow...' She shuddered. 'I've just spent the morning scouring Brussels for you. And when I couldn't find you anywhere, I had visions of you lying collapsed in some gutter somewhere. And where do I find you? Strolling about the park as though you haven't a care in the world!'

'I'm not exactly strolling.'

'Don't be so pedantic! You know what I mean! You said—' her lower lip quivered '—you said you loved me! Tom,' she said reproachfully. 'Is this your idea of *love*?' Her eyes grew luminous with burgeoning tears. 'To abandon me, just when I need you the most?'

'Need me the most?' His determination to resist her vanished under a wave of dread. He stopped walking, turned to face her, and seized her arms. 'Has something happened? Your brother? Lord Randall. Is he...'

'I have no idea how he is. It isn't that.' She gulped. 'You said you loved me. I thought you meant it. I actually thought...' Her mouth twisted into a bitter line. 'And then you left. Left me *alone*. I have nobody in Brussels, Tom, don't you realise that? Justin is probably dying and Mary won't let me anywhere near him. Seems to think she has to protect me from him. And Gideon is lying in that revolting coffin, in that hideously cold chapel. Even B-Ben ran off the moment Adam snapped his fingers. I thought at least I could rely on you, Tom.'

'You *can* rely on me,' he said. 'Can't you see that I'm trying to do the right thing by you? If I'd stayed with you any longer, now that I'm getting well, I don't know how long I could have resisted you.' He gave her a little shake. 'Just once in my benighted life, I wanted to do the right thing.'

'I don't *want* you to do the right thing.' She stamped her foot. 'I don't want you trying to behave nobly. It isn't *you*, Tom. And I want *you*. And if...' She lifted her chin, though it was quivering. 'If *you* really did love *me*, you wouldn't dream of leaving me here alone. Knowing I'd have no alternative but to slink back to Antwerp with my tail between my legs and beg everyone's forgiveness. And I *won't*. I won't. I didn't do anything wrong!'

'No. You didn't. You haven't, not yet. But don't you see? If I stay with you any longer, we'll become lovers. I can't resist you any longer. I want you too much. That's why I had to leave. *Because* I love you so much. I want the best for you, Sarah.' He gave her shoulders a gentle squeeze. 'And I'm not it.'

'How do you know what is best for me? Have you ever asked? No.' She gave a bitter little laugh. 'Nobody ever does. Everyone always think they know what is best for me. But they don't. *You* don't.'

'Perhaps you are right.' He let go of her arms and drew himself up. 'But I do know it isn't a cur like me. Sarah, you deserve so much better.'

'No, I don't,' she said defiantly. 'If you knew what I'd done this morning…' She turned her head away briefly and swallowed. 'I was so cross with Adam. So sure it was all his fault.' She shook her head. 'Tom, you keep talking as though you think I'm some sort of paragon. But I'm not. I'm just a woman, that's all. Given to flights of fancy and tantrums, and fits of spite. Not the angel you keep telling me you thought I was when you were in that fever. I started to think…' Her shoulders slumped. 'I thought you knew me, but you don't really. So all your talk of love? It isn't true at all, is it?'

She drew herself up and looked him in the eye, hers flashing with pride.

'Go, then. Leave. After what I've just done to Adam, my own brother, I deserve to be on my own.'

'No, Lady Sarah, you will find someone, one day, who will be worthy of you.'

'I thought I'd found him,' she retorted. 'But I

was clearly mistaken. As mistaken as you were when you said you loved me.'

'No!' He took her hand again. 'I do love you. Don't ever think I don't.'

She lifted her chin. 'A fine sort of love,' she said scornfully. 'The sort that leaves me broken and alone.'

An elderly couple who were strolling past caught her words and gave Major Bartlett a scandalised look. Clucked their tongues, and hurried on.

'Sarah,' he said in an urgent undertone, pulling her off the main path and into the shadow of a stone lion, 'the last thing I ever wish to do is hurt you. I didn't think I *could* hurt you. I thought leaving was for the best. It's not as if you care for me all that much.'

'That's all you know.'

'What?' He seized her hand. 'What are you saying? I know you only took me in to prove something to yourself. And then you kept me because you needed the excuse to stay in Brussels so you could find out what happened to your twin. I've been convenient, until now. But—'

'Yes. That's all true. I've been utterly selfish. Until you said you loved me, I *was* only thinking about Gideon. But since then…'

'What?' His heart was banging against his ribs. 'Since then, what?'

'Since then, I started to wish for something I'd never thought I wanted before. To belong to someone, other than Gideon. To belong to *you*.'

'I want that more than anything,' he said, raising her hand to his lips. 'But it cannot be.'

'Oh, for heaven's sake, Tom, stop talking such fustian! So, you've been a rake. So, your background contains a bit of scandal. I don't care. I don't care about any of it. What I do care about is what you think of me. That's all. Because you're the only person never to have condemned me. Or tried to order me about. You might even...' her breath hitched in her throat '...be able to forgive the wicked things I've done,' she ended, gazing up at him with eyes full of hope and longing.

'You couldn't do anything wicked. I don't believe it. If you have done something you *regret*,' he added swiftly when her face fell and he recalled her saying something about deserving punishment because she'd done something dreadful to Major Flint, 'I would know that you didn't mean any harm by it. Or if you did, that you were sorry, afterwards. Sometimes, we all do things, in the heat of the moment, we shouldn't. That doesn't make us bad people. Only human.'

'Well, I suppose at least this has made you stop saying you think I'm an angel,' she said sadly.

His face worked. 'Yes. But that doesn't change what *I* am. Why do you think Lord Randall selected me to become an officer in his unit? It's because I've always been so good at causing trouble wherever I go. And leading others into it.'

'The way you formed those village lads, the ones who taunted you with that horrid song, into a gang who followed you into all sorts of enterprising adventures?' She curled her fingers into his. 'You are a born leader of men, Tom. Why can't you see that it's a good thing? Why do you talk of it as though it is some kind of crime?'

'You speak of me as though I'm some kind of...' He shook his head, unable to find the right word.

'To me, you are, Tom,' she said with a soft smile. 'The best man in the world.'

Her words sucked the breath from his chest. Made his legs start shaking. 'And I can't bear the thought of you leaving. Please, Tom, don't leave me.'

Chapter Thirteen

'I can't fight you,' he said, bowing his head over her hand as he pressed it fervently to his mouth. 'Not as well as my own desire. But it's wrong of me. If I come back with you now...' He looked up at her and what she saw in his eyes made her heart thunder. Naked desire. Agonised longing.

For her.

'Tom,' she breathed, 'I'm already as good as ruined. There is no point in you fighting some sort of rearguard action by leaving me.'

She stepped up to him, slid her arms round his neck and kissed him.

And his brain simply dissolved. He couldn't have formed a rational explanation for why he should stop her from kissing him, had his life depended on it.

'Disgraceful,' he dimly heard somebody say. A swift glance over Sarah's shoulder confirmed it was the same elderly couple who'd walked past a few moments ago. They must have doubled back to make sure they didn't miss anything.

With a low growl, he pulled Sarah closer into his body and gave them something really worth watching.

He stopped kissing her only when his head began to spin.

'Take me home, Tom.'

Home. He lifted his head, eyes closed, and swallowed back what felt like a sob. From now on, wherever she was would be his home. And to think she'd spoken of their little room as home, too.

'I very much fear,' he confessed, once he could breathe steadily again, '*you* are going to have to take *me* home,' he said. 'My legs are shaking so much.'

'Oh, I'm so sorry,' she said, instantly snaking her arm round his waist and wedging her shoulder under his. 'Come on, let's get you back to bed.'

They began to weave their unsteady way back up the slope, and on to the Rue Royale.

They said nothing more during their short walk back to the lodging house in the Rue de Regence. Tom hadn't the breath for it, for one thing. For another, he was too stunned by her declaration she needed him to know what to say.

'You fought for me,' he said as he collapsed to the bed, having only just made it up the stairs. 'You always have done. Right from the first. That is what made me fall in love with you. '

'I will always fight for you, Tom,' she said, bending over him to plant a kiss on his brow. 'Because you are worth fighting for.'

'I'm not. But your faith in me makes me wish I could be the sort of man who was.'

'I don't want you to change,' she said, stroking his cheek tenderly. 'I love you exactly as you are.'

He snaked his arms round her waist. 'You make me feel as if I belong. As if I'm exactly where I ought to be.'

'You are, Tom,' she said softly. 'You're with me.'

'And what,' he said with a rakish smile, 'do you intend to do with me, now you've got me?'

'Do you know, I've been thinking about that,' she said, with a little frown. 'When you left me, one of the things that made me really cross was the fact that I've gained the reputation of being a fallen woman, without actually experiencing any of the pleasure that would have made it worth while. So, Tom, do you think you could show me?'

'Show you?' He swallowed.

'Yes. What is the point of falling in love with a rake, and knowing he's had so many other women, and being the only one to leave his bed still a virgin?'

'Because you're not like any of the others,' he said.

'Are you going to tell me they meant nothing to you?'

'No. Not that. I've been grateful to every one that's been generous enough to share a few moments, or hours of pleasure. I like sex, Sarah. I won't deny it. I like it a lot. It chases away all thoughts of who you are, and where you are, and replaces it with sensation. Glorious sensation. And leaves a sort of peace in its wake. A peace that enables a man to sleep without having to numb his brain with liquor. But this, for me, will be completely different.'

He sat up and clasped her hands. 'I know that you are feeling rebellious, and lonely, and will be seeking comfort and a sort of thrill. And there is nothing wrong with any of that. Those things have driven me to indulge in liaisons, in the past.'

He gazed deep into her eyes.

'But if I make love to you, Sarah, it will be really making love. For the first time in my life.'

She didn't know what to say.

He bowed his head over her hand, and kissed it. 'Lord Randall would say I'm not worthy of this,' he said, kissing each knuckle in turn. 'And I agree. I don't have the right to claim it.' He slid his tongue between her first and middle finger. She gave a little gasp, because for some reason the slide of his tongue sent sensations spiralling from her stomach to the juncture between her thighs. 'But you have asked me, very politely—' he turned her hand over and bit down on to the mound of flesh at the base of her thumb, turning the spiralling sensations to an insistent throb '—to show you the kind of pleasure that fallen women experience.'

'Are you going to?' Her voice came out like a sigh. He'd already started. And if this was how he could make her feel just kissing her hand, what would it be like when he really got going?

'No power on earth could stop me. Not today,' he growled, surging to his feet and pulling her into his arms.

'Tom, oh, Tom—' she panted between kisses '—you are shaking. You aren't well enough for this. Today was your first time outside since the battle. We should stop.'

'I have strength enough for what I have in mind,' he said, sitting on the edge of the bed and pulling her on to his lap. 'But,' he continued, as he deftly undid the ties at the back of her gown, 'if I need to, I can always lie down, can't I? And you will lie down with me.'

She opened her mouth to agree, when he started kissing his way down her neck to her shoulders, which he could get at easily now that he'd loosened her gown. And all that came out was a little sound halfway between a gasp and a groan.

'I think,' she panted out, when she was able to form thought into words, 'we should lie down right now. Just in case.'

'Not yet,' he pleaded. 'I want to get your clothes off first. May I?' His hand went to her neckline.

'Oh, yes, please.'

The dress fell to her waist. He tugged her breasts free of her chemise. Cupped one gently in his hand, while he kissed and suckled at the other.

'Tom—' she gasped. 'Oh, Tom.' She kneaded at his shoulders, her head rolling back as the delicious sensations he'd already started grew and blossomed, so that she felt full, and ripe, and ready for…something.

He slid his hand up under her skirt, caressing the soft skin he found at the top of her thigh, above her stocking. And then a little higher.

And when his fingers began to work at her

there, it was as though he unleashed some kind of storm. As he skilfully removed the rest of her clothing, flashes of lightning flickered up her spine, lit up her blood, dazzled her every sense. And she was naked, on her back, and he was beside her, stroking her, kissing her, nibbling at her neck, her breasts, her belly. Making her gasp with shock, moan with pleasure.

And then he shifted further down the bed, bent over her and fastened his mouth to the spot that was at the very centre of the storm. Pushed his finger into the heart of a maelstrom of sensation. Lashed her with his tongue. Lashed her into a frenzy.

'Tom, I can't, I… Oh, Tom…oh, oh, oh!'

Pleasure exploded through her. Ripped her from her moorings. And gently floated her back to shore.

For a moment or two, she was so stunned that all she could do was breathe. Drag in one breath after another and wait for the world to stop spinning.

But then she managed to just about open her eyes.

To see Tom, crouched over her.

Looking at her not the way she thought a lover should look at all. But like a warrior. A warrior who was about to face a mortal foe.

'Tom,' she breathed, reaching up to cup his cheek with a tender hand. 'What is it? What's wrong?'

What was wrong? He sucked in a sharp, painful breath. There she was, lying there in the afterglow of the pleasure he'd given her. Still virgin.

He'd thought he could do this for her. Thought he could give her the pleasure she'd asked him for—and leave her intact.

But the thought of some faceless man, a man they'd think worthy of marrying her, seeing her like this, having the right to go where he hadn't, it made him want to howl. With rage. With pain. The agony of imagining her with any other man was worse than any physical pain he'd ever suffered.

The temptation to ruin that smug, worthy man's hypothetical wedding night by making sure he wouldn't be her first was almost overwhelming.

He gritted his teeth. It was wrong. It was wicked.

But, hell, when had he ever been anything but wicked?

And hadn't she said that he wasn't any use to her when he tried to be noble? She didn't want him to do the right thing. She wanted him to do the wrong thing. He tore open the fall of his breeches. Had *asked* him to do the wrong thing.

She shifted a little. Parted her legs. Caressed his shoulders.

And the last sliver of resolution melted away. Right now, she was his, utterly his. Whatever happened, tomorrow, or the next day, nobody would ever be able to take *this* from him.

With a shout of defiance, he surged into her. Surged into the only heaven a sinner like him was ever likely to know. The fleeting, carnal paradise of becoming one with the woman he loved.

She rose under him, murmured his name. Shivered with renewed pleasure as he sought his own satisfaction. He slowed down, waiting for her. Wanting to make it last. For as long as he could.

But at length her own rising excitement infected him. When she shuddered round him, gasping out his name, he lost all control. Did the very worst he could have done to her.

Not only did he deflower her, he spent inside her, too.

And he wasn't sorry.

So why were tears streaming down his cheeks? He buried his face in her neck, in her hair, clinging to her as tightly as he could without hurting her. And she, darling that she was, hugged him back. Rocked him as though he was a lost, lonely child.

'Tom,' she murmured. 'What is it?'

'I deserve to be shot,' he growled into her neck. 'For taking your virginity.'

'You didn't take it. I gave it to you.'

'I should have stayed strong. I should have stopped. I should have—'

'Shh, shh. You did exactly what I wanted you to do. You made me feel wonderful. And I don't mean just physically. For the first time in my life, I feel wanted. Really wanted.'

He held her more tightly. If only he could preserve this moment by clinging to it. This moment when everything felt perfect. Just bask in the sensation of her running her hands up and down his back, pressing kisses to his shoulder. His neck. Stroking her foot up and down his calf.

If only he didn't have to burst this perfect bubble with the ugly lance of truth.

'You don't understand,' he forced himself to say. 'I didn't stop when I should have done. I could have dropped a baby inside you. I've ruined everything. I'm sorry,' he said, raising himself up so he could look into her face. 'We'll *have* to get married now.'

For a moment Sarah just froze. But then a stricken look leached her face of colour.

'No.' She shoved him hard, but he didn't move

off her. 'For heaven's sake, Tom, haven't you listened to me? I have told you I don't know how many times that I don't want to marry. And nor do you, to judge from that horrid expression on your face.'

'You are right. The thought of marriage—' He swallowed. Before today, he hadn't really thought about it, not in relation to himself. It just hadn't entered his mind that one day he would meet anyone like Sarah. But now, well, even though he hadn't thought beyond the mutual pleasure they could bring each other, it...it made sense.

'But surely, this changes everything?'

'This?'

'The fact that you might be with child. We can't just condemn a child to being labelled a bastard all it's life. I have to give it my name.'

A mutinous expression came over her face. 'No, you don't. My own name is perfectly adequate.'

'Not for my child, it isn't. I don't want it to think I walked away from the responsibility of bringing it up.' The way his own father had done.

'Well, I'll tell it that it was my fault, then, shall I? That should salve your conscience.'

'No, it won't, because—'

'I should have thought you,' she interrupted, 'of all men, would agree that it's better for a child to have no father at all, than a bad, or a reluctant one.'

She didn't think he'd be a good father?

He withdrew. You couldn't have a fight with a woman when you were still inside her, your body still throbbing in the aftermath of release. He had no answer to that clincher. Because he knew it was true. Their own childhoods had been marred by their respective fathers.

She pulled the sheet up to her breasts and scowled at him over the top of it.

To think he'd promised her she'd feel peaceful afterwards. She'd never felt less at peace in her life. And from the looks of it, nor did he.

Marry her just in case there was a baby, indeed! That wasn't a reason to get married. The only reason to get married was if you felt as if you simply couldn't live without the other person. If you wanted to be with them more than you wanted your next breath. If they made you feel as if you didn't care about anyone or anything else but being together.

A little sob caught in her throat. For that was how she felt about Tom. That was why his guilt-ridden proposal had hurt her so much.

A cold fury began to replace the icy stab of hurt. She was almost as bad as Mama—falling for a rake who looked on marriage as the ultimate sacrifice. She'd never understood how Mama could do such a foolish thing, until now, when she'd just had an experienced rake turn her into a puddle of lust and longing.

Except she *had* managed to retain the strength to turn down that half-hearted proposal.

And at least Tom *had* proposed. He wasn't the kind of man to turn his back on a child of his. Not like Papa. Not like Papa at all. Papa had littered the countryside with his own natural children and never cared tuppence what happened to any of them. Or their mothers.

It felt as though someone drew a curtain away, flooding her mind with light. All her life she'd believed marriage was the worst fate that could befall a girl. It had made her reject Tom's proposal in a kind of sick panic, even before she'd registered the reluctance in his voice. She'd always thought marriage meant becoming some man's property, being obliged to watch him have affairs, while bearing him son after son until she was worn to a shadow.

But now she could see why her sisters had been so keen to see her follow them down the aisle. It wouldn't be awful being married to Tom, not if he'd wanted to marry her. Really wanted to.

The way Graveney had wanted Harriet. The way Blanchards doted on Gussie.

But he didn't. He'd only proposed because he felt he'd behaved badly and now wished to make amends.

Guilt made her insides squirm. Because Tom had only done what she'd asked him to do. What she'd begged him to do. Why, he'd even tried to escape her and she'd hunted him down and dragged him back to this room.

'None of this is your fault,' she said. 'Even before we came to bed, you warned me that it was only to show me the pleasure a fallen woman could experience. You reminded me that you aren't the man to either ask for, or be granted, my hand in marriage.'

'And you said you would always fight for me,' he growled back. 'Was that just words? Do you even know what you meant when you said you loved me just as I am?' He gave a bitter sort of laugh.

'I do love you, Tom.'

'But not enough to marry me.'

'Oh, but—'

'No, don't bother saying any more. You're young. This is your first love affair. You're confusing the physical satisfaction for something else.'

Was she? She'd already worked out that it was the physical attraction her mama had for her father that had made her make so many poor judgements. But she wasn't the same as her mother. And Tom wasn't like her father.

'There's nothing to fight about, is there?' he said, flinging himself back into the pillows and staring fixedly at the ceiling. 'We're in agreement. Neither of us wants to marry. We've both been clear about that from the start.'

Yes. They had. Though now she was the only one who thought marriage might not be so bad, if entered into for the right reasons.

Unless—could he have changed his mind, too? Might there be more to his proposal? Was that why he'd seemed so hurt and angry when she'd turned him down flat?

Perhaps she should give him a chance to explain, if that was so.

'It was sweet of you to propose, then, when you really don't want to marry me. All for the sake of a baby that might not even have been made.'

'It wasn't just that.'

Her heart bumped into her throat.

'I shouldn't have gone so far. I know you maintain you wanted to gift me with your virginity, but I needn't have taken it. I could have given you pleasure, and taken it, without leaving you in no state to marry anyone else.'

Guilt. It was only guilt, after all, that had prompted him.

'I don't want to marry anyone else!' Her eyes were burning so hot she had to blink rapidly. 'I was ruined and facing scandal, just for staying with you here unchaperoned. We talked about it— how I was going to live on a small estate somewhere and withdraw from society. I'm happy to do that. With or without a baby.'

All of a sudden she couldn't bear being so close to him while they were fighting. She rolled out of bed, grabbed her crumpled chemise and dragged it over her head. Then went to pour herself a drink.

So. She thought he was good enough for a quick romp, but not for ever. And any child that might spring from this coupling would be better off living on an estate, somewhere, hidden away in shame, than having him for a legitimate father.

How could she maintain she loved him? She didn't know the meaning of the word.

He watched her pour a drink and tip it down

her throat in one go, with a kind of reckless desperation.

He'd done that to her. Not one hour ago, she'd been sweetly purring, anticipating the pleasure he'd promised her, and now she was all stiff and wary again.

Just because he'd suggested they marry.

She was staring into the empty glass now, as though searching for an answer that eluded her.

If only he could be her answer. But she'd been completely honest with him, right from the start. He could understand, really, why she'd refused his proposal. And it wasn't only because of who he was. It was because of who she was. Who she wanted to be.

She wanted to be free. She'd told him she hadn't spent four Seasons avoiding marriage, only to surrender now, when freedom, total freedom, was finally within her grasp. If he persisted in speaking of it, or took some step to force her to comply with his will, for the sake of a child that might not even have been conceived, he'd feel as if he was slamming the prison door shut on her.

It was probably only because he'd said he wasn't the marrying kind that she'd trusted him to become her lover. Maybe giving him her virginity was one more step she'd needed to take, to make sure no other man could shackle her with legal ties.

Maybe he should look on all this as a tremendous honour.

Maybe— Oh, to hell with it. He didn't know what to think. He just hurt so much he wanted to howl with pain.

For Sarah had become his lodestar. His anchor. His every single blessed thing in life that was worth hanging on to. If she didn't want him the way he wanted her, then…

He groaned. God really must want to punish him. He'd spared him eternal damnation only to cast him into a living hell. The hell of falling in love with a woman so elusive she might just as well have been an angel.

Sarah stared down into her wine glass, unable to so much as look at Tom, or the way he was lying there with his eyes screwed shut, as though he couldn't bear to look at her.

How had it all gone so wrong? He did still love her, didn't he? A chill snaked down her spine, even though the room was as hot as an oven.

She went back to the bed. And found she couldn't just climb in next to him and snuggle into his side. Not while there was all this anger, and hurt, and confusion swirling between them.

'Tom?' She perched on the bedside chair, twirling the glass between her fingers. 'You aren't angry with me, are you?'

He flung his arm to one side and turned to look at her through dulled eyes. 'With you? No,' he said wearily. 'Only with myself.'

With himself? For proposing? For losing control so that he felt he had to propose?

'Please don't be,' she said in a small, rather tremulous voice. 'Don't let anger and regrets spoil this.'

A look of contrition flickered across his face.

He sat up. Reached for her face. Cupped her cheek.

'Forgive me. I have spoiled it already, haven't I? By bringing the spectre of marriage into our bed. Let's forget it, shall we?'

A spectre? She flinched away from his caress. He thought of marriage as something deathly? Then she'd been right to refuse his proposal. She didn't want a husband who looked on marriage as a grisly fate.

Heaven alone knew what she might have said had not someone knocked on the door.

His gaze roamed her body, her tousled hair, in

a way that made her feel very conscious of what they'd just been doing together. That made her feel like a…well, a fallen woman.

Well, that was exactly what she was. What she would always be now she'd made him retract his proposal. And she'd better get used to people looking at her like that. With a toss of her head, she marched across the room and flung open the door.

'Yes?'

Standing in the corridor was Robbins. With a letter in his hand.

Looking more than usually grim.

The cold pool in her stomach froze into a solid lump.

'Justin,' she whispered, wrapping her arms round her forebodingly chilled midriff. Something terrible had happened. She could feel it.

Felt as though she deserved it.

Chapter Fourteen

'Is it Justin?' she finally managed to ask. 'What has happened? He hasn't…'

'No, miss, he's on the mend,' said Robbins as she snatched the missive from his fist and tore it open.

The shock of fearing the worst made her instinctively head for the nearest chair and sit down on it. A wave of giddiness assailed her even after she'd scanned the letter that was penned in Mary Endacott's neat, precise hand. Because even though Mary had assured her that Justin was well enough to do without her, she'd ended the letter by wishing her well in the future, just as though they were never going to see each other again.

'What did he do to her to make her leave?' Sarah blinked up at Robbins in bewilderment. 'After all Mary did for him, too.'

'Couldn't rightly say, miss,' said Robbins.

'Won't say, you mean,' Sarah muttered. The man must know why Mary, who had loved Justin enough to go searching for him in the hell that was the aftermath of battle, was leaving him now she knew he was out of danger. But he was loyal to Justin, so Tom had said. So loyal he wasn't going to publish Justin's idiocy abroad.

'Don't know as how this,' said Robbins scathingly, 'is going to affect him, when he finds out.'

He'd come in, shut the door behind him and eyed first the disordered state of the bed, then Tom's insolently lounging nudity and finally her own *déshabillé*.

'Well, it's only what he's been accusing us of getting up to all week,' she retorted.

Tom covered his face with his hands. And groaned.

Which just went to confirm her suspicion that he'd only asked her to marry him because of what others were going to think, not because of what he felt for her at all.

Sarah glared from one to the other. 'No need to worry,' she said to them both. 'Now that Justin is well enough to survive a visit from me, I will come and make a clean breast of it.'

'No! If anyone goes to tell him it should be me,' said Tom.

'It sure as hell ain't going to be me,' muttered Robbins darkly. 'I'll just tell him you will come to see him then, shall I?'

'Yes,' said Sarah.

'No,' said Tom at exactly the same time.

As they squared up to each other, Robbins sighed.

'The note weren't from *him* anyhow. Nor I needn't tell him I've been here. No need to tell him anything at all.'

'Just so. Thank you, Robbins,' said Tom, without taking his eyes off Sarah. 'We need to discuss just how to break it to him that...'

Sarah lifted her chin, though her cheeks went so hot she was sure they must have turned scarlet.

Robbins beat a hasty retreat.

'I'm not afraid of Justin, if you are!'

'It's not a question of being afraid, Sarah. Or not the way you think.' Tom flung aside the sheet and stalked, naked, across the room to take hold of her shoulders.

'It's just that, once we own up to Colonel Randall that we have become lovers, he is bound to put a stop to it. One way or another.' He'd either split them up altogether, or force them into marriage somehow. Neither of which things were what Sarah truly wanted.

'Sarah, I know you have been anxious about his health. I know you wish to go and see with your own eyes that he is recovering, but, please, I beg of you, don't go right now. Leave it until morning. So we can have tonight. Just one night together, that's all I'm asking.'

One night as lovers who'd chosen each other. Lovers who hadn't been coerced in any way, by anyone or anything but the feelings they had for each other.

Her heart leapt. He still wanted her!

Of course. It wasn't *all* about duty and appearances, or he wouldn't have made love to her in the first place. She'd only slid into that maelstrom of doubt and fear because it was so hard to believe anyone could really love her, after a lifetime of accepting her unimportance in anyone's life.

She bowed her head and rested it on his chest. Tom was the only person—apart from Gideon—who had never made her feel like a duty, or an encumbrance. He might only be asking her for one more night together, but after all, one night was more than anyone else had ever begged her for.

'As your lover,' she said. Marriage was a step too far, for either of them. But hadn't they both kept saying that they should seize the moment? To just live in the present?

'My lover,' he grated. Then closed his arms round her and held her so tightly she could feel his heart hammering against her cheek.

She bit down on her lower lip. If she'd been more like other women, she would be his fiancée now, not his lover. They could be looking forward to a lifetime together, not just one night. If only she hadn't been so afraid she'd end up like her mother she'd refused his proposal in such terms he'd admitted he hadn't really meant it.

Fortunately the Latymor pride rushed to her rescue. The pride that would never let anyone suspect they'd hurt you. The pride that enabled her to lift her head and give him a saucy smile. 'Well, if one night is all we have, we'd better make the most of it.' Laying the palm of her hand in the centre of his chest, she pushed him towards the bed. 'You are trembling,' she said, tilting her head to one side. 'Does this mean you are not up to the task in hand?'

He sat down heavily, and pulled her on to his lap. Buried his face in her neck. Breathed her in deeply, though tremors kept on running through his magnificently muscled body.

'It means,' he said, at length, 'that I can't believe this is happening. Am I dreaming? Am I in a fever?'

She laid her hand on his forehead. Then placed a kiss where her hand had been.

'This is real, Tom. You are not dreaming. You have no fever.'

'You have really just agreed to postpone visiting your brother, to spend a night in my bed?'

'I really have. And we have all night.' She tiptoed her fingers along his shoulder, then slid them down his beautifully sculpted arm.

His eyes took on a slumberous quality. 'Up to the task, indeed.' he huffed. 'Did I disappoint you last time?'

She pretended to think. Then shrugged. 'I have nothing with which to compare it, as you very well know. So how can I possibly judge?'

For the first time since they'd been intimate, the frown melted from his brow. His mouth curved into a wicked smile. His rakish smile.

'Do I detect a challenge?'

She shrugged with feigned insouciance, though her heart was beating a rapid tattoo.

'Well, I'm always up for a challenge.'

'Ooh,' she murmured with approval, glancing down at his lap. 'Indeed you are.'

'You will have plenty to compare that first time

with, before this night is through,' he promised
her. 'It will be a night you will never forget.' If
she wouldn't marry him, if she only saw him the
way other society women did, as fit for a night of
pleasure but no more, then he was going to make
sure that she would never know pleasure like the
pleasure he was going to give her, tonight.

No other man would ever measure up.

Through the gathering shadows of evening, and
into the moonlight, he exerted all his strength, and
all his considerable expertise, into living up to his
vow. He woke her, time and time again throughout the night, sometimes to pleasure her, sometimes to feed her or bring her drinks to replenish
her strength.

When she woke the next morning she ached in
the most unusual places, but not in a bad way.

On the contrary, she felt a pleasurable lassitude
throughout her whole body. For the first time in
her life, she was tempted to yield to the heaviness
weighing down her limbs. She had never lain in
bed late of a morning. Even if she'd been dancing
all night at a ball, she would be out in the stables,
getting her horse saddled before anyone else in
the house was stirring.

But after one night of Tom's ministrations, she felt completely undone. If she wasn't so determined to face Justin, she would have rolled over and gone back to sleep.

Instead, she yawned and stretched like a cat.

'You are awake?'

She opened her eyes, turned her head on the pillow and found Tom gazing across at her. He had a lock of her hair twined round his fist. But he held it so gently she hadn't even noticed.

'I think the church bells must have woken me,' she said.

It was Sunday. Exactly one week since she had fled Antwerp, and the respectable safety she'd known all her life, to come searching for Gideon. One week that had changed her into a different person. Gone for ever was the self-effacing, eager-to-please girl who was scared of men, of passion, of life itself.

'I should be thinking of going to church,' she mused. 'I missed going last week. But I cannot possibly take communion.'

'Because you've sinned?'

'Because I can't pretend to repent. Because I'm not sorry. Not about the time I've had with you, at least. And I don't think you can make a partial repentance, can you? Oh, dear.' She sniffed.

'I promised myself I wouldn't cry. No, don't hug me,' she said, scooting out of his reach and scrambling out of bed. 'And don't look at me like that. As though you regret what we did.'

'It isn't that. I just can't bear to think I've made you cry.'

'You haven't,' she said, lifting her chin. 'And you won't. No, don't go being all sympathetic,' she said, stepping further away when he made as though to reach for her again. 'I need to be strong, now, to face Justin. And if you encourage me to lean on you I shall probably go to pieces altogether.'

'You are going to see him, then.' Tom sank back into the pillows, his face drawn.

'Yes. I have to, don't you see? All my life, I've done my best to avoid scenes. I've never let anyone know what I really think, or feel. I've just gone along with what they told me I must do, behaved the way they said I must, so that they would leave me be. My house was one long battleground, growing up. If it wasn't Mama and Papa at daggers drawn, it was Gideon getting into a scrape, or Harriet spouting radical principles. I took delight in being the good girl. It was the only thing about me that was of any comfort to Mama.' She shook her head. 'But now it's time to take a stand.

To face Justin. To face life squarely, instead of getting my own way by stealth. And I shan't be able to do it if I'm breaking my heart over you.'

He frowned. 'Breaking your heart?'

'Oh, Tom. Don't you know how much I love you?' Good heavens. Where had her Latymor pride gone this morning? Although, if she was determined to start being honest and forthright with everyone, then where better to start than with the man who'd become the most important person in her life?

'I'm sorry if you don't like it, but I really wish we could have had more than one night. If only there was some way we could be together for longer. If only we...'

She lifted her chin, scurried back to the bed, stooped over and kissed him swiftly on the forehead.

'Even marriage might not be too high a price to pay.'

Having lobbed that grenade at him she went out, presumably to get washed and dressed. Leaving him reeling in shock.

What was all that about him not liking it? Hearing her say she wished they could have one more night made him want to crow with sheer joy.

And when she'd said marriage might not be too high a price to pay?

He sat bolt upright.

There was a chance, then. A slim chance, but a chance, none the less, of persuading her that marriage wouldn't be any kind of penance at all. If only she'd consent, he'd spend his *whole life* making her feel wanted. Treasured.

When she came back...

Hell. By the time she came back, Ramrod Randall would have talked sense back into her.

He flung himself back on to the pillows again, ready to howl with despair.

'Tom?' Sarah poked her head round the door, twisting her hair up out of the way. 'You will still be here when I get back, won't you? You won't go doing anything stupid like trying to report for duty again. Not until I've had a chance to speak to Justin first. Explain that all this has been my fault. I don't want him to punish you. Strip you of your rank or have you cashiered out of the regiment or anything horrid like that. I know that your career is all you have.'

'Don't do anything out of fear for my career, Sarah,' he growled. How many women would have thought of that? At a time like this, most women would surely be fretting about their own reputation. Their own fate.

But not his Sarah.

'And don't go pleading for mercy on my behalf,' he growled. 'You mustn't worry that Randall might destroy me. He can't. There are always other avenues for a man like me.' He smiled grimly. There were always revolutions going on in distant corners of the world, where men with his experience, his skills, could earn their living. Perhaps not honourably. But if he lost Sarah, he didn't think he'd care about honour any more.

He frowned. *Any more?* Where had that stray thought come from? When had he ever cared about his honour, or what anyone else thought about him? Hadn't he been perversely proud of being picked to hold command in a unit that was so disreputable they'd come to be known as the Rogues?

And yet, somehow, the thought of selling his skills to a foreign power suddenly felt wrong. As though he would be letting Sarah down. As though he would be staining this time for her. If she ever heard news of him, he wouldn't want to have become the kind of man she would regret having taken as her first lover.

Hell's teeth! He was going to have to spend the

rest of his life proving he'd been worthy of spending last night in her arms, whether he ever saw her again or not. Making love with her had changed everything. He'd never be the same man again.

She came fully into the room then, though a little hesitantly.

'How do I look?'

She was wearing the least favourite of her three gowns. It had a high neck and a lot of unnecessary frills. It made her look prim. Over it she'd pulled on her new black coat.

When Sarah saw his expression, her own face fell.

'I really should have bought a black bonnet, as well.' She sighed, pulling on her blue one and deftly tying the ribbons. 'And as for this stupid parasol,' she said, picking it up and looking at it in a puzzled fashion, 'it is of no earthly use, yet I wouldn't feel properly attired for church without it. I don't know why I didn't pick up a black one while I was buying my gloves,' she said, drawing them on.

'Because you have been thinking about things that are more important than your appearance?'

'Sacrilege!' She shot him a brave smile, but didn't approach the bed. 'If Gussie could hear you now, she would rap your knuckles with her fan. Which would, I assure you, complement *her* outfit to a nicety.'

'You don't really care, though, do you? Not deep down?'

She cocked her head to one side. 'Actually, no. I don't. I have found it liberating, not having to consider every single aspect of my dress. Or changing three or four times a day.' She clapped a hand to her mouth. 'Don't tell anyone, will you? That I don't give a fig for my clothes? That, I assure you, would scandalise the *ton* almost as much as discovering that I'd taken a lover.'

Her face wavered. She pressed her lips together as though she was trying to keep them from trembling.

'I am going now, Tom. Wish me luck.'

'I don't think you need luck, Sarah. You are equal to anything.'

'Oh, Tom, don't. Don't say such things. You will make me cry.'

'I shan't apologise. You *are* equal to anything. Even attending service at the Chapel Royal in a mismatched outfit.'

She laughed. Dabbed at her eyes with a handkerchief she pulled out of a little pale-blue reticule and hurried from the room without looking back.

Chapter Fifteen

How much difference a week made. The Sarah of one week ago would have been quaking in her shoes at the prospect of bearding Justin in his den. In fact, she reflected as she knocked on the door of the house in the Rue Ducale where he was staying, she wouldn't have come here at all. She would have stayed hidden away with Tom, hoping that by the time Justin was well enough to get up and come round, something would have happened to avert disaster.

She wasn't even all that nervous. In fact, if anything, she was looking forward to clearing the air.

Robbins said nothing as he showed her to Justin's room. Before she went in, however, she took a large white handkerchief from her reticule and extended it before her, waving it like a flag.

Justin's grim expression didn't falter.

'I hope that ridiculous display signals your unconditional surrender,' he said, in a voice that was so reedy she could barely make out the words.

'Not a bit of it,' she replied firmly, even though his attempt to both breathe, and speak, was clearly something of a struggle. She went across to the bed in which he sat propped against a bank of such snowy-white pillows they made his complexion looked positively grey. No wonder Robbins had been so angry with her.

'I was given to understand that even the bitterest enemies,' she said sadly, 'could conduct negotiations under the flag of truce, though.'

'I am not your enemy, Sarah.' He drew another breath. 'I have your best interests at heart.'

'Yes, well—' she sighed, settling herself on a chair at his bedside '—that is a matter of opinion.'

'No such thing!'

'Justin, don't get yourself into a pucker,' she said, pulling off her gloves with as much nonchalance as she could muster, given the shock his weakened appearance had given her. 'I am aware you *think* you have my best interests at heart. The only trouble is that, like everyone else in my family, you have no real idea what that would be.'

'It most certainly isn't that...' His lip curled. 'That libertine Bartlett.'

'Now, there we shall have to disagree. However—' she raised one hand to stop him when he drew in a sharp breath to remonstrate with her '—I didn't come here to talk about Tom. I know that my taking up with him has upset you and for that I am sorry. Most dreadfully sorry that hearing about our association caused you to become so dangerously ill. Oh, Justin, I never dreamed anything I did could cause you any harm.'

'I know that. But—'

'No. Let us speak no more of it, not today. Please, Justin, if you love me. I know you are angry with me for all sorts of reasons, but when I heard that Gideon had died, I—' She sucked in a short, sharp breath, blinking rapidly a couple of times in order to stop the tears before they could gain hold.

Justin reached out his hand, his gaunt face softening just a touch.

'You foolish child,' he growled. 'What on earth possessed you to leave the safety of Antwerp? And at such a time. Gussie must be out of her mind with worry.'

'No, oh, no.' She took the hand he offered and held it firmly. 'I have been writing to Blanchards, from the very first, with very carefully worded reports of what I have been doing. And you know how he dotes on Gussie. There is no way he would have let her know I was in any sort of scrape, even if he suspected it.'

'You really are the most cunning creature.' He frowned. 'I would never have suspected you of such duplicity. Or of such reckless behaviour. Gideon was always the reckless twin.'

She smiled at him impishly. 'You should have known that, as a member of the Latymor family, I had it within me to act in the most reprehensible, reckless manner. It was just that, until they told me that Gideon had died, I never had sufficient motive to step beyond the bounds of what is considered proper. I wasn't really interested in anything but what Gideon was doing. I lived for his letters, or for him to come and tell me what he had been doing. It was as if,' she pondered out loud, 'he was the one who went out and lived life for both of us.'

'But what, precisely, did you think you could achieve by coming to Brussels?'

'I don't know.' Her voice wavered. 'It was just that I couldn't believe Gideon was dead. It was too dreadful. He *was* my life. Without him…' She shook her head. 'I don't expect you to understand, but I felt I should have known if what they said was true. We always had this connection, you see.

I was sure that if it had been broken, by death, I would have been aware.'

When she saw his lips twist cynically, she added hastily, 'And then again, there was the Duke of Brunswick.'

'The Duke of—?'

'Brunswick. They brought his body to Antwerp. Laid it out in the inn for everyone to see. So I couldn't understand why they hadn't brought Gideon, too. But you all spent so much time telling me not to bother my head about things, whenever I used to ask questions you didn't want to hear, that I got out of the habit of trying. I could see Blanchards patting me on the head, so to speak, and telling me not to make a fuss, because he didn't want Gussie upset. And of course, it would have been unforgivable to have gone and wept all over Gussie and plagued her with all my worries while her own health is so uncertain. So there was nobody. I had nobody. But then I thought *you* would be bound to know the truth. Or would be able to find it out for me. So I came looking for you. Only when I got here nobody knew where you were, either.'

'Did you really have to come right out to the battlefield to look for me, though?'

'No.' She sighed. 'As usual, my presence was

pointless. Mary already had the search well in hand.'

His face went carefully blank.

'She couldn't rest until she'd discovered whether you lived or died, you know. Because she loves you as much as I love—loved Gideon.' He turned his face away at that. But she couldn't let the matter rest. Justin had behaved like an idiot where Mary was concerned. She had to at least try to make him see what he'd lost.

'Of course, she is a far better, more sensible woman than I. She even went inside the barn that they told us was full of dead bodies, refusing to believe their report of your death. Though I wasn't brave enough to go in with her. It made me feel so ill that I went over the wall into the orchard to be sick in private. That was the moment when it occurred to me that you might be trying to protect me from distress. If Gideon had been as mangled as some of the poor wretches I saw lying all over the fields, you wouldn't have wanted me to see him like that. For my last memory of him to be so gruesome. It hit me, when I couldn't even bear the thought of seeing *you* dead, or wounded. And we've never been exactly close, have we?'

He looked at her again. 'So you do accept that I act in your best interest.'

She sighed. 'I accept that you *try* to, yes. But as I said, I haven't come here to argue with you. Justin, Tom told me that you were with Gideon, at the end. Will you…will you tell me…?'

If she'd thought he looked ill before, that question made him look positively haggard.

'I know,' she added, 'you cannot tell me all, but I do want to hear as much of the truth as you think I can bear.'

'I can tell you what he wanted you to know,' he replied with a nod. 'His last thoughts were of you. *Tell Sarah I died well, Justin,* were his last words.'

'Oh!' She'd promised herself she wouldn't cry. But discovering that her twin had sent her a message, with his dying breath, was more than her resolve could stand. She reached for the handkerchief she'd brought to use as a flag of truce and held it to her face.

'I promised him,' said Justin more gently, 'that you would know you could be very proud of him.'

'Could I?' She looked up, her stomach lurching with hope and dread and grief. 'I have been so afraid that he threw himself away doing something foolhardy. I'd been so worried about him, in the days before the Duchess of Richmond's ball. I always know when he is planning some mischief and I had this awful presentiment that he was about to do something even worse than usual.'

Justin looked sceptical, but he only said, 'He died bravely. He died well.'

'Can—?' She hiccupped. 'Can you tell me... how?'

He frowned. For a moment she thought he was going to fob her off with the usual excuse of her not needing to trouble her empty little head with the ugly realities that should more properly be taken care of by men.

But then he surprised her by saying, 'Major Sheffield's unit got cut off by a party of French chasseurs. When I came across them, they were penned into a town square.' He paused to draw in a couple of breaths. But she didn't fill the silence with questions. She could see he was gathering his strength to tell her the tale in his own way.

'Bennington Ffog's troop,' he continued, 'were holding off the French, while Lieutenant Rawlins was attempting to get the Rogues to turn the guns round so they could make their escape. Gideon saw him struggling to control the men. They'd lost heart when Major Sheffield was killed. Gideon rallied the Rogues, got the guns turned and then stood and fought a rearguard action. I...' He paused again. There was something in his face that told Sarah he was right back in that town square all over again. With what looked like an effort, he continued.

'For a while, Gideon and I fought side by side, blocking the street so the French couldn't pursue the guns and their crews. We fought until reinforcements came. But by then it was too late for your twin. He was badly hurt.'

'Cavalry sabres,' she said in the ghost of a whisper. 'I've seen what they can do.'

'Yes. I'm sorry. Though if it helps, he didn't take long in dying. I tried to stop the bleeding, but...' He stopped when she gave a choked cry and buried her face in the handkerchief again.

'Sorry, that was tactless of me. I just wanted you to know he didn't suffer for long.'

'Thank you,' she whispered. 'I have been tortured by the thought of him lying out there, slowly dying, like so many of them did. Alone and in pain.'

'He died in my arms. He died bravely. Saving my men, and the guns, to fight the next day. The day we defeated Bonaparte once and for all. He won't come back to tear Europe to pieces again, Sarah. And the way Gideon died made a contribution to that outcome.'

'Thank you,' she said once she'd regained command of her voice. 'For not spinning me some sugary confection to make my grief easier to swallow. For—' She sat up straight, and gave him a searching look. 'You say he actually had command of your men? If only for a short time?'

He nodded.

'Oh, Justin, if only you knew what that would have meant to him.'

'I think I did. We had a chance to speak a little, at the very end. He told me that he wanted me to return to Chalfont and manage the estates. That Mother is struggling, but won't say anything. He even stole the sword, thinking that without it, I wouldn't go into battle—'

'Oh! So *that* was it. I wondered… He'd been acting so very…so very…well, the way he always did when he was planning some mischief.' Thoughts were teeming, nineteen to the dozen, through her brain. 'Yes, of course,' she breathed. 'He saw the chance to prove he could be as good an officer as you. Of course, he had to *steal* the Latymor Luck so that he could wear it into battle.' She shook her head. 'And you blamed Mary for taking it. I heard you. Oh, Justin, how could you?'

'Do you think I don't know what a terrible mistake I made?'

'You made another very grave error, too. About

the night of the Duchess of Richmond's Ball. It was entirely my doing that Mary was there. She didn't want to go, you know. I positively compelled her to go with me. I was absolutely determined to see Gideon. And Gussie was too ill to go. So I went straight round to Mary, spinning her such a tale that she felt she had no choice but to go with me. And then you had the gall to accuse her of—what was it?—*ingratiating* herself with your sister?'

Justin's lips firmed as though he was biting back a pithy retort. But before he could utter it, Sarah plunged on.

'It was the very opposite. I tried and tried to make friends with her, but she simply wasn't interested. You were the only Latymor she cared about. Even after you were so beastly to her that night she still came to the battlefield to find you. And wouldn't let anyone else nurse you back to health. What I should like to know,' she said with reproof, 'is what, exactly, you have done now, to drive her away? Surely you know that you'll never find anyone who loves you as much as she does?'

'I thought you came here under a flag of truce. I thought we were not going to argue about our private affairs.'

'It is not a private *affair*, what you have with Mary. You should marry her.'

'As you plan to marry Bartlett?' His lip curled scornfully. 'The man is a rake. A scoundrel. You know I didn't want you to so much as speak to him, let alone marry him!'

'I didn't say I was going to marry him. But I'm most certainly not marrying anyone else. Not after what—' she lifted her chin, and though her cheeks felt hot, she made sure to look her brother straight in the eye '—not after what we have been to each other.'

'You don't know what you are saying,' he spluttered. 'You cannot ruin your whole life because of one stupid, mad interlude.'

She glared at him. 'Tom has not ruined my life. I will always be grateful to him for what he's shown me this week.'

When Justin looked as though he was about to explode, she laid a restraining hand on his shoulder. 'And I don't mean *that*. Please, try to understand. I told you that I only ever lived through Gideon, before. And, well, it is as if, since he has died, I have started living my own life, at last. This week, for the first time, I have started to ask what I want from life. I've learned more about myself, of what I'm capable of, of what I truly think, than I have in the whole of the preceding twenty-two years, when I was content to just sit at home, like Rapunzel in her tower, watching life through her window.'

'Don't try making Bartlett out to be some prince, climbing up to your turret and setting you free. This is no fairy tale, Sarah.'

'No. It is my life. And I know full well that Tom is just a man. You aren't really listening, are you? You are fixated on Tom.'

'Fixated on *Bartlett*?' He gave her an indignant look. 'Nothing of the kind.'

'Good. Then you do accept that it was Gideon dying that shocked me out of my stupor.'

'I know it was certainly a shock to you, yes,' he conceded. 'But—'

'But nursing Tom,' she interrupted, 'living with him, a life so very different from anything I've ever experienced before, has opened my eyes. I know what I want now.'

'I dare say he can make any woman want *that*.'

'I dare say he can,' she replied loftily. 'But that isn't what I meant. When he asked me to marry him—'

'Do you honestly expect me to give him my permission? And don't forget I have control of your inheritance. Let's see how much he wants to marry you without it.'

'You would cut me off without a penny if I married Tom without your permission? Ooh, you... you...' If he wasn't so ill she would have shaken him. 'You think I'm hen-witted enough to accept a proposal from a rake?' She got to her feet. 'And so unattractive that he wouldn't want me without my fortune?'

'Wait. You haven't accepted his proposal?'

'You can keep my money, Justin,' she cried, ignoring the relief washing the tension from his face when she'd said she'd turned Tom's proposal down. 'I don't need or want it. I can earn my keep.' She could. Surely she could. Somehow. After all, Mary did. And it would mean she wouldn't be dependent on any man, any more, not even to manage her fortune. She really would be able to take control of her life.

'I could become a teacher.'

'Have some sense, Sarah,' he said, with that all-too-familiar tone of exasperation. 'No school would hire a woman who's been ruined and put her in charge of impressionable girls.'

She flinched. She wasn't used to being spoken to like that any longer. Tom never treated her as though she was an idiot. If she'd told *him* she would be a teacher, he would probably...

'Now sit down,' said Justin sternly. 'And calm down. We don't need to fall out, not if you aren't going to marry Major Bartlett.'

'I don't see why you are so against him,' she said huffily, though she did sit down again. Justin had gone alarmingly pale when she'd started talking about marrying Tom and she really didn't want him to suffer another relapse on her account.

'He isn't a bit like Papa, you know. He would never treat me the way Papa treated Mama. Because Papa never pretended to love Mama, not even at the start, did he? It was one of those dynastic unions, arranged by our grandparents, wasn't it? And Tom does love me.'

'Not the way a gentleman should love his wife. Or he wouldn't have ruined you. The man's a rake and a scoundrel.'

'I cannot see that Tom's behaviour has been any worse than yours,' she retorted. 'Or Gideon's. There is a vast difference between a single man enjoying his freedoms, and a married one breaking his vows, is there not?'

'You really think he'd be able to stick to his vows? A man like that?'

'I don't know,' she admitted ruefully. 'But one

thing I have learned is that not all men are like our father. Some men do truly fall in love with their wives. And cherish them. You only have to look at the way Blanchards is with Gussie. Or consider how happy Harriet is with Graveney. And she always swore she wouldn't marry, either.'

'Either?'

'That's right, Justin. I swore I wouldn't end up like Mama, chained to a man who treated me with less consideration than his horse or his hounds. In fact—' she gave him a straight look '—I've come to the conclusion it would be much better to be a man's mistress than his wife. And only stay with him as long as he treated me well.'

'No, it wouldn't! Look…' He struggled with himself, as though determined to keep his temper in check. 'I suppose I can understand your aversion to marriage. I have my own reservations, after all. Because of Father. I am his son and I would never be sure…' He grimaced.

'You are not a bit like Papa, Justin. Not in that way.' She stretched out her hand and laid it, briefly, against his gaunt cheek. 'You wouldn't treat Mary badly. You are not that kind of man. So marrying her wouldn't be a disaster. Thank you, Justin.'

'What for?' He eyed her with misgiving.

'For helping me to reach a decision.'

'I don't like the look in your eye. Dear lord, you've never looked more like your twin when he was plotting some mischief.'

She smiled. 'Thank you.'

'It wasn't meant to be a compliment.'

'I know. But you see, when I came here, I didn't know what to do about Tom. And now I do.'

'You agree to leave him? And return to Antwerp?'

'No. I'm not ready to leave him. I love him, you see.' To soften the blow, she bent to kiss his cheek.

'He cannot marry you without my permission,' growled Justin. 'As his commanding officer.'

'He may not want to. As you've taken such pains to point out, marriage isn't for every man.' She stuffed her handkerchief back into her reticule. 'So I shall ask if I can stay with him, on terms he can accept.'

'As his mistress, do you mean? Sarah, you cannot possibly—'

'Well, I'm probably, sort of, his mistress already,' she mused. 'I was certainly ruined the moment his men laid him in my bed, in the eyes of society. And I've been with him for a whole week since then.'

He drew a rasping breath with which to voice a protest.

'I don't think we should discuss this any more,' she cut in. 'I don't wish to make you unwell. And your face is going a most unhealthy shade of puce.'

'Is that surprising? At least Major Bartlett had the decency to propose. Whereas you—'

'I was rash enough to turn him down. I was afraid of marriage then. And worried he wasn't offering because he loved me, but out of guilt.'

'That makes no difference. At least he didn't attempt to get away with sullying your reputation without offering to pay the penalty.'

'Interesting to hear you think of marriage as the price you have to pay for getting a woman into bed. Is that why Mary has left you?'

'We are not talking of me, but of you and that b—Bartlett!'

'We aren't talking about anything, any longer,' she said serenely, getting to her feet. 'Or I shall be late for church.'

She had been worried about going to church, but she now felt as though she could use a period of reflection before returning to Tom. Her conversation with Justin had made her look at certain aspects of her past in a new light and she wanted to mull over them before dealing with her future.

It hadn't been until Justin had challenged her behaviour, and her motive for coming to Brussels, that she'd seen that while Gideon had lived, she really had behaved like a sort of modern-day Rapunzel, locked up in a tower. A tower that was entirely of her own making. She'd seized on the story their nurse had spun, about how she and Gideon were but one soul, inhabiting two bodies, and used it as an excuse for not struggling to break free of the strictures her parents had placed on her, because she was merely a girl. It hadn't seemed worth the bother of enduring a scene, such as the ones Harriet had caused when she came back from school, to get her own way, when she could tell herself that in some sort of mystical way, she was sharing Gideon's adventures so long as he told her about them.

But now he was gone. He couldn't do all the living for both of them. It was—it was her turn.

If this was Gideon, in love for the first time in his life, would he let fear of potential disaster stop him? No. Why, he hadn't even hesitated to steal the sword, go into battle and lead Justin's men, to prove what he was worth.

He'd always believed life was for living.

And she was in love. Deeply in love with Tom. And just because they both had reservations about marriage, that didn't mean they couldn't be together, in a way that suited them both, did it?

She hesitated on the church steps, noting that only a few people had started arriving. There was just time to go to the vault and visit her brother before the service commenced.

'Gideon,' she whispered, depressed by the gloomy silence that pervaded the vault. 'Gideon.' She reached out and lay one black-gloved hand on his coffin.

She closed her eyes and pictured him stealing the Latymor Luck. Strapping it on to his sword-belt. Taking control of Justin's men, even if it was only for half an hour. Fighting side by side with the big brother he'd alternately adored, and emulated, and chafed against, all his life. Then finally confronting Justin with his choices. *Eldest sons should stay at home, run the estate and set up their nursery,* he'd said, oh, often and often! *It's for the younger sons to go out and become heroes. He has to have it all, damn him! Well, I'll show him, Sarah. You see if I don't.*

Well, he'd shown Justin, right enough. And died in the process.

'Oh, Gideon,' she sobbed. 'Why did you have

to prove yourself to him? Why couldn't just being you be enough?'

She was glad, of course, that he hadn't died alone, or in some terribly painful, lingering way, or as the result of some stupid blunder.

But it didn't change the fact that he was still dead.

Sealed inside this coffin. Silenced for ever.

Worse. He'd stolen the Latymor Luck without telling her what he meant to do. And she hadn't known. Hadn't guessed. That stark truth snapped the last frayed thread linking them together.

At the exact moment that the bells began tolling to warn churchgoers that the service was about to start.

She stumbled to her feet, dabbed at her eyes and blew her nose one more time.

And went to sit through a service which was going to be of no solace to her at all.

She wanted Tom. She wanted to run to him and pour her woes into his ears, and have him soothe her with his loving words. Feel the strength of his arms holding her close to his heart.

Because when he held her, she wouldn't feel as if she was all alone in the world any longer.

She raised her head, staring sightlessly straight ahead as the words of the service washed right over her. Talking to Justin had helped her to get some things clear in her mind. She loved Tom. She did. Not just because he was handsome and charming, either. He'd become her friend. Her confidant. The one person she could trust with the secrets of her heart. The man she wanted to live with, grow old with, even have children with.

Even when he'd first warned her he might have got her with child, she hadn't minded. She'd pictured herself bringing up a sturdy little boy with green eyes like Tom's and a thatch of blond hair like hers. And loving him so much it wouldn't matter if his father wasn't around. She would have been all the child needed.

Except—her breath hitched in her throat at a sudden image of Gideon, hanging out of a tree branch, holding out his hand to help her climb up.

If she denied her child a legal father, then it couldn't have any brothers or sisters.

It would grow up alone.

It was all very well thinking she could endure scandal, if it meant she could stay with Tom. But was it fair to condemn her child to a lifetime of loneliness, as well?

She'd have to talk to Tom about marriage, again. In the cool light of day, not in the heat of passion, while he was weltering in guilt and she was reacting from a bone-deep habit of avoiding it at all costs.

She was still a little afraid that he held the same view as Justin—that marriage was the price a man had to pay for taking his pleasures unwisely. But even if that was so, even if he didn't love her the way she loved him now, she was going to have to tell him how she felt. She was going to have to face him, and tell him exactly what she wanted, and why.

And then deal with the consequences like a… like a…

She sat up straighter, and squared her shoulders.

Like a Latymor.

Chapter Sixteen

Tom soon grew tired of alternately pacing and looking out of the window. So he dragged a chair to a vantage point from where he could spot Sarah the moment she turned into the street.

His heart leapt at his first sight of her. Though he couldn't tell anything about her mood from the way she was walking. She might have been any society miss, returning demurely home from church.

Which just went to show how deceptive appearances could be.

'Well?' He fired the question at her the moment she came into their room. 'How did it go?'

'About as well as anyone could expect,' she said with a wry smile as she drew off her gloves.

His heart plunged like a horse refusing a hedge. That little touch of sadness in her brave smile was like an alarm bell, clanging in his head. He wasn't going to like whatever she was about to tell him.

'Justin…well, at least he told me how Gideon died. More or less everything, I think, which was surprising, considering the way he has always brushed me aside before. Oh, not that he was ever actually unkind. It was just that his eyes would always skate over me, as though he had neither the time, nor the patience, to bother with such an insipid little goose.' She smiled wryly as she untied the strings of her bonnet and tossed it carelessly on to a side table.

'And I also managed to speak to Adam after the service, and apologise for what I did to him—or at least,' she corrected herself with a frown, 'the mischief I *tried* to do him yesterday.' She shot him a rueful glance. 'And don't ask me to tell you about it, because I am so deeply ashamed of myself I couldn't bear to repeat it. And by the looks of things, I didn't succeed in my aim, anyway. Though how a man of his calibre has ended up linked to a girl of *that* sort,' she muttered darkly, 'I cannot think.'

His heart was thundering against his breastbone now. 'But what did Colonel Randall say about us? You did talk about us?' He dismissed the cryptic comment about Flint getting tied to some light-

skirt. It was what had passed between Sarah and
Colonel Randall that concerned him. It had been
a risk, letting her go and speak to her brother on
her own. Heaven alone knew what arguments the
Colonel would have used to induce her to leave
him. None of which he could refute, that was the
hell of it. Sarah shouldn't have lived on terms of
such intimacy with him this week. Let alone actually permitted him to become her lover. If he was
her brother, he'd order her to return to Antwerp
at once, then do whatever it took to salvage what
he could of her reputation.

'Of course I did. Oh, Tom,' she said, before
flinging herself on to his chest and wrapping her
arms about his waist. He closed his arms round
her, hard. Perhaps for the very last time.

'I thought that knowing how Gideon died would
help,' she said in a muffled voice, since her face
was pressed into his shirtfront. 'And I suppose at
least Justin did allay the worst of my fears. But it
doesn't really change anything. He's still dead. I
don't think I'm ever going to be able to come to
terms with that.'

'And why do you think you should? You are always going to feel as if a part of you is missing,'
he said, rocking her gently.

'Oh, Tom, I knew you would understand. You

always understand,' she said, lifting her head to gaze up at him with her blue eyes full of what looked very much like adoration.

'How is it that you understand, when nobody else does? You don't have a twin. You don't have any family—so how is it that you know what my grief for Gideon is like?'

'Because I know what I will feel like when you leave me,' he grated, past the huge lump that had formed in his throat. 'A part of me will always grieve your loss. There will be a great gaping wound inside me that will never heal. That I will never *want* to heal,' he said fervently. 'Oh, I will wear a smile on my lips so that the world won't know that I'm bleeding inside. I will flirt with women and no doubt, knowing my nature,' he said with a bitter smile, 'I will take fleeting solace in their beds when the loneliness gets too much. But none of them will be you.'

'What are you saying, Tom? Why should I leave you?'

'But—you said you wouldn't marry me.'

'Ah. Well...' She took a deep breath. Turned bright pink. 'Actually, I've changed my mind about that.'

'Have you?' He shook his head, which seemed

to be filled with a strange buzzing sensation. 'Are you sure?'

'Yes,' she said firmly. 'If,' she added, looking suddenly very young and vulnerable, 'only if you really do want to. If you really love me. You do love me, don't you Tom?'

'You know I do. I would die for you.'

'Much good that would do me,' she said rather tartly. 'I have no wish for anything but that you should live with me. And,' she added, a bit hesitantly, 'the way you just spoke of what it would be like to live without me gives me hope that you would like it, too.'

'Yes, I would, more than anything.'

'Well, then, I need not be afraid to marry you. Even though you have the reputation of a rake. You wouldn't dream of being unfaithful, or humiliating me by fathering natural children all over the place, would you?'

'Absolutely not!'

She sagged into him with relief. 'Oh, that was so much easier than I'd hoped. I've regretted refusing your proposal ever since the words left my lips.'

'You did?'

'Yes. But you looked so...' She shook her head. 'And I was still so scared, Tom. Or at least, in the habit of being scared of marriage. The refusal came to my mouth without me even thinking about it, really. But when I'd said no, I didn't feel relieved at all, or as though I'd escaped some terrible fate. I just felt as though I'd made the biggest mistake of my life.'

'Why didn't you say so?'

'Oh, Tom...' She sighed up at him. 'It was the way you asked me. As though you were worried about a child, or my reputation. I didn't want to make you marry me for such reasons as those. Marriage is such a big step for both of us to take, we have to go into it for the right reasons. The kind of reasons that made Harriet marry Graveney, in the end, except without all the books. I want you to love me the way Blanchards loves Gussie—' She gave a swift frown. 'But without all the smothering. I think you do want to marry me for the right reasons, don't you, Tom, or you wouldn't have said all that about no other woman being able to replace me in your heart, even if you did take them to bed, would you?'

'I thought you only wanted to be my mistress. I thought...' He grimaced, swallowed and shook his head.

'I would rather live with you as your mistress than live without you, that is true. But whichever future you choose for us, Tom, I am certainly not going to abandon you to the fate you just spoke to me of. Going around with a brave smile on your face, sleeping with all sorts of women whose names you won't even remember because they won't be me, bleeding inside from a grievous wound.' She clucked her tongue in disapproval. 'So much unnecessary suffering. Besides the guilt you will always bear for breaking my heart.'

'Breaking your heart? No, Sarah, I would die before harming so much as a hair on your head.'

Their eyes held for a moment, and then, on a surge of mutual relief and joy, they kissed.

'There's just one thing you should know,' said Sarah, dragging her lips from his. 'Justin is set against our match. And he's going to cut off my allowance. I don't know if he can stop me from laying claim to the capital when I reach thirty years of age, but I wouldn't be surprised if he doesn't at least try to prevent you from touching one penny of my fortune.'

'Fortune? You have a fortune?'

'Yes. Rather a substantial one. You didn't know?'

'Oh, good God, he's going to think I'm a fortune hunter now on top of everything else.' Tom groaned.

But she began to smile. He hadn't known a thing about it.

'Why are you smiling?'

'Because the thought of my fortune doesn't tempt you. Not one bit. When it is all any of the other suitors got excited about.'

'Well, they were all idiots,' he said gruffly, tightening his arms about her. 'If they couldn't see what a treasure you are,' he added, huffing into the crown of her head.

She hugged him hard.

'Tom? You really do love me, don't you? You don't care about me coming to you without a penny to my name.'

'Well, it won't make any difference to me, will it? I've never had a penny to my name. But you…' He put her away from him a little, so he could look down into her face. 'It's going to be very hard for you, living on my pay. I won't be able to give you any of the things you're used to.'

'You will be giving me things I've never had, though. Like respect. And confidence. And the knowledge that I'm loved, really loved, just as I am.'

'Of course you are.' He cupped her cheek. Gazed into her eyes in such a worshipful manner that she melted with longing.

He kissed her again. With a reverence that made her feel so strong, she could conquer the world.

'You do realise,' he said, after all too brief a time, 'that your brother, as my commanding officer, is not likely to give his permission, don't you? I will have to resign from the British army.'

'Oh...' She pouted. 'Actually, he *did* warn me about that. But, I wonder...' She glanced up at him through her lashes. 'After the way I threatened to become your mistress if you weren't of a mind to marry me, he might change his mind about that. I should think he will be extremely relieved we intend to make things respectable.'

'Well, that's just where you are out. For one thing, we wouldn't be *respectably* married. The shame of my background would mean you would always be subject to gossip—'

'Pah! Much I care about that.'

He shook his head sadly. 'Tell me, did he look as though he was keen on my marrying you, when you left Lord Randall? Or was he foaming at the mouth and uttering threats of what he'd do when he got his hands on me?'

She looked abashed. 'Well, yes, he *was* very angry whenever I mentioned you, in any capacity. But—'

He shook his head again. 'The only way we

are likely to be able to marry is if we elope. Your family may cut you out of their lives, Sarah, for defying them. And I will have to exchange into another regiment. Or even, God forbid, sell my services to some foreign power. And since there has already been one traitor to the crown in the family, we will become notorious, I should think. Could you live like that?' He gripped both her hands in his and looked her straight in the eyes. 'Could you become a disgraced exile from your family, your country? Just so you could be with me?'

She sucked her lower lip between her teeth. 'Are you trying to back out of marrying me, Tom? Is that why you're painting such a bleak picture of our future?'

'No. Goodness, no! But I really would be a rogue,' he bit out, 'of the worst sort, to casually condemn you to such a life. I knew it, the moment I'd proposed. *That* was why I didn't press you,' he said, grasping her shoulders gently. 'Not because I was unwilling, or only proposing out of guilt because I may have made you pregnant, but because I really, truly believed you would be better off without me. I didn't want you to feel trapped and dragged into a future of shame and penury.'

Tears slowly welled up in her eyes. His insides

hollowed out. He'd made her see, at last, what the cost of marrying him was going to be. He'd made her face reality. What a foolhardy thing to do! She'd leave him now, for sure.

But then, to his amazement, she flung her arms round his waist again.

'I have lost Gideon.' She sobbed into his chest. 'I absolutely refuse to lose you, too. How could I just walk away, and go back to Chalfont and a life that is no life at all, knowing you are walking around somewhere, smiling bravely, taking other w-women to b-bed? I can't. I can't! And I won't.'

'Then your fate is sealed. For I cannot let you go, Sarah. I cannot break your heart this way.'

No. Instead, the way they would be obliged to live would grind it down, insult by insult. Until the day came when she would look at him with loathing.

He crushed her to his chest and buried his face in her sweet-smelling hair.

At least, until that day came, she would be his.

And even after that, he would always be hers.

He took her to bed. And spent the rest of the day showing her how much he loved her.

And then spent the night, while she slept, watching her. Just watching her beloved face with that sweet, contented look on it, fixing it in his mind against the day when lines of discontent would bracket her mouth and regret would stamp grooves into her forehead.

In the morning, he rose early and went along the passage to the small dressing room, where Gaston shaved him and helped him into his dress uniform.

When he went back to their room, Sarah was sitting up in bed, sipping some hot chocolate, her hair delightfully tousled. Her eyes roved over him appreciatively.

'Tom Bartlett, if I wasn't already in love with you, I declare I would fall for you on the spot. Though—' Her face suddenly fell as comprehension dawned. 'You wouldn't be all dressed up like that if you weren't going out.'

'That's it,' he said, coming to the side of the bed and raising her hand to his lips to kiss it. 'I'm going to visit your brother. Always pays to look one's best when facing a boll— I mean, when about to get a rare trimming.'

'Oh, Tom. Do you want me to come with you?' She made as if to get out of bed.

'No. By no means. I need to speak with him man to man.' When she didn't look at all convinced, he added, 'Apart from anything else, I need to report for duty.'

'You aren't well enough. Don't go. You don't need to visit him today, do you?'

'No sense in putting it off. Best to get it over with quickly. And then we can get on with living our lives, however it turns out. Besides,' he said with a wicked grin, 'you cannot seriously try to persuade me I'm not well enough to report for duty after the shameless use you made of me yesterday afternoon?' He turned her hand and placed a hot kiss on the inside of her wrist. 'And into the night?' He trailed kisses up her arm to the crook of her elbow.

She blushed. 'No, I suppose you are right. You certainly wore me out. I ache all over.'

He gave a quick frown. 'Was I too demanding? I didn't hurt you, did I? I know once or twice I was a bit...'

'You were perfect.' She sighed. 'I wish it could have gone on for much longer. No wonder,' she said with a very sultry look, 'you have gained such a reputation. I only wish I had more stamina.' A sudden look of insecurity flashed across her face. 'It isn't going to be easy for you to be satisfied by just one woman, is it?'

'Now stop right there,' he said sternly. 'If you can't trust me to be faithful, then—'

'No! Oh, no.' She knelt up and flung her arms round his neck. 'It isn't that. I just wish I was more experienced, that was all. That I knew how to please you.'

'Couldn't you tell how much you pleased me?'

She bit on her lower lip and nodded, though a little uncertainly.

'And you will very soon become experienced,' he promised her on a low growl. 'And besides, it isn't the same with you as it has been with any of the others. Because my emotions weren't involved. It was just—' he shrugged '—a sort of appetite that had to be met. The moment I'd finished with them, I left their beds. I have never wanted to hold a woman in my arms all night and just watch over her while she slept.' He brushed a strand of hair from her forehead.

'You just—'

He nodded. 'Did the deed and left. I didn't even want to *speak* to them again. But please don't think of the others, Sarah. They were all before I met you. Just know that from now on there won't, ever, be anyone but you.'

She subsided into the pillow, a frown pleating her brow.

'No, there won't. Because if I ever got so much as a whiff of you betraying me with another, I would...I would...' She crossed her arms. 'Well, I don't know exactly what I'd do, but I most certainly wouldn't turn a blind eye, the way Mama always did.'

'Really?' He grinned at her. 'I must say I'm flattered by this display of jealousy. Even if it is slightly insulting of you to assume I might be so inconstant. Because it means you care.' He sobered as it hit him again what a lucky dog he was. 'You really care.'

'Of course I care. Can't you tell by the way I'm willing to be cut off from my family, and live in some foreign land while you command some revolutionary army? On your wages, too, once Justin cuts me off.'

'Yes.' His face fell. 'Loving me is going to condemn you to a lifetime of penury and disgrace. I wouldn't blame Colonel Randall if he reached for his pistols the moment I set foot in his room.'

'Then take me with you. He won't shoot you in front of me.'

'No.' His face set in harsh lines. 'I'm not going to hide behind your skirts. Nor let him think for a moment I would do so.' He bent and gave her a swift kiss.

And, having set his jaw with determination, strode from the room to face whatever punishment Colonel Randall decided to mete out.

It was awful, being alone in this room, knowing Tom was facing Justin's wrath. Now she knew how he must have felt yesterday, when she'd been the one to go out. She lay in bed, for a while, imagining all the dozens of methods Justin could employ to part them. Though he couldn't, legally, prevent them from marrying. She wasn't under age.

She flung the covers aside in vexation. Tom might have worked himself into such a state that by the time she came home, he'd convinced himself she was going to leave him, but she was a Latymor. She would never, never, fail.

So she would just have to find something to do to keep her mind off Tom's interview with Justin. Though what?

And then she thought of Mary Endacott. Probably breaking her heart somewhere, over Justin. Because it sounded as though, even after all she'd done for him, Justin had been perfectly beastly to her, or she wouldn't have sounded so utterly defeated in that note she'd written. There wasn't much she could do about Mary's broken heart.

Only Justin could fix that. But she could at least go and apologise to her, properly, for her part in it.

She rang for some hot water. Apologising probably wouldn't do any good. Mary had never responded to any of her overtures of friendship even before the disaster that had been the Duchess of Richmond's ball. But she wouldn't feel right if she didn't make the attempt to offer what comfort she could. And explain Gideon's motives for stealing the sword that had become such an issue between Mary and Justin.

Besides, if she stayed in this room all morning, wringing her hands and worrying over what Justin was doing to Tom, she'd end up positively demented.

Chapter Seventeen

His collar was too tight. There was a smudge of dust on his left boot. His bandages made him look ridiculous.

Good God. For the first time in his life, Tom actually cared what the person about to give him a trimming thought of him.

'You can go in now,' said Robbins, more dour-faced than usual.

'Well?' Colonel Randall glared at him from a bank of snowy-white pillows. With eyes that were so very much like Sarah's. 'What have you to say for yourself?'

Where to start? He ought to be giving an account of his movements. Report that he was fit for duty.

'I'm in love with your sister, sir,' he blurted, his normal laconic attitude towards superior officers totally deserting him. 'I'm aware you must think it a great piece of impertinence.'

Randall gave a low growl.

'I suppose I'd better resign my commission.'

Randall's eyes narrowed.

'She's already told me you intend to cut off her money,' Tom explained. 'So there's no point in asking for your blessing, is there?'

'None whatever.'

'Even so, I do ask you for it. Oh, not for me. I know I don't deserve it. I know I'm not fit to fasten her boots, let alone marry her. But, have you considered how unhappy it will make her, to be so entirely cut off from her family? She says she doesn't care, but I'm not sure she fully understands what it would mean.'

'There is an obvious solution. Give her up.'

Tom gave a wry smile. 'Do you think I haven't tried? She hunted me down and dragged me back when I tried to do the decent thing. She's even said she'd rather be my mistress than live without me. Naturally, I couldn't treat her so shabbily. No, I'm going to have to marry her, sir. With or without your blessing.'

Randall glowered at him in silence for so long that Tom could hear his heart pounding in his ears.

'She says she needs me, sir,' he added. 'It's because she's lost Gideon, you don't need to tell me that. She clung to the dog to start with. I suppose you might think I've taken its place in her affections. She certainly picked me up out of the mud the same way she rescued that flea-bitten cur. And you may not believe me, given my reputation—' he could feel his cheeks heating '—but I would be as faithful to her as a hound.'

Randall snorted. 'I'd warrant that the dog left her though, didn't it, the moment Major Flint came on the scene?'

'Well, yes, but the dog was always his, more than anyone else's, wasn't it? And I grant you that it wasn't a very good comparison to make, except that, well, the dog may have spread its favours widely, when Major Flint wasn't around, but in the end, it belonged only to him. The way I shall only belong to Sarah, for the rest of my life.'

'You expect me to believe that Tom Cat Bartlett is suddenly going to reform? Because of my sister?'

'Yes, sir.'

'And you fully intend to elope with her if I refuse to grant my permission?'

'Yes, sir.'

'And oblige her to live on your pay?'

'She says she's perfectly happy to do so, sir.'

'She has no notion of what that means. Why, you couldn't keep her in gowns for a month!'

'She doesn't care a rap for gowns. And if you knew her better, sir, you would know she would rather be out on horseback than being dragged from one modiste to another by her mother or her sister.'

'It won't hurt to acquire a wealthy wife, though, will it?'

'It wouldn't if I cared for money. Which you know I don't. I've always contrived to live well within my means. And anyway, she won't be wealthy, will she, not if she marries me. You have said so.'

Colonel Randall made another of those low, sort-of-growling noises.

But—was he imagining it, or had Randall's frown turned a touch less angry, and a tad more thoughtful?

'At least you haven't debts,' he finally conceded. 'Or a gambling addiction.'

'Given the way my father ended, you should know why I abhor gaming of all sorts. Although,' he added thoughtfully, 'in one respect, I believe I am more like my father than I ever knew.'

'Indeed?'

'Yes, sir. It only occurred to me, on my way here, this morning. I know now why he ended so badly. It was because he loved my mother so deeply. When he lost her, nothing else mattered. Not his title, not his position, not even his own son. Without her, his entire life ceased to have meaning. For the first time, I can begin to contemplate what he felt like. For I would feel like that, too, should I ever lose Sarah. And so I regret to inform you, sir,' he said, drawing himself to his full height and looking his commanding officer straight in the eye, 'that nothing you can do, or say, will make me give her up.'

'I suppose you had better marry her, then,' said Randall.

'What?'

'I have not the energy to repeat myself,' he said wearily. 'I have thought of little else since she visited me yesterday.' The line of his mouth softened into something almost resembling a rueful smile. 'The women in my family are strong-willed. Stubborn. Once they get a notion in their heads there is no shaking it. If she's set her heart on you, then have you she will, by hook or by crook. Heaven help you,' he added with a shake of his head.

'Yes, sir. Thank you, sir.'

'Well, then, since you are to become my brother, you may as well be the first to know that I shall be leaving the army. It is past time that I returned to Chalfont and took up my duties there. All of them,' he added, in a rather more determined tone. 'Randall's Rogues may be disbanded. But if they do continue, in whatever form, then I have complete confidence that I may trust them to either you or Major Flint.'

'Sir!' It struck him that it was particularly fitting that the next commanding officer would be either the half-brother or the brother-in-law of the man who'd originally formed the unit.

'It will mean promotion, of course. Better pay.'

'Sir!' He couldn't credit it. He'd come here expecting to get cashiered out of the regiment and instead he was looking at a possible promotion. How on earth would they work out which of them would land the job, though? Normally promotion would have gone to the officer with the most seniority. But it would be devilish hard to work out which of them that was, given the way the unit had been formed. Both had exchanged from other regiments. There was probably some clerk, somewhere, who had a formula for working out such things.

Not that he would object to serving under Flint, if it turned out he was the one who had seniority. On the contrary, he admired Flint for the way he'd worked his way up through the ranks. It took an exceptional man to do that.

'Bartlett!'

'Sir?'

'Stop standing there like a stunned sheep and get out of my sight.'

He just about had the presence of mind to salute, before turning on his heels and leaving.

Sarah was going to be so pleased.

With a broad grin, he skipped down the stairs and out into the bright June sunshine.

'Tom? It's good news, isn't it? I can see by your face.'

'The best,' he said, catching her up and swinging her right round.

'Tom, you lunatic. Put me down this instant!' Even though she was shrieking with laughter, so that he must know she didn't mean it, he complied at once.

'So, Justin gave us his blessing? I don't believe it.'

'He did more than that. He has given me command of the Rogues. At least—'

'What? Is he going to go home, then? Oh!' She clapped her hands to her cheeks. 'It was Gideon's last wish. Mama needs him, you see. And now that Bonaparte is trounced, I dare say he feels he can go back. And oh—' she squealed '—they always hand out honours after such a decisive victory, don't they? I shouldn't be a bit surprised if you got something. A knighthood at the very least.'

He shook his head. 'Only those already in favour get distinctions of that sort. And I won't be in favour. My action, in seducing the sister of my commanding officer, will outweigh any credit I may have gained by whatever small part I played in the battle itself.'

'Nobody will think that. We are going to be married. And once you become his brother-in-law, Justin is bound to put in a good word for you in all the right places. And before you say he is just an artillery officer, he is also an earl and has the ear of some very powerful people. He could even,' she said on a burst of inspiration, 'petition for your grandfather's title to be restored to you.'

'What if I don't get any honours, though, Sarah?

You have to face the possibility. Are you sure you will be content to follow the drum? The life of an army wife isn't an easy one, you know.'

'Oh, Tom, how can you say anything so absurd? I've felt more alive these last few days than I ever have done. More...*me*, if you know what I mean? At last, I feel as if my life has some value. Some meaning. I am going to be such a good wife to you. And just to prove it, I have been busy this morning, showing everyone that I am *not* a silly, frippery, fashionable ninny.'

'And just how,' he said with a grin, 'did you do that?'

'I volunteered to help in Mary's hospital. What used to be her school is full to the rafters with wounded men. And Bertrand said I would be a valuable addition to the staff, only think of that!'

'Bertrand?' She thought he stiffened a little. His smile had certainly slipped.

'Yes. The doctor who comes in every day to oversee Mary's work. You need not worry about him. He's in love with Mary. So even if Justin has made a complete mull of it at least she won't be on her own for ever. But never mind them, Tom, the important thing is that this proves I can be a good officer's wife. I will never, never fail you, Tom.'

'You don't need to go working in a hospital to prove anything, Sarah. I don't want you to have to.'

'But *I* want to. I felt so badly for all those poor injured men and wished I could do more for them. Well, now I can.'

He frowned and took a breath, as though about to say something she wasn't going to like.

'You aren't going to be a disagreeable sort of husband, are you? Forbidding me to do things I want to do?'

'No.' He smiled. 'I'm not going to forbid you to do anything. I want you to be happy. But I also want you to be safe. We are going to have to employ a maid for you. And probably some form of male servant to watch over you. I don't like the thought of you wandering about on your own.'

She burst out laughing. 'Oh, Tom, as if I haven't been wandering all over Brussels this week without so much as a groom in attendance. My word, I never dreamt you could say anything so stuffy!'

'It comes of having been a rake, I expect. I know how very bad men can be. So I want to protect you from all the others. I,' he said, pulling her close, 'am going to be the only rake who gets his hands on you from now on.'

'Yes, Tom,' she said demurely. And then ruined the effect by adding, with a twinkle, 'You may put your hands wherever you like.'

* * * * *

Don't miss the third story in the fabulous
BRIDES OF WATERLOO *trilogy*
A ROSE FOR MAJOR FLINT
by Louise Allen
Coming November 2015

MILLS & BOON®

Why shop at millsandboon.co.uk?

Each year, thousands of romance readers find their perfect read at millsandboon.co.uk. That's because we're passionate about bringing you the very best romantic fiction. Here are some of the advantages of shopping at www.millsandboon.co.uk:

* **Get new books first**—you'll be able to buy your favourite books one month before they hit the shops

* **Get exclusive discounts**—you'll also be able to buy our specially created monthly collections, with up to 50% off the RRP

* **Find your favourite authors**—latest news, interviews and new releases for all your favourite authors and series on our website, plus ideas for what to try next

* **Join in**—once you've bought your favourite books, don't forget to register with us to rate, review and join in the discussions

Visit **www.millsandboon.co.uk**
for all this and more today!